CW00869485

MISS KATIE

Jack Barry
Miss Katie Regrets

A Dublin murder mystery

A Brandon Original Paperback

First published in 2006 by Brandon
an imprint of Mount Eagle Publications
Dingle, Co. Kerry, Ireland, and
Unit 3, Olympia Trading Estate, Coburg Road, London N22 6TZ, England

www.brandonbooks.com

ISBN 0 86322 354 0

2 4 6 8 10 9 7 5 3 1

Mount Eagle Publications/Sliabh an Fhiolair Teoranta receives support from the
Arts Council/An Chomhairle Ealaíon.

Cover design: www.designsuite.ie
Typesetting by Red Barn Publishing, Skeagh, Skibbereen

To Brian

Chapter One

THE STORY OF the blue-rinse transvestite, the Provo in the fawn Lacoste sweater and the government minister started off with just a little splash of pee-pee and a couple of shouts on a clammy June night in the summer of 2005.

"It's chucky our ducky time, Mr McMenamin!"

It was all very East LA, in a lowlife WOMA (West of M50 to you, that is) sort of way. Nothing to get that excited about. *Let them kill one another.* At least that's what the other lawmen liked to say in the day room, though myself and Squirrel didn't really buy into it that sort of bull, because when the drug retailers started topping one another out in the suburban Bantustans of Dublin, it was suddenly Colombia meets the Quiet Man. Only there was no one saying top-o'-the-morning to anyone any more.

The killee, this particular night in June, didn't see the witness to his murder because she was cowering behind a big yellow builder's skip (SKIPPY SKIPS – WE FILL YOU EMPTY!), with her drawers around her ankles. It would all end up down a cyber cul-de-sac at kissmyass.com. Catherine James was just minding her own business, wheeling home after a wild night on the town with the girls, when her bladder gave out. Now, no one likes to hear menacing male voices late at night, and especially northern Irish ones, so Catherine James just pressed her little blonde head back against the yellow skip and cut the operation short. With her head low as a Larne Catholic, as my scaredycat father used to say, she closed her eyes and wished they would all go away. She didn't budge a millimetre, even when the three shots from the big black Walther rang out – a sound that would have made most men permanently incontinent. Which was where we came in.

It was Squirrel who took the call that night. The sincere, blue, bulldog eyes and droopy ginger moustache looked over the phone at me. The tall, thin frame was crammed into a traumatised grey suit that was short at the ankles and tight at the elbows. Squirrel's long, lean face was chomping on a piece of pizza we had picked up from Mario's on the way home from sorting out a row in a pub in Harold's Cross. I was flicking through stuff from the Arland Properties case, the one I had, in the background, helped set in motion with old documents from the 1970s. I should have been prepping myself for the trial of the decade, but I was really going over the separation papers that had arrived in the post that morning. Unhappy Differences Have Arisen. All that kind of legal bolloxology. Squirrel nodded at me, brushing pizza crumbs from his red moustache.

"There's been a shooting behind Rathmines Barracks."

"Anyone we know?"

Squirrel glanced around him, then looked me straight in the eye.

"Larry McMenamin."

"You're not serious?"

"Do I look like I'm joking? Come on, Barrett, let's see what's left of the poor bastard."

I had just time enough to stuff the separation papers in my inside pocket and check my gun. The quality were stumbling out of the little Thai restaurant on the Rathgar Road as we zoomed past. Any other night, we might have amused ourselves with them, but we just carried on for the barracks. All we knew, at that stage, was that someone had heard shouts, a northern accent, then shots.

Maybe some unemployed Provo doing a nixer.

A couple of young soldiers were standing around the skip with their mouths hanging open. Squirrel, all six foot two of him, in his shirt, tie and suit, was first out of the car. The little army boys straightened up respectfully.

"I'm Detective Murray. Anyone know the story here?"

It seemed very odd though, right from the start. The late Larry McMenamin, God be good to him, a northerner who was big in the anti-drug crusade, was lying behind the skip with the thinking part of his head blown off. I was caught off guard when I saw the condition he was in and brought Mario's pizza up pronto. I had only been speaking to McMenamin on the phone a few days before. McMenamin had provided the receipts, cheque stubs and all the other stuff that had been used to start up the Arland bombs-for-property investigation, a trial that would reveal how a little cabal of southern politicians and hangers-on had bought out bombed property in the north, in the early seventies. A property company based in Dublin, Arland Properties, had been used as a cover. Through a series of front companies – Arland Properties being the main one – this property passed into the hands of speculators in the south, who, presumably, would then resell it when the great revolution was over and property prices rose again. And it got worse: some of McMenamin's evidence showed that there was a sort of *à la carte* bomb-and-buy service, where certain republican elements bombed on demand. I thought McMenamin was phoning because the case was finally coming to trial with my *bête noire,* Mr Brian Toomey, TD, in the dock. But McMenamin seemed edgy on the phone, like someone was breathing down his neck. I had told him to take it easy, that no one would dare touch him now, but he didn't seem convinced. I remember the breathless voice on the phone.

"Just lift Tommy Ellis, Barrett. You're going to find out something that will make even Arland look tame."

"Is this more evidence on Brian Toomey?"

"Just lift that little toe rag Ellis, but do it quickly."

The army boys smirked at me as Squirrel passed me a handkerchief. I almost dropped the separation papers with the signature of my ex-wife-to-be – *Anna M. Barrett* – scribbled in the margins, in the puke.

Detective Thomas Barrett was beginning to get used to living back in Mammy's house, with all the lodgers. After my father's death, the house had been converted into our bit downstairs, an "open" flat on the first floor – where my mother had lived until she had to go into the home – and three bedsits on the second floor. It gave us a few bob extra and provided company and creative contention for my mother, because it had, suddenly, become a lonely house without the tormented spirit of my father filling every room. My mother had the ground floor living quarters, I had the first floor, and the top floor was divided up into three bedsits. Mammy was, at that moment, in the red-brick Eden convalescent home in Killiney, where she was not, strictly speaking, convalescing but dying. I was back in my old family home, and it looked like I would be staying there indefinitely. So myself and Anna now had a house each, I passed her on some maintenance each week, and we had sorted out the arrangements with Aoife in a civilised, grown-up fashion. *Yeah, right.*

The uniform boys arrived then, along with a snotty, curly-haired little wanker from *The Irish Times*, who appeared out of nowhere, full of cleverboots college-boy questions. The smell of sick was still in my mouth, but the sourness came from somewhere else.

"Listen, don't get in the way here. You might contaminate the scene."

The Dublin middle classes were obviously developing a taste for local crime, in between the stock reports, Doonesbury and the letters page. What would my late father, the great journalist Jack Barrett, have done? Probably snivelled, deferred to myself and Squirrel and written some harmless account of the murder in the next day's paper. *Harmless*. The worst word, beside paedophile and politician, that I could apply to anyone. It's hard when you come to the conclusion that your dead dad was just a hopeless old wanker, though. It means you spend half your life trying to get your own back on the rest of the world, on his behalf.

But where was I? Ah, yes, myself and Squirrel were just hoping against hope that it wasn't politicos who had killed Larry McMenamin – retired Provos looking for a golden handshake – because it was easier with the local unwashed and the local brainless who, thank Christ, lacked the group ethic of the politicals. In a way, that's how it all looked at first. Something exotic but essentially local. Maybe in connection with McMenamin's little anti-drug crusade. Since he hadn't managed to get the Brits out of the north, Larry McMenamin thought he would have better luck as an anti-heroin hero. Maybe a hired out-of-town hand had been brought in to top him. Myself and Squirrel were good on guesses that night, but, all ballstalk aside, we knew, in our heart of hearts, that we must treat this killing a bit more seriously than the others up on the board. We were hoping against hope that the killing had nothing to do with the forthcoming Arland trial – a political hit, in other words. But what did McMenamin mean when he said, "You're going to find out something that will make Arland look tame"? I found it hard to believe that McMenamin had been taken out by one of his own, for whatever reason. For one, he was still on cover from his old republican friends. And for two, he was a sort of hero for some of the liberal journalists around town. And for three, the blowback would be just too much for whoever had ordered it.

By the time Breen, the tubby little coroner with the bow tie, had arrived from his batchelor's mansion out in Castleknock, it was all hours. We didn't get back to the station until nearly four. When I slipped into the bathroom to douse my face with cold water, I took a good look at myself, reluctantly. Face firm enough. Slightly thinning black hair on top. Sallow skin I had inherited from my father. Little dodgy Norman DNA along the line somewhere. With the five o'clock-in-the-morning shadow, I might have passed for a wandering Italian. Nothing love, a strong laxative or a good night's sleep wouldn't sort out. I drew myself up straight. Must lose a few pounds here and there. Get round to ironing the odd shirt, that sort of thing. Might be reasonably presentable then.

It was half five by the time I got back to my lonely old house in Drumcondra. Where I had become so uptight and emotionally dead that I even suffered from wanker's block. I slung Papa's battered briefcase with the Arland Properties papers on the floor beside me and kissed Aoife's photo goodnight, like I had done every day for the past year since I had moved out of the family home. All I wanted to do was go back to the house in Rathfarnham: to my wife, who was sick of me, my daughter, who seemed to be slowly forgetting me, and a nasty Jack Russell called Georgia. Then I collapsed into sleep, forgetting all about the man with half a face, the cold pizza and the separation papers, and slipped gently into sleep.

Chapter Two

TWO DAYS AFTER Larry McMenamin was topped, I was in the witness box at the Arland bombs-for-property trial. Court 18, in the Four Courts complex, was abuzz with legal vertebrates: snotty senior counsels snorting at one another across the courtroom and My Learned Lord shifting uneasily on his perch. The paying public, in the gallery, were belching and farting and rubbing their hands with glee. I had to give evidence of the raid on Merrigan's, solicitors. I felt like a slow learner, a little Christian Brothers' boy thrown in into a lions' den of big lads from Belvedere, Gonzaga and Clongowes Wood. When I dressed up, I always felt like Tallaght-in-a-suit. My arms and legs just seemed to come from separate assembly lines. Still and all, myself and Squirrel were the ones who had bypassed all the tribunal bullshit and ratchetted the whole business up to the level of a criminal investigation, which is what it should have been in the seventies, when my faint-hearted father was still around. Maybe now we were finally going to see some politicians in the dock. I really wanted to see some of the high-class scumbags slopping out their cells in Mountjoy, instead of quaffing Earl Grey down in Shelton Abbey – the gentleman's jail for yuppie criminals down in Wexford.

In the crowded public gallery that very first day, I caught a glimpse of old Tom Hunt. He looked grey and stooped and he squinted as he scanned the courtroom. Now, Tom Hunt was one of my father's heroes, even if my father wasn't one of his. He was the goody-two-shoes superintendent who had tried to take them all on in the seventies and who, for his troubles, got sent to the damp Gulag of Kerry, to a little station beneath Mount Brandon where, on a nice day, you could see the American tourists getting pneumonia in the mist. I didn't think Hunt copped who I was at first, then I saw the eyes narrow and he gave me a little wave, like you'd give a nervy child on its second day at school. It was just in and out of Court 18 that day, which gave me time to go over my case notes again, see the solicitor about the separation deal and make a few more laid-back inquiries into the Colombia-style execution of the late Mr Laurence McMenamin.

There was a big confab back in the station that afternoon. Lots of lukewarm coffee and cigarettes. Inspector Daly, with his coronary-in-a-can face, came all the way from town just to sit with myself and Squirrel and our station sergeant, O'Leary. O'Leary, all rheumy, seen-it-all-before eyes, fiddled with a pencil and looked straight ahead, as if he was being interrogated himself. All together in the royal room for a chat on matters pertaining to. O'Leary was a squat, unimposing little man for a station sergeant. At times, when he turned around to catch my eye in the day room, he reminded me of a depressed frog, with his bulbous eyes and neckless head and his big, broad, mother-of-twenty arse. I learned early on to play ball with him. Even depressed frogs can be humoured.

Squirrel poured coffee for us. It was all suspiciously civilised. In hindsight, I should have spotted Squirrel's involvement straightaway, but what you don't want to see, you can't see. O'Leary was anxious to show Daly that the Arland case was not allowing us to forget matters closer to home. He tapped his coffee cup with a spoon, his big thick shoulders shaking with the effort, the sweaty bald head bobbing up and down.

"Detectives Barrett and Murray have already interviewed . . . how many, lads?"

"Fifteen, to be exact."

"I see."

"And we're coming up with a picture are we, Tom?"

Tom O'Leary nodded. Then we all repeated the standard mantra that it looked like a case of the local lads taking out an anti-drugs activist who had got too cheeky. Daly let on to get real serious. Real seriously.

"But why take such a big risk in killing him, Sergeant Barrett?"

"Well, with a hired hand from the north, it would be much harder to trace."

"Oh, spare me those northern bastards! We had enough of them down here during the hunger strikes."

Daly was all for a United Ireland, Squirrel often said, just as long as it was united with Bongo-Bongoland, and not with us. Daly was an unrepentant Free Stater to the core and revelled in it. When he said Sinn Féin, he meant it one hundred per cent: ourselves alone and screw the north.

Daly stood up suddenly and slapped his thighs. He was a tall, well-built man with a generous, well-groomed head of grey hair that instilled respect and caution in his inferiors. Coupled with a keen Cork accent and an ability to frown on demand, he had made his way swiftly through the ranks, pausing only to pat a head, here and there. Daly said he would be passing through again towards the end of the week. The word from the top was that there were to be no latchico manouevres that might prejudice the outcome of the Arland bombs-for-property case. The government was anxious to show foreign investors and the EU lot that, if we had skeletons in the closet, we could dance with them publicly. Openness, accountability, transparency and all that kind of ball-sology. Any unauthorised and excessive action could blow the whole thing and end up with the case of the decade being thrown out of court. Or worse, being turned back into just another time-wasting, money-wasting tribunal. Daly looked straight at me.

"The source of the Arland evidence is likely to be dragged up by the Arland defence shortly."

"You mean the material Larry McMenamin gave me?"

"Indeed I do, Detective Barrett. The shit will hit the fan when they realise that the material came from an ex-Provo and that he was blown away just before the trial started."

"That won't make the evidence inadmissible."

"No, I'll grant you that. But if we're too busy with the McMenamin murder investigation, it will draw undue attention to ourselves. It might even compromise the evidence."

"I understand."

But I didn't, because it was bullshit. I sat behind with Squirrel in the red room, putting the finishing touches to the cartoon I was drawing. It went something like this:

You looked at it one way and you saw O'Leary. You looked at it another way and you saw Daly. Two cheeks of the same asshole.

But Squirrel was away in space, chewing on his ginger moustache and thinking devious Squirrel thoughts.

"Read out to me what this Catherine James one said again, Barrett."

I took out my blue notebook and flipped it open in great style. Then I went through the whole scenario again. Catherine James. Single mother with one small child, in her early twenties. Out for the night, probably meeting the likes of disenfranchised men like me. Heading back home at about one in the morning and can't make it to the house. Pauses in the laneway to pass water. Has just relieved herself when she hears loud voices and someone being threatened by a northern voice and another voice. Larry McMenamin knows it's curtains for him.

There is a clanging of the killee's head off the big yellow skip. Now Larry McMenamin is crying. Then another clang as his head whacks off the skip again. Our man must be half-unconscious by now. The northern voice says, "Chucky our ducky, Mr McMenamin!"

Then *Blam! Blam! Blam!* And footsteps flying down the laneway. There is no sound from the late Mr McMenamin. Our witness waits a while, until she is sure they are gone. She runs past the skip without looking down, and drops her keys on the path outside her flat. The babysitter comes out of the flat when she hears the commotion. Catherine James gets rid of the babysitter, then phones us. End of story.

Squirrel was standing by the window, doing his looking intense routine.

"Couldn't have anything to do with Arland now, could it, Barrett?"

"Because of McMenamin's evidence? I don't know, Squirrel."

"You don't think it's just marginally possible that one of Brian Toomey's old associates took out a contract on McMenamin? As a favour to Brian Toomey?"

"Why would he bring the house down on himself?"

"It's coming down on him at the Arland trial anyway, Barrett."

"But we're talking about murder here. Do you think a bomb-and-buy conviction is worth the risk of taking someone out?"

"Maybe Toomey thinks it is."

"No one is that stupid, Squirrel."

"That's what they said the week before Veronica Guerin was killed."

"I don't see any connection, and if you do, I wouldn't go mentioning it around anyway."

"So you don't want to check out the Tommy Ellis connection, Barrett?"

"I'm saying, let's be discreet, Squirrel."

"I can do discreet."

"So, let's let the dust settle a bit and then check him out, though I don't see how a little waster like Tommy Ellis can have anything to do with anything. Shallow end of the gene pool."

We chatted aimlessly for a while then, mostly about the great Mr Brian Toomey, TD, a plummy, chummy, gentleman's gentleman who had been up the holes of the highest in the land for more years than he cared to remember. But we live in liberal times, so it was no business of ours whether the ex-minister for justice sank his shaft into half the cabinet. All I knew was that I wanted Toomey. The man who had shot my pa, metaphorically speaking. Squirrel crossed the room, took up my little cartoon and scrunched it up slowly. Then he put his hand on my shoulder and smiled down at me. Papa Squirrel. Baby Barrett.

We had a couple of drinks in the Carlton House that evening. No chance of running into any of our lot there. Too classy for them. Then I headed back to my mother's house in Drumcondra. Now that my mother was in the nursing home and wasn't coming out, I had moved downstairs and rented my old pad, on the first floor. If you wanted advice on renting property, there was any amount of property-owning guards who could give it. Squirrel had a couple of flats in the gentrifying slums of the south inner city and a house in Crumlin. O'Leary himself, though he wouldn't discuss it with the likes of us, was supposed to have a couple of houses too. But I never wanted to get into the property game, even with all the contacts on the force. One house full of tenants was enough for me.

The Kerry girl, the Spanish girl working in the travel agency and the Irish student were company and gave me something to worry about, beside myself. The Kerry girl, Máire, was a fine cut of a Department of the Environment civil servant who had discovered what passed for nightlife in Dublin. I often heard her wander in it all hours of the morning. Christina, the Spanish girl, a penny-wise Catalan who wouldn't squander her substance on fairs and fiestas, kept to herself. The student, a young, surly male from the midlands, went home to Mammy at the weekends, which suited me fine. Too much male about the house was a bad thing. There was a faucet gone in the upstairs bathroom and someone had called to cut off the Cablelink. Great.

Squirrel said he would drop into the nursing home the following morning and say hello to my mother to give me a bit of a break. He knew Anna was back in my thoughts again and I was going a bit nuclear. Too nuclear to be listening to my mother going on and on about my stupid father as she slipped in and out of her mind.

I tried my best not to think of Larry McMenamin. Underneath everything, however, I felt the faint throbbing of guilt: had Larry McMenamin died for Arland, so to speak? Or, to be more exact, had the material I had anonymously-so-far passed to the bombs-for-property investigating team cost him his life? Maybe little Tommy Ellis, out in WOMA, would be able to shed a little lowlife light on things.

Chapter Three

I REMEMBER MY father saying to me once, as he chewed on a Woodbine, his eyes masked by a velvet blindfold, "That little pooftah has balls of brass, Thomas."

It was late 1973, or thereabouts. Brian Toomey was the little pooftah with the balls of brass. Our own gentry. The admiration in my papa's voice was unmistakeable. Here was someone who had screwed the Brits, without having to dismember any bodies. We were sitting together in what passed for a study: the downstairs bedroom, lined with bookshelves and beauty board.

We were playing my father's favourite game: blindfold chess. It was a gimmick he had learned when he was interned in the Curragh, for being a republican fellow-traveller, during the Emergency, otherwise known to the rest of the known world as the Second World War. It went like this: if the game had got to the stage where more than half a dozen of the pawns had been knocked out, you memorised all the positions and donned your little black velvet blindfold. Needless to say, I never managed to beat my father at blindfold chess. And I developed the unhealthy habit, into the bargain, of fussing too much over worthless pawns. In later years, when an investigation took a sudden dip, I would think: *Here we go again, blindfold chess.*

My father was particularly full of admiration for Toomey's

going public and putting his "peculiarity", as my grandmother down in Cork called it, on the public record. Of course, my father wasn't exactly behind the door in the whole affair. He was the Dublin journalist who had first mooted the possibility, among his cronies in the Scotch House, of an interview in a sympathetic British newspaper. No Irish paper would carry the story. There were no homosexual politicans in Ireland in those days. Not even common or garden homosexuals. The headline, when it hit the streets of Manchester, Dublin and London, said simply

Éire Politician Admits to Homosexual Affair

Not that the scribes in the Scotch House, around the corner from the old *Irish Press*, could get their molars round either the word or the concept. I watched the whole thing from the background. There had been vague talk that Toomey was going to be shafted by the British establishment because he had been too negative on extradition. The story was that if, as minister of defence, he couldn't see his way to handing over the odd Provo to London or turning a blind eye to SAS incursions, they would out him as a homosexual. In the end, Toomey decided to out himself and call their bluff. There was a crisis meeting of the party *apparatchik*s in the West County Hotel, on the heels of the threat to Brian Toomey. There were basically two options, from the old stagers' point-of-view. Either

Toe the Establishment Line
OR
Tell the Brits Where to Go!

But Brian Toomey, sitting sipping his favourite tipple – a brandy and port – chose a third option. To tell the truth. Without informing any of the mohair suits around him. Game, set and match to the pooftah with the balls of brass.

The interview with the *Guardian* took place in Mama and Papa's house in Drumcondra sometime before the summer of '74. It was around ten at night when the taxi with the journalist pulled up. I was watching a horse opera on television. I had just turned ten. On the threshold of unreason, so to speak. The journalist, John Reed, was a big, blocky fellow with a north of England accent. Shirt and tie, jacket and briefcase. The real thing. He wasn't going to let poor Paddy down. The *Guardian* was very "understanding" of the Irish in those far-off days. We were, after all, an oppressed minority like the Palestinians, the South Moluccans and whatever-you're-havin'-yourself. The little matter of the fussy million Protestants who wanted no part of our ramshackle Republic wasn't up for mention at that stage. My father waved me into the sitting room, and my mother went off to boil water. It was all very hushed, though I could hear John Reed's booming Geordie accent against my father's little Dublin whimper.

"The great and the good usually get their way in Britain, I'm afraid, Mr Barrett."

"They usually do here too, if they're let."

It was around midnight when the phone rang. A few minutes later, a car with a serious-sounding engine drew up on the far side of the road. I didn't actually see Brian Toomey that night; I only saw the sulky Special Branch man who was hooshed into the sitting room with me. My father had given in to my request to stay up late. Maybe he thought letting me in on this bit of history might turn me into some version of the *Guardian* journalist. It didn't. It turned me into something closer to the Special Branch man.

It was a year or two later that my father realised he had been sold a pup. Sure, I came to know, years later, that he had been browbeaten, somehow or other, out of investigating Arland 1 because he was compromised over his defence of Toomey, but I could never understand the depth of his bitterness. There were many journalists in Dublin, from the fifties to the eighties, who had to put up and shut up about nasty political secrets. Why did my father have to descend into drink-sodden self-loathing? It was a question I had never managed to figure out. And the letter he had left before he died threw no light on it either. He showed his bitterness mostly in my mother's company during nasty, drunken, vicious exchanges that showed how little he liked himself and how he felt he had been gulled. I always felt there was more to it than Toomey's outing and the early Arland, but you can't bring a dead daddy in for questioning. Mr Brian Toomey's fingerprints were all over the bombs-for-property scandal, of course. And poor old Superintendent Hunt was shuttled off to Kerry for sticking his red nose in too far. And the *Guardian*, that great liberal toe-rag, waded in like an indignant idiot to provide covering fire, to distract everyone. And my daddy, Mr Jack Barrett, was the go-between in the love-fest between Toomey and the *Guardian*. The little pooftah had balls of brass, indeed. And a neck like a jockey's bollox too. So Toomey outed himself and the suspicions about bombs-for-property were carefully swept under both the British and Irish carpets. But it still didn't explain why my dear daddy had drunk himself into an early grave. Did it? Maybe. Maybe not.

I had just arrived in the station from the solicitor's office when I found Squirrel's note about dropping out to Tommy Ellis's house in the wild west of WOMA. I can't say I was much in the mood for it, especially after the warning from Daly. The meeting with my own solicitor, Sullivan, earlier that morning, was enough aggravation for one day. Sullivan, in his pink shirt and navy tie, was polite and terribly courteous though. We met in his well-appointed office in Fitzwilliam Square, where a lot of the guards went when their ex-wives were bent on fleecing them. He smiled through the John Lennon glasses and ran his hand through the blow-dried grey mop.

"There's no point in rushing into things, Mr Barrett."

I imagine he wasn't really that eager to have me on the books, seeing as how I had raided one of his fraternal solicitor's offices the previous August, in the name of Arland. *They really are a little priesthood*, I thought to myself as I sat there. The priesthoods in Ireland went something like this:

Fifties-Actual priests

Sixties-Politicians

Seventies-Republicans

Eighties-Economists

Nineties-Solicitors and Barristers

New Millenium-Journalists

I instinctively mistrusted all the priesthoods, whether they were made up of goody-two-shoes liberal journalists or die-for-Ireland politicians. There would have to be more phone calls between him and Anna's solicitor, he said. There was no reason why things mightn't be settled before the court. And my ex-wife didn't really sound like a vindictive sort of person. She had a job, after all, a house and custody of the child. She would probably be happy with a reasonable amount of maintenance and an agreement on special expenses.

I glanced at Squirrel's scribbled note again: "Give me a bell,

Cyril." I was just about to do that when the Yosemite Sam moustache appeared around the corner.

"Let's go and pay our new best friend a visit, Barrett."

WOMA. West of M50. New estates, old problems. Now, I don't like afternoon raids in working-class estates. The junkies and the dealers and the other losers are usually up by then. We crossed the bridge in Clondalkin and swung right. I scanned the knackered-looking shopping centre at the roundabout and the walking dead lounging around the street corners.

It was Thursday. Dole day afternoon. The Elms would be full of wasters and talk merchants. The tough boys wouldn't appear in the bar until later, though. We swung sharp into Leamington Gardens, an ass's fart from The Elms. If Squirrel's contact was right, bollocky Bill would still be in bed. Points docked for garden maintenance (none); points docked for frontage maintenance too (none). I rang the dead doorbell, then knocked politely. Squirrel slipped around the back, just in case our man tried to do a runner. Which he did, of course. In the shake of a lamb's tail, the three of us were all cosied up together in the sitting room, just running over things. Tommy Ellis was a long shot, though, but maybe not so far removed from the boys who might have put the contract out on McMenamin, all the same. Maybe McMenamin had already been warned before they topped him. There was a lump of hash on the dressing table upstairs and a little white powder in one of the drawers. Besides the smell of booze all over the place, the house was reasonably together.

"You must have a good cleaning lady, Tommy."

I left Squirrel chatting away to Mullarky downstairs, licking his lips and wondering whether he should agree to go down to the station or brazen it out here. There was no silly talk about rights or warrants or all that stuff. Tommy Ellis knew the score. Give us a little leeway here and we'll leave you alone to get back to your loser's life and father another few bastards for the state to suckle.

Upstairs in the boudoir, I stumbled over beer bottles and cast-off ladies' clothing from the night – or the week – before. The second bedroom seemed to be the mail room. The two single beds were piled high with leather jackets, pirated CDs and fake Nike jackets. The alternative economy. But the box room was a different matter altogether, when I shouldered in the door. A little techno den, quite out of character with the rest of the des. res. There were CD copiers, a tape slave and a fairly hefty computer standing in the middle of the whole lot. Tommy Ellis's nervous little voice called up to me.

"Don't break anything up there!"

"Detective Barrett is a very scrupulous sort of person, Tommy."

I flicked through the CDs while I waited for the computer to boot up. Garth Brooks, Fleetwood Mac, Cher. A demand-driven operation. A model of free market enterprise. And all so nicely arranged that I knew well Brainless down below hadn't much to do with it, which also explained his edginess about me entering the sanctum. He was more the hash-dealing, gun-renting type. Holidays in Santa Ponsa twice a year. Fights in The Elms every Friday night. Knew when to change his underwear when it stuck to the floor. Squirrel might to be on to something though, seeing as he was one of the few to have constant contact with our northern friends.

I started checking the computer files. The CD copying software was all there, everything neatly filed and arranged. There must be a second room, somewhere else in the city, that served as the nerve centre of the whole operation. Small beer really, though. I would have logged on to the internet connection only my eye was taken by a couple of rather large files tucked away in the Windows Explorer. There was a series of photo files with shots of young men in their late teens. No names. Just numbers. Suddenly one of the faces caught my attention: a young fellow who had been attacked and left for dead, somewhere around Blackrock. I suddenly realised I was in rent boy territory. Maybe we had just stumbled on the tail end of a rent boy ring, an online one.

"Squirrel! Get up here! Quick!"

There was a note of panic in scumbag's voice below deck, as Squirrel's long legs skipped up the stairs.

"Don't touch that stuff man! It's not fucking mine."

"I certainly hope so, cowboy, for your sake."

I was convinced we had strayed into rent boy country now. Squirrel glanced back down the stairs.

"What will we do with this idiot downstairs?"

"Get a reaction. Then arrest him."

Now, at least, we had some sort of hook on your man downstairs. Squirrel dragged Tommy Ellis upstairs. This boyo wasn't about to do a runner out the door. His eyes widened when he saw what we saw.

"I've nothing to do with that! No fucking way, man!"

"It's on your property, Thomas."

"I thought she was only doing CDs."

"She?"

"The woman who comes here every few days."

"I think you're involved in some sort of male prostitution racket, Tommy?"

"Are you fuckin' mad! I wouldn't have anything to do with them dirtbags! Fuckin' steamers, I hate them!"

"Ethics are a great thing, Tommy. Now get your gear and let's go for a little jaunt in the mo-mo."

We went back to base with Mr Ellis. We didn't put on the blinky-blinky light until we were on the M50. No point racing around on those Third World roads and making shite of the computer in the back. Not that anyone was going to hear much about the computer haul yet. As of the moment, this was just a case of pirated CDs. Me and Squirrel were keeping quiet on this one. Just for the moment. Rent boys. Never know who might be doing business here.

Tommy Ellis wasn't exactly the sharpest knife in the drawer. The likelihood was that he got to do the pirate CDs and DVDs and flog them locally, in return for using the Clondalkin computer as a dead drop for someone else. But who? There was always a possibility that we had scared off whoever was pulling little Tommy's string by raiding the kip in the first place.

I was late phoning Anna that evening, and she ate the arse off me. There was a television blaring in the background. *Bad day at the civil service computers, dear?*

"You were supposed to pick Aoife up at six. I have an appointment."

"Look, I'll be over in ten minutes."

Hump her appointment, I thought, *whoever he is. Touching my ex-wife! Her lovely, long, silken blond hair. And her soft, sensual skin. Looking into those beautiful blue eyes of hers. Bastard!* But I cooled down before I got to Rathfarnham. Aoife bounded into the Audi with her nightbag and her Walkman. I got a big hug and let her sit in the front seat, illegally. Then we dropped out to Killiney for a quiet visit to Granny in the nursing home. Granny wasn't the best and it showed. Cerebral ataxia. Life having the last laugh. Aoife was gawking out the double-glazed window over Dublin Bay when mother gestured towards the front page of *The Irish Times*. There was Mr smoothie Toomey. The man that gulled my da. The headline said,

Toomey to Testify on Arland Tomorrow

which was the first I'd heard of it. As far as I knew, he wasn't due to appear for another week.

Mother smiled at me. I only half caught what she said, through her weak lips, but it went something like, "Wasn't your father a real soft idiot, Thomas?"

But I didn't get in the pool. I had done that often enough, over the years. I promised to call in on Friday and then got Aoife out of the place as fast as I could. I had no intention of phoning Squirrel, because I wanted to spend some talk-time with Aoife. It seemed like a month since we had met, though it was really only a week. But Squirrel must have been thinking his Squirrel thoughts, because he phoned sometime after eleven, when Aoife was in bed and only one lodger was stomping about. But it wasn't Toomey he wanted to talk about. It was about the Clondalkin business.

"There is even more stuff on this computer. Like possible customers."

"Any names we know?"

"Maybe . . . maybe."

I peeped out the door to make sure my daughter wasn't ear-wigging, then I disconnected the phone and plugged it into the sitting room socket. Squirrel had got one of the technos to check out the internet connections and e-mail addresses. Something interesting had come out. Squirrel thought we should discuss "the ramifications" over coffee in the Swan Centre, the following morning. Ramifications. Another bullshit word.

"You're keeping me in suspense, Squirrel."

"No reason why you should sleep and not me. Anyway, not over the phone line."

And so, it had to wait until morning. And so did the ramifications. Whatever that meant when it was at home.

Chapter Four

THERE WAS A tailback all the way from Drumcondra to town the next morning. I tried my best to work my way around it as Aoife jabbered away in the back. It was all caused by a big yellow truck that had gone belly-up at the corner of Dorset Street and North Frederick Street. The road was covered in broken pallets and straw. I stayed in the car and let the uniforms get on with it. I didn't reach St Ide's NS until around ten o'clock. The schoolyard was empty. The only sound was a child's voice chirping away at show-and-tell in one of the infant classes. Aoife goaded me into accompanying her to the classroom. To explain everything and show her daddy off. I hadn't seen the schoolmarm, Ms Deirdre Dunne, in a few months. I tended to let Anna handle that sort of thing. It was mammy territory. And teachers, especially women teachers, found it hard to bullshit the mammies. Deirdre Dunne almost seemed pleased to see me. I remember thinking: *What's wrong in her life?* I took in the black sweater, the black cords, and the giddy Alannis Morisette eyes. I liked bright-eyed, long-legged women. Still. The children were bent over their work when we arrived, filling in workbooks with scrawly, earnest writing. The scratching of thirty pencils amused me. I couldn't help comparing and contrasting the scene with the puke I had dredged up on the Clondalkin computer the day before. Another world altogether.

And always gentlemen behind it. If they weren't doing it with a gun, they were doing it with a knife. If they weren't doing it with a syringe, they were doing it with their dicks. I was beginning to sound like a shrivelled-up seventies feminist with a grudge against the newer girls on the block. And anyway, hadn't Tommy Ellis mentioned a "she", before he clammed up? There were bad bitches in the world too. I oohed and aahed over Aoife's school copybooks, listened with half-an-ear to what Alannis Morrissette had to say, then headed for work .

Reality met me on the doorstep of the station. And it wasn't even ten o'clock yet. Byrne and Guildea were bringing in a couple caught shoplifting.

"Leave him alone, you moxy cunt!"

I smiled at Byrne and Guildea and threw my eye over the charming pair. The young woman's eyes were dim. Not much going on behind them. But El Hombre's aspect was rougher. Postnatal abortion needed there. Dick, knife, gun, syringe. I strode slowly over and rested my hand on mutt's shoulder.

"Don't I know you from somewhere, Mr Fogarty?"

I stayed like that a moment, forehead to forehead, just staring into the bloodshot eyes. Real Christian Brothers schoolyard stuff. You see, I was in the A class in the Christian Brothers, in the seventies. Not the D class, with the dumb and tough ones, but the A class, where a large section of my peers were smart AND tough. But this one hadn't the brains of a basking shark. The scruffy head pulled away from me. Byrne and Guildea wished me a cheery good morning and I followed them in.

Squirrel was out on a call in Ranelagh, but he had left a little blue envelope for me. It was a three page list of e-mail addresses with one address highlighted in yellow: 0.223.887.@hotmail. com.

Or something to that effect. I pushed the envelope to one side and went over the notes I had made the previous day on the Clondalkin raid. Now that Tommy Ellis had been released without charge, I could give a tidy ending to the whole thing. We couldn't do him for soliciting, or being a party to such a thing, without mentioning the computer. I made no mention, in the report, of the computer. Tommy Ellis wouldn't be looking for it back, and we didn't need to tell O'Leary about it. I got myself mentally ready for the meeting that had been arranged with O'Leary and the man from the DPP then. I was halfway through my cup of coffee when the summons from above came.

The man from the Department of Public Prosecutions had a sensitive faceful of stubble and a pair of steel spectacles. Terenure College, I thought. Middle middle class. Certainly not a Jesuit man. Too earnest. Too desperate for success. O'Leary passed me an ashtray. He nodded at the visitor.

"Mr Doherty here has important tidings."

I smiled. No politician would be seen dead near a garda station until the Arland case was done, but someone from middle management had to be sent with the messages. Off the record, no notes, no phonecalls.

"The department and the DPP are very anxious that the Arland case isn't compromised in any way."

O'Leary ran his tongue around his mouth. He took up a copy of the Clondalkin file that I had left on my desk the previous afternoon. In his blustery way, he said that we all had a great service to perform here. This would go into the history books. (Not into mine, it wouldn't. I preferred American Civil War history and Second World War history. Not Dublin scumbag stuff.) Grey suit said that this was a crossroads for the whole state, the first criminal case of its kind. The message was not to muddy the waters. He was rambling on with this sort of shite when a uniform stuck his head around the door and said that there was a taxi waiting outside. Grey suit was gone in a flash. He had delivered his message and, doubtless, was off to his office to make a secret minute of our meeting. Just in case it figured in some future investigation and someone, somewhere could say: "I told you so." O'Leary looked as me as I stood to leave.

"This was all off the record, Detective Barrett."

"So it won't be in the history books, then?"

O'Leary grinned his evil father grin. The grin bad daddies gave when they came in drunk on payday, full of jokes and singing songs, then beat six kinds of shite out of Mrs Daddy when they found the dinner was burned to a frazzle. O'Leary tossed the Clondalkin file at me. He emphasised again that we were to back-pedal on things for a bit. Anything even vaguely connected with Arland had to be referenced upwards to Daly and, from there, to divisional and so on.

Squirrel appeared in a short while later. He had been off sorting out some old doll who had suffered a break-in, down in Rathgar. A grandnephew would liaise with the Neighbourhood Watch crowd about bringing Mrs Wilfred Harrington into the new century and familiarising her with the key concepts of burglars, alarms and locks. Squirrel was gnawing on a salad roll.

"Want a bit, Barrett?"

"No, thanks."

"Where did you get to this morning?"

"Got held up leaving Aoife into school."

I waved the letter with the list of e-mails in front of his nose. Things were quiet around the shop at that moment. Tom Conway was dealing with a passport application at the hatch. A younger uniform was typing something into a computer. Squirrel parked his arse on the desk and dropped his voice an octave to a conspirator's pitch, which sort of made me nervous. He told me that he had had one of the technos do a quick run-through the Clondalkin computer. The e-mail addresses had all been sussed out. They were mostly addresses on hotmail.com. Squirrel said they were dead letter boxes. But one address, accessed only once in the whole year the Clondalkin computer had been running, was pegged to a certain Alannah Harris.

"And who the fuck is Alannah Harris, when she's at home?"

"Ah, Barrett, do you not remember the eighties?"

"I was drunk at the time. I know people who do, though."

Now, if Squirrel had been the melodramatic sort of copper, he would have pulled out an old file photo, there and then. But that wasn't his style. Instead, in his own roundabout way, he made me run through my own mental book of newspaper cuttings, knowing that a journalist's son would have more press cuttings in his head than the average editor.

Now, in the seventies, everything was black and white: marriage, religion, the north, television. It went something like this: you were married, or you weren't. You were a Catholic, or you weren't. You cheered for the Provos and Manchester United, or you didn't. And you still watched an old B/W Bush or Pye, into which the north was poured every night, at around teatime. Remember that stereotypical, over-the-shoulder shot of soldiers sheltering behind a Saracen or a Landrover? Then the camera zooming in as the car bomb went

Ka-BOOOOOOOOOOOOOOOOOOOOOOOOOOOOOM!

The TV camera jerking towards the sky as half a street was

taken out. You rarely saw shots of arms and legs or viscera amid the ruins, of course. (Except, that is, on Bloody Friday, when a big decision was taken in RTÉ to show human offal being shovelled into plastic bags.) You never really saw close-ups of stiffed Taigues and Prods either. Or family photos of the thousand slashes that preceded the merciful release. Or the crumpled up penis stuffed in the mouth to add sexual insult to sectarian injury. Everything was in B/W. Clear and simple. Until the Dublin bombings of 1974, that is, when it suddenly went colour for us down here. 625 lines. And everyone suddenly seemed to know someone's cousin who had been killed or maimed, or had passed one of the three bombs just seconds before. Bombs weren't objects of amusement any more. But why was Squirrel getting me to kerb-crawl through the seventies again?

"Do you remember all the photos of Toomey leaving the Dáil, after the *Guardian* gay article was published?"

"And all the bogmen baying for his blood because his mickey wouldn't stand up when a lady entered the room? Sure."

"Well, do you remember the woman with the dark glasses who walked a few paces behind him?"

"Jackie Onassis?"

"Come on, Barrett! Think, man!"

I closed my eyes and bit into the Styrofoam cup. The images shuffled about before my eyes. Shots taken from the railings around Leinster House. Long focus shots that flattened everything out and seemed to bring the woman in the black glasses closer to the front. A woman with a bouffant hairstyle that was, even then, more than passé. Brave, bold-as-brass Brian Toomey, with his unctuous little solicitor at his side. Mr Laurence Walsh, who would later cream it off in the nineties at all the useless little tribunals the rich and powerful arranged to show that justice really was being done. Until his fat-clotted heart finally gave out, as he lay on top of a paramour, in a Dublin hotel. Squirrel clapped his hands together.

"That was her, Barrett."

"That was who?"

"Alannah Harris. Brian whoring Toomey's sister!"

"And your point is, Detective Murray?"

"This is Alannah Harris's e-mail address. What's it doing on this scumbag's computer?"

"Do we really need to know this, Squirrel? Didn't you hear what Daly and the DPP said?"

Just at that point, we were called out to a little number near Harold's Cross Bridge. Small matter of a junkie wielding a syringe in a sweetie shop. As we rounded the corner and pulled up on the pavement outside Mina's Confectionary, Squirrel looked into my eyes.

"You don't really think the McMenamin thing has anything to do with Arland, do you, Barrett?"

"In my professional opinion, Sergeant Murray."

"Come on, let's leave it, Barrett! Let's nab this mutt."

When I had calmed down poor Mina – she was really a little spinster called Miss Attracta O'Neill – I lashed out into the garden to see Squirrel standing with his gun over a man with a loaded syringe. But it was scissors cut stone. Squirrel was pointing a loaded revolver at him.

"Drop that syringe, my little friend, or I'll ram it back up your arse."

"Get away from me, pig!"

"After I've put a bullet in your leg first."

The spike dropped into the uncut grass, among the red pansies and yellow piss-the-beds. We trussed up brainless and headed back to the station.

That evening, there was a letter waiting from my solicitor with a draft outline of the agreement with Anna's solicitor which I couldn't be bothered going over. I did a real clever thing then: slung it in the deep-freeze until I was in the mood for it, the next morning. Then I dragged out some of Papa's old books of cuttings from the shelves. As I pored over the many shots of Toomey and his sis and the late Laurence Walsh, solicitor, striding out of the Dáil, I began to long for the black-and-white days, where everything seemed so clear and simple. When everything wasn't really so clear and simple. It was just that, in those days, you couldn't see who was in the shadows.

Chapter Five

I WAS NEVER that good at spotting the red lights flashing in my face, little things like my father's final depression, my mother's slow slide into the fog and the disintegration of my marriage. Especially the disintegration of my marriage. Because I was always busy, busy, busy. Always not there, weighing myself down with work so as not to have to think about things, I didn't notice the flashing sign that said, "GAME OVER! GAME OVER!" until it was too late. Until Anna had given up on me.

We first met through pictures and colours. She was giving an evening class in watercolouring at an institute on the southside. I was smitten by her girlish grace, the smile and the quick words. It was love at first daub. I forgot all about magenta, ochre and burnt sienna, dropped the woman I had been dating for six months and made a beeline for Anna, the civil service computer operator with the flair for watercolours. One year later, we were married. Another year later, Aoife was born. And then, somewhere around the fifth year of our marriage, the decay set in. Arguments turned to silence, a septic, sullen sort of silence that went on for a year. The cartoonist and the watercolourist no longer had anything much to say to one another. The shadow of a dead papa snuck up on me like a thief in the night. My mother began to lose her mental moorings and drift out to sea. I went into a sort of silent tailspin. Didn't see the ground rushing up to meet me. The whole thing broke a week or two after Aoife's communion.

A sunny south Dublin Saturday. Aoife was staying overnight with a cousin. Anna called me into the sitting room, where she was working away at this sketch of Bullock Harbour she had started the week before. She slowly wiped the charcoal from her hands and, looking over her shoulders, said almost as an afterthought, "I want to get out of this marriage, Thomas."

"I beg your pardon?"

"I've made up my mind."

"Is this some sort of a joke, Anna?"

But it was anything but a joke. Whoever said that women think with their emotions got it arseways. Women plan months, if not years, in advance. Anna had her contacts firmed up, legal stuff set in motion, support network of girlfriends accessed. She looked me right in the eyes – a cold, distant look – because I just wasn't there. Hadn't been for a year or more now. I might have been fourteen again, being told I was surplus to requirements, at the back of the tennis court.

"Let's face it, it's over . . . dead . . . deceased. OK?"

"You can't be serious, Anna?"

"It's just a question of burying the carcass."

"What the fuck are you on about?"

There were months of little emotional tableaux after that, of Aoife weeping buckets and me drinking myself to a standstill. And Squirrel listening to any amount of nonsense out of me. The closer I tried to get to Anna, the more she pulled back now. Revenge, when it was served, wasn't served at room temperature. By November of that year, I had agreed to move out of the family home.

Mother had gone into the nursing home by this stage. By January, I had begun a revenge affair with a woman garda from Donegal, newly separated herself. I buried myself even more in work, drink and in the biddy from Donegal, who couldn't, even on her best days, hold a candle to Anna. And, in the back of it all, I felt I was being done over again. It wasn't a question of whether you got screwed in life but of who did the screwing. Squirrel tried to call me to order, one tipsy night in the Cat and Cage.

"You're in denial, mister."

"Don't go all Californian on me, Squirrel."

"OK, then. How about, you're telling lies to yourself. You love Anna, right?"

"Maybe."

"And you can't have her. Face it."

"Who says so?"

"Sure. Have it your way, Barrett."

It was too late by then anyway. It was now over a year down the line since the afternoon with the charcoal sketch of Bullock Harbour. I wasn't in denial any more, just deeply pissed off about life and living. I was crying quietly, when I wasn't panned out from overwork. I couldn't get it up enough to satisfy a seventy year old any more. With love went lust. And once the lust was gone, everything went. My Donegal rose was well away by this stage. There was just me, the three wise lodgers, the weekly visit from Aoife and the visits to my mother. At least I was back to drawing cartoons. That much was a good sign. Squirrel thought so too. I did pictures of Disney characters, with Dáil politicians' faces, and even made a few bob doing caricatures to order from photographs. I sold cartoons, from time to time, to *Magill* and *The Phoenix*. It was loose change for beer and cigarettes. It helped me pretend that everything would one day be right again, but it would never be right again without the watercolourist with the blue eyes. Ever.

As I recall, my first full session at the Arland trial was a severely sunny day. Guards in short sleeves. Girls without goosepimples. A melatonin-challenging sort of day. The Brits were there, with the Germans and the French – all our EU buddies – just to see that Paddy really was washing his dirty linen in public and not doing the tribunal caper again. I slept in my suit on the sofa the night before. I reckoned that, if I slept my way into the suit, I might feel more natural in it. I still felt nervy in front of the legal savants though. The opposition were the best hired guns in the land. They had the shivering balls of any number of senior politicians, bank personnel, solicitors and other assorted worthies in the palms of their grubby little hands. If things went wrong, someone might actually end up doing time over the bombs-for-property scandal. A strange concept in Ireland. Or, as O'Leary kept repeating, as he chuckled into his coffee, "It's our own Lester Pigott, lads."

I didn't want to see Brian Toomey go down alone. There were a few more I wanted to see done, like that bastard barrister Keenan, for a start. He was the one who had fired the shot over my father's bows when the penny finally dropped about Arland, way back in the seventies. Served a few personal writs on him. I knew there had been rumours around, which I heard about much later, that my father had been threatened out of investigating Arland any further, but I was still left with the question of why my father had chosen to drink himself to death over a noble silence. In other words, should you really kill yourself over property? I was hoping that the mangy bank manager, Callaghan, who had salted a lot of the dosh away in the Cayman Islands would do time. A right jolly gem with a gut on him must have done grievous bodily harm to many an American Express card. And there were at least two politicians still living, apart from Brian Toomey, who were up to their brass necks in it. It would be good to see a nice liquorice allsorts done down. In other words, I wasn't going to do anything to prejudice the outcome of Arland, including looking awkward in my old wedding suit. I pictured my mother's smirking face in the nursing home. The badly applied lipstick. The skittish eyes.

"Wasn't your father a right fool, Thomas?"

I shared a lunchtime sambo with Squirrel in Coman's in Rathgar. Squirrel had been on a stake-out for a wages hold-up at an electronics warehouse down in Bluebell. As it happened, no one showed up for the appointment. Either one of the gang smelled pork or there was a tip-off. It was taken as read that the bad guys couldn't break into the secure phone and mobile lines any more, but I was never entirely convinced of that. The office slaves around us started drifting back to their desks. We could stretch our legs a bit now and pump up the volume. The barmen were only too happy to leave us alone, having been run off their flat feet over lunch hour.

"When's the trial, Barrett?"

"What trial?"

"The separation thing."

"It's not a trial. I haven't murdered anyone. I might have wanted to, but that's no basis for a trial."

"All right, when's the case then?"

Squirrel adjusted the awful blue polka-dot tie his wife had bought him. He glanced around him, tweaking his moustache.

This meant he was getting to the point, but what point? I suddenly noticed the clock.

"Christ Jesus! We're late for the CAB meeting, Cyril."

"Now?"

"Ten minutes ago."

"Ah Jaysus, Barrett, you could have told me."

It was half two by the time we were driving in through the big black gates of Harcourt Terrace. Squirrel had already dealt with the boys in the bureau just before Christmas, in connection with the Mulhuddart heroin seizure, the biggest raid we had been involved in. I ran my finger over the snazzy little brass plate by the door.

Criminal Assets Bureau

Our own little gang of Eliott Nesses. How well we couldn't have done it before Veronica Guerin was topped.

Squirrel opened the door in front of me, and we swept in, full of apologies. Redmond, the head honcho, kept us waiting precisely the same amount of time we had kept him waiting. Outside in the office, we sat sipping expensive spring water, bottled and sold in the wettest country in western Europe. Sand to the Arabs, ice to the Eskimos, water to the Paddies. The door finally opened and the great man appeared. Maurice Redmond looked like a building society manager, the sort who could foreclose on a mortgage with a smirk and a friendly word.

"Detective Barrett and Detective Murray, isn't that correct?"

"That's right."

"Sorry for the hold-up, lads."

Redmond had no fuzzy edges. He was the type who never broke his watch in school. And a nice, shiny office it was too: a big computer with a big screen on a big desk, filing cabinets, shelves of box files and everything in apple-pie order. This was where they tried to seize the big bucks from the major dealers. Not the pocket money of the undernourished, tenth-generation losers in WOMA. No, this operation was where the accounts of the smart bad boys were looked at, because everyone was dead keen on taking the money from the bad boys now. We had finally understood that jailing them, humiliating them, harassing their wives and children counted for nothing. But take their money and toys away and they became distressed. Even the Brits were flying in to see how it was done. Learning from Paddy. Oops! But the truth was that without the murder of Ms Guerin at Newlands Cross, a few years earlier, none of this would have happened, because the politicians were quite happy with the status quo in "the ghettos". But when Ms Guerin snuffed it, shivers went down the spine of the Superquinn mummies. *It could be us!* It was the only time I had ever really seen Anna irrationally angry.

"They should shoot the bastards who did it!"

"Aren't you the one who doesn't believe in violence?"

Now we were all in the firing line. So, hey presto! The toughest anti-drugs legislation in Europe.

Maurice Redmond invited us to sit down, with a wave of his manicured hand.

"I've been asked to run through our take on the McMenamin business."

The call for this session with Redmond and the CAB had come all the way down the line, from Inspector Daly through O'Leary. No doubt about it. Still, I instructed my brain to listen and shut up, although anything Maurice Redmond would have to say probably wouldn't be worth much. I threw back the last of the

Kerry water. I had drunk better tapwater in Drumcondra. Squirrel was given special permission to light a cigarette, although we understood, of course, that this was a government office. Redmond adjusted his honeysweet voice.

"McMenamin may have been going to blow the whistle on a few boys in the south inner city."

"I see."

Myself and Squirrel went all sincere. And sincerity, as the saying goes, is the most important thing in life. If you can fake that, you can fake anything. Redmond turned the computer monitor around on the desk. There were dates and numbers on the file, records of meetings and phone calls. It appeared that the late, great Larry McMenamin, through an intermediary, had been in touch with the bureau. It was all above board, of course. I stared at the screen. The dates started about four months earlier, then stopped a few weeks before McMenamin was topped. I glanced at Squirrel, who paid no attention to me.

"Now, why would Larry McMenamin be telling you what you knew already?"

I glanced at Squirrel again. Why was he bothering his arse asking such a thing? Maurice Redmond swung the screen back towards himself. He was a cop who didn't like being questioned by the police, apparently. This was his little fiefdom. And yet, in a niggling sort of way, the whole exchange seemed awfully rehearsed.

"We never refuse information, Detective Murray."

"Of course not."

"So, we just let him talk, and we ended up with a fresh list of names for cross-reference."

"Ah . . . cross-reference."

"Yes, we have programmes that do all that now."

It got a bit rambling after that. I started doodling in the corner of my *Irish Times*. Hexagons and octagons and pentagons and every other type of gon. Anything, not to start drawing faces, Redmond's face in particular, because I felt a caricature coming on and I could hardly keep it in. It would have to wait though. The gist of the thing was that Redmond, along with his colleagues, felt we were in a punishment shooting scenario. Perhaps whoever ordered it had only meant to scare McMenamin. After all, who would want to kill a gentle, retired Provo, with friends still "on the force", so to speak. Squirrel smiled his fake half-wit smile.

"Am I missing something here?"

"Yes, Sergeant Murray?"

"How does shooting someone three times, in the face, constitute a warning?"

Redmond got a bit touchy at that point, because he thought he had the answer. Or he was letting on he thought he had. His thesis was that the northern hired hand had lost the run of himself, being used to blowing away other people for anti-social behaviour and so on. We both nodded enthusiastically then, on cue. I said that it made a certain amount of sense. But where did that leave our investigation?

"Well, now, Sergeant Barrett, I'm not going to tell you how to run your investigation, but personally, I have a feeling that . . ."

"Yes?"

"That Mr McMenamin may have well known his killer."

"Ah, and why do you say that?"

"Well, from the evidence of Ms James, and let's face it, these northerners all have the same alma mater: the Maze, Magilligan and Crumlin Road."

We stood up and shook Redmond's clammy hand. He prom-ised us help in locating any files we thought relevant. He passed us a few pointers on Mr Thomas Ellis from Clondalkin – good old Tommo, who was lying very low now – but it didn't look like much of a lead. Squirrel blinked, but said nothing. We could have nipped over to the Harcourt for a coffee then, but since the gardaí had been bugged by subversives from that side of the street only a few years before, it seemed reasonable that the gardaí themselves might keep a weather eye on the other side of the street now. There was no point in chatting in the station or on the phone later. So myself and Squirrel took a detour by Sandymount Strand, where we sat sipping coffee in the car like a non-communicating married couple out for the day, watching the rich old dolls out promenad-ing their dogs and the children playing in the sand. And the power station stacks pumping sulphur dioxide into the air over Dublin Bay. Squirrel slung his plastic cup out the window.

"Have you no breeding in you, Detective Murray?"

"It was beaten out of me, so it was."

Squirrel picked at his teeth and made that funny face of his. He spoke without looking at me. "You don't buy all that bollox, do you, Barrett?"

But I was busy drawing a cartoon on the side of an envelope. A cartoon of a man in a shirt and tie, sitting by a computer screen, with a word balloon coming out of his mouth. I offered Squirrel the chance to fill in the word balloon. He took the envelope and wrote, in his cramped little Christian Brother's hand: "Piss off my patch, lads!" Then he scrunched the envelope up and sent it fly-ing after the plastic cup.

If I had checked the general computer mail that day, I might have noticed the e-mail that had been sitting there a day or so.

My name was spelled wrong on it: "Det. Serg. Barett". I always hated that second R being left out. As I say though, I didn't get the message.

Myself and Squirrel still hadn't reached a decision on what to do about the Alannah Harris e-mail address. Sure, it connected McMenamin with Toomey with Tommy Ellis, through McMenamin and Alannah Harris, Toomey's sister – but what did that say? It was all up in the air. Which had nothing to do with the fact that, later on that night, having visited Mother in the nursing home, I had a real skinful in the Cat and Cage. When I rolled home at about twelve, I insisted on phoning Anna, pleading with her not to go ahead with the court business. With my trial, as Squirrel called it. Anna's voice was calm and cool and collected.

"It's all about finality, Thomas . . . closure."

"Closure? What am I, a fucking limited company?"

I didn't even want Anna to consider taking me back. I would agree to any conditions she wanted in the agreement between the solicitors. Just no court. No closure. To leave some hope that we just might get back together. There was silence at the other end of the line. Anna said, slowly and carefully, "I'm leaving down the phone now, Thomas."

"Well, I'll phone you again."

"And if you do, I'm phoning the guards."

"I am the guards."

"Don't push it, Thomas. Go to bed. Grow up, be a big boy."

Anna was going ahead with the "trial", that much was clear. The truth was that she had once loved me and she needed the whole court production to prove to herself that it was all over. Like that friend of Squirrel's on the New York Fire Department who was obliged to take the pulse of jumpers on the subway tracks, even if their bodies had been cut in two by the current. I woke the next morning with a mouth on me as dry as a camel's armpit. Cursing my stupidity, I rolled out of bed and drove, still half-drunk, for the station.

Chapter Six

MYSELF AND SQUIRREL still kept a weather eye on grumpy little Tommy Ellis, with his Saddam Hussein moustache, out in WOMA. We got permission for a few phone taps here and there. Not that we were really expecting anything. Maybe a few juicy phone calls or a few interesting numbers on the phone tracking system that might show up the names of a few possible clients. We kept the dope charge and the possession of pirated goods charges hanging over Thomas Ellis though. He needed to know we cared. Then we let him off, to go back to his girlfriend, his dope and his fake Nike jackets.

The Arland trial was up on the blocks for a couple of days because a question of admissibility of evidence had gone to the High Court, so I had a little more space to deal with Larry McMenamin's killing. Mind you, the papers were happy enough to believe that the killing was just another case of the muck killing the muck, so we were left alone to get on with it. We hadn't decided what to do with the information about Alannah Harris though, whether to bury, burn it or nose about a bit more. But the shadow of Arland fell on everything, and when we got a bit jumpy, we realised we should probably let it go. It was one thing to bust a solicitor's office and bring down a government. It was another thing entirely to go down in the history books as the ones who had fluffed the pass. But I strayed from protocol, in the end. I'll admit that now. I didn't want to make a big deal of it to Squirrel. And Danny Mulhall was my own contact, after all, the one who had put the late Larry McMenamin my way, with his Arland information. Mulhall was a suave republican hero from the seventies, an old contact of my father's who didn't figure in the headlines any more but who was still there, oiling the wheels behind the scenes.

I spent that Saturday afternoon holed up in the house in Drumcondra. Tenant B, the male postgraduate, had just finished his doctorate and was off to the States on a fellowship. An ad in the paper had brought out dozens of potential tenants from under the rocks. Viewing time was between eleven and twelve. I sat into the sitting room and spread the English papers out in front of me: the *Guardian*, *The Times* and the *Independent*. An old habit of my father's – the English papers at the weekend. I munched on a slice of toast, sipped my coffee and thought, "Things could be worse."

There were quite a few visitors that morning. First was a young couple on social welfare with their very first illegitimate child and a look that said: trouble down the line. No, thank you very much. Then a couple of women students who were working in town for the summer. I shortlisted them. Even if they were out riding the range all night, they would keep the place clean. A scruffy yoke on a motorbike turned up then, but as soon as he smelled cop from me, he lost interest in the room. I made a mental note of the motorbike reg. The one I took, in the end, was an Italian woman in her fifties, with steel-grey hair, who was here to do a Joyce splurge for the summer. Her main qualifications were her age, lack of social welfare status and the fact that she didn't have any *illegitimati* with her. And she was paying cash. Angelina

Marcusi had the sort of sunny disposition that came of living in a better climate, with good food and drink. I left a message on the answering machine, saying that the room was gone, then brought Angelina into the kitchen for a coffee. That much I had learned from Anna, along with how to use a washing machine, how to fold my clothes and how to do bills. I liked the idea of having an intelligent, warm-hearted woman around the place for a while. A house wasn't a home without a woman wandering about, commandeering things. I looked my new lodger up and down. Angelina would have the "open" flat on the first floor, which meant she would be using my kitchen and living room. I would be, in a manner of speaking, half-living with a woman again. After the fashion of women scanning another woman, tip to toe, I did a silent recce of Angelina as she stood there. Fiftyish. Fine features and a gentle smile. Black, pearly eyes that spoke smartness coupled with kindness. I knew, right away, that I would get on with Angelina Marcusi. I could feel myself warming up already, because a little panic alarm was already ringing in my inner ear: *Steady as she goes, Barrett!*

Angelina left her little leather briefcase down on the kitchen table.

"I am going to give a new course in the university on Joyce and the city, in the autumn."

"And you're going to take a course here first?"

"My course will be my feet, Mr Barrett. I will walk the streets and read and talk to the people."

"Call me Thomas. Most people don't read Joyce, you do realise that?"

"This is the same with all great writers. In every country. I have this map of Dublin in my head . . ."

"Well, I've got one in my head too – I'm a policeman – so I can help you a little."

I dropped Angelina off at the corner of Parnell Square later that morning – she wanted to talk to someone in the Writers' Museum – then I headed north to meet my man. Not too far north, of course, because Detective Thomas Barrett wasn't about to cross the international border with the United Kingdom of Great Britain and Northern Ireland, just for a chat with an out-of-season Provo. Not as much as an inch across the border. Nice semi-literate headline it would make:

Arland Detective Stopped by Northern Cops with Provo Boss

Danny Mulhall obliged me by meeting in an ugly barn of a pub near Balbriggan. The Black and Tans, as history records, had burnt the town of Balbriggan, but they had only half-finished the job. That's the trouble with having ex-cons in your auxiliary force. I was sitting at the bar when he entered. The whole place seemed to sense, at once, that this was someone. The little huddle at the bar drew closer. They hated Mulhall, on the instant, and feared him, the way a cat will rasp at a dog at the same time as its hair stands on end.

Danny Mulhall was a youngish man when my father first met him, right at the start of the troubles. In those days, no one in the south believed the Provos had plenty of sectarian bastards among them. When journalists wanted to give credit for statements given to them by some thug in a Dublin bar, they would say, "*Sources close to the movement state that . . .*" It was all very gentlemanly. The Provisional IRA had neglected to mention that, Godspeed and the Devil tarries, when they were finished up north, they would be down to sort the southern quislings out. I never had much time for northerners, Catholic or Protestant. To me, they were all fundamentally lacking in a sense of self-criticism, were either playing orange flutes or doing Irish dancing, and gave you a pain in both ends when you sat in a bar with them. Still, they never really had to take on the south for, if they had, they would have found us twice as unenthusiastic about their cause as the other lot up north. We would have wiped the floor with them – gloves off; no British Queensbury rules – like we did with more than a few of them on the back roads, in Dev's time. As Mulhall himself once said to my father, "Scratch any southerner and you'll get a Free Stater."

Danny Mulhall was under no illusions where my sympathies lay. Like Daly, back in the station, with ourselves alone, and a plague on both their whorehouses up there. In his sports jacket and tie, with the close shave and well-groomed head of hedgehog hair, Danny Mulhall might have been a school principal on the first day of the school holidays, heading for the golf course, his mind free of whingeing children and whingeing teachers.

"Thank you for coming, Danny."

I was still the da's boy all the same. I knew you had to lick their arses before you licked your reporter's pencil. Danny Mulhall smiled fleetingly. We got straight to the point. He knew the basic details of the McMenamin thing, of course. Without, oh dear me and pass the smelling salts, knowing exactly who was at the top of the chain of command of the various republican cabals at that particular moment. Danny Mulhall must know chapter and verse about the principals involved at the height of the Arland business, the reptiles who had offered to bomb places for profit. Not that bombing them for a cause would make any permanently maimed shopgirl whose face was scarred for life feel any better. Some of the seventies lot were dead, of course, killed in action or stiffed by a cocktail of the ubiquitous Ulster fry and booze, but many were still around. Only a couple of Mulhall's actual colleagues were mentioned in despatches in Arland. Mulhall's hands were clean on that much, which was why he was able to authorise McMenamin to shovel all the documentary evidence in my direction that started up Arland. I never quite got my head around what was in Arland for Mulhall, beyond making himself appear squeaky clean in the new post-conflict Ireland. Maybe he really did feel my father's memory needed to be rehabilitated. Mulhall said he would check up the bits and pieces I asked him and get back to me, through the usual channels. He sipped at his orange juice and crunched on the ice.

"Great spot of weather. Are you a golfing man at all, Thomas?"

"I sometimes have a few drinks up in the club . . . Edmonstown."

Mulhall cast his eyes around the bar. Everyone was studiously being seen to be not listening to us.

"Great game, golf. Gives you time to think. Relax."

Great interview that would have made for my father, in the seventies, when they were all in thrall to the Provos after Bloody Sunday. I thought of the sort of craven headline my father might have written.

Top Provo Says: A Good Round of Golf Relaxes Me!

Five minutes later, I was on the road back to Dublin, just marginally uneasy about Mulhall's surprising willingness to travel down to see me. Wondering what was in it for him. Perhaps putting some distance, for the future, between himself and Arland days. I asssumed that he had some bit of business to do down south too. Spot of Provo golf with a baseball bat afterwards maybe. I knew that he would check things out for me though. Discreetly. Now that peace was in the air. And now that peace was both profitable and popular.

I was late back to the house because of dropping in to see my mother in Killiney. She was in good enough form. She was very bothered about the whole question of some new sort of poll tax being brought in. Hadn't the English already done that and thrown it out? That was the great thing, I told her, about having the Brits next door. Bigger economy, bigger projects, bigger mistakes, from which we could learn. Ergo, we only had one serious attempt at high rise flats in Dublin, and those, Ballymun, were being pulled down. When I arrived back in Drumcondra, Angelina was sitting on her suitcase, surrounded by bags. I apologised, telling her I had forgotten the time. I told her we could work out the finances later and dragged her down to the kitchen for a spot of tea. Then I nipped across the river to the station and picked up the diary I had meant to take home when my shift ended the day before. One of the young lads doing cover told me there was an e-mail waiting for me. It was surprising there weren't any more. I read it as I headed back out the door.

Netherlands CIB
Dept of External Affairs
Amsterdam
Ref: SRJ/OS/283
Dear Det Sgt Barett,

Please contact me at the earliest in connection with the above ref. Thank You,
Det. J. Wollenweider

I couldn't be arsed phoning there and then, so I left it until I was home with my feet up on the coffee table, watching *Match of the Day*. For good luck, my Dutch counterpart was in the office late that day. He was a chipper sounding bloke with that unnatural sounding English that comes from early immersion courses and too many American sitcoms. It appeared that Declan, aka Dekko, Tierney, an Irish thug arrested almost a year previously in Holland, was scheduled for extradition the following week. He had been an old and close associate of Mr McMenamin's in Dublin. Before there had been a parting of the ways, that is. There was a suggestion that he might know something of the current case. As I was in charge of the case and it was a standard extradition (relating to a seizure of heroin out in Mulhuddart), Wollenweider suggested I might be interested in travelling to Holland to bring the boy home. *Home is right*, I thought. It was the first I had heard of Dekko Tierney's impending extradition, and I was a bit caught off-guard by it. I told Jon Wollenweider that I would get back to him before the evening was out, which I did, having spoken to O'Leary at his home number. I was given the green light to travel, without any great to-do. I was to travel with with Detective Sherwin, rather than Squirrel, as Sherwin was the one who oversaw all the legal stuff on our side.

I must have been feeling *flaithiúlach* that evening, because I made a great show of bringing my new Italian guest for a spin around the city – with a map, of course. Then I capped it all by bringing her for a meal to a little restaurant off Suffolk Street that myself and Anna used to frequent, a long, long time ago. A few days later, with Arland still being debated in the High Court, a jolly Dutch detective would be doing the same for me in Amsterdam. After all, we were all in Europe now. When it suited us.

Chapter Seven

TOO MUCH THINKING about flying is taboo. But, no matter how hard I try not to think about it, when I take off in that aluminium tube, I always expect the tail of the plane to scrape off the runway. To see trillions of sparks, hear a terrible scream of metal and concrete and then

Kaboom!

It doesn't of course. And I'm not really interested in finding out why not, having been stupid enough to listen to a boozy pilot in a bar in Howth once, going on about V1 and V2 and how a plane can abort take-off if it hasn't passed the V1 mark. But pass V2, however, and it's commit to take-off time. And I was always poor at the commitment carry-on. Then, of course, there's that stomach-churning business of the plane banking on take-off, to break up the G-forces, so that the thing doesn't do a loop-the-loop and end up, a heap of sophisticated wreckage, on the runway. I should never have listened to all of that stuff, because it made flying even worse. I was thinking all these fine thoughts when myself and Sherwin, the legal shotgun, took off from Dublin for Amsterdam that morning and mulling over the fact, at the same time, that I hadn't gone into the whole thing with Squirrel. He would have caused too much V1 and V2 panic in me.

There was lots of turbulence crossing the Irish Sea, as per usual, and loads more crossing the North Sea. We touched down at Schiphol in the late, grey afternoon. During the flight, Sherwin, busy with the extradition documents and the little matter of scumbag's last-minute appeal to the Dutch courts, had scarcely spoken a word to me, because Dekko Tierney was coming home to the bosom of Mother Ireland, the new Ireland of the Criminal Assets Bureau. Tierney, we had discovered, had made several threats in Larry McMenamin's direction, in the year before his death, and had been implicated in a scare-shooting too. It wasn't a lot to go on, but a little pressure might do wonders. I was still surprised that O'Leary had agreed to letting me go so readily. Maybe this was my little reward for learning to be case sensitive. At last.

The fast train in from Schiphol was full of dope-eyed Dutch dippers. You could spot them a mile away. When I tapped Sherwin on the shoulder at one stage, a couple of hostile eyes scanned mine. We were ruining business. Like a rooster in a hen house who has sniffed the fox on the night air. We took a taxi to the hotel in the Jordaan area, a sort of gentrified working-class district, and I threw a couple of post-flight beers into me. It was around six that evening when the phone rang in my room. Our friendly Dutch bobby was down in the lobby. Jon Wollenweider was a little, fair-haired thirty-something. No beer-gut and no beard. He just wouldn't have fitted in back home. When Sherwin had to scuttle off to the midnight court because scumbag Dekko was pulling out the last legal stop, myself and Wollenweider headed downtown to the cop shop. It wasn't the best time to visit Amsterdam though. The North Sea was shipping in a lot of non-Euro weather, and the streets were streaming with cold, sleety rain. Still,

I wasn't there for the climate. Wollenweider's office was on the third floor of the police building. It was as immaculate as Redmond's back in the CAB office in Dublin. Wollenweider ran through the whole story about the charming Irish gangs who were to be found in Amsterdam, Rotterdam and the Hague.

"You know, Holland is a very small country. Smaller as Ireland, Thomas."

"So I hear."

"But we have a very big population."

"Standing room only, they say."

"Pardon?"

"Nothing, nothing."

"But we have good intelligences into the Irish community. Fortunately, they drink a lot and we hear things."

It seemed that Dekko had come to light because of a drunken row in a Thai restaurant in Rotterdam. An argument over the bill, a lot of swearing, and then idiot goes and pulls a piece. Doh! No marks for subtle thinking there, Paddy. And that coincided with Dekko's name appearing, on our side, in the Mulhuddart heroin inquiry. Then in the McMenamin investigation. So a Dutch special unit, wearing natty black balaclavas, nabbed scumbag on a street in Rotterdam. Leapt out of van, with their Heckler and Kochs at the ready and slipped a black hood over Dekko's head. And – oh, dear, the shame of it, back home! – Dekko went and scuttered his pants. Right there, on a spic-and-span Dutch street. *More of this*, I said to myself, *and they'll be throwing us out of Europe*. Wollenweider offered me a cigarette and we lit up together.

"Very embarrassing for him, of course."

I explained to Wollenweider that, in Dublin, there had always been an overlap between criminal elements and paramilitary elements. That a certain symbiosis existed on the fringes of both groups. This led to occasional co-operation on bank robberies, securing untraceable weapons, protection money and drugs. But, sometimes, the arrangement broke down. The interface over drugs was one such area. The politicos wanted to be seen to be hard on drugs, but too much gun-play in working-class areas would have the opposite effect. Not to mention causing a turf war on the streets of Dublin's housing estates.

"So, Mr Tierney is in the middle, somewhere?"

"Well, we believe Declan Tierney was involved in this earlier attack on McMenamin; that he may know who did the killing, even helped with the logistics."

We sucked on our cigarettes solemnly. There was a moment for reflection, then Jon Wollenweider stubbed out his Marlboro in the ashtray.

"But Tierney was in Holland, in this time."

"You think?"

"We know, Mr Barrett. On the other hand, as you say, he may know things."

"Did I say that?"

We took a tram towards the centre of the night-life in Amsterdam and, pushing our way through the crowds, dodged in and out of doorways as the sky broke over us. Wollenweider went through the shortlist of names, most of whom I knew: chaps who lived between Holland and Ireland, when they weren't spending their hard-earned euros on the Costa del Sol. Most of them, they just kept an eye on. The rest, dumb fuckers like Dekko or ones who were wanted by us, were shipped back ASAP.

"Let's have a drink, Thomas."

We were in the door before I realised it was a gay bar. The whole trappings: leather, lights, action. But this was Holland, and everything was in the right place, like a Swiss hippy's backpack. Even the strobes at the back of the bar seemed strategically placed. Wollenweider called for a couple of lagers.

"Loosen up, Barrett. You'll get your man. This late court session means nothing. He'll lose. Enjoy yourself!"

Out of the place I thought I'd never get. I was terrified, in case my awkward posture at the bar would be read by some roaming Romeo as a coy come-on. A couple of dark-skinned charmers nodded at Wollenweider along the bar. They had to know he was a cop, of course, but then, this was probably his style. Nose up every nook, so to speak. No wonder they had the drunken Paddies so well sussed. When we finished up our drinks, we walked on in the rain towards the red light district.

"Look, I'm too old for this sort of stuff."

"I'm just showing you my town, Detective Barrett."

There were quite a lot of porn shops open, even at that time of night. The fevered cock knows no clock, of course. Wollenweider dragged me down a side street into one, nodding at the middle-aged man behind the counter. It was the usual fourteen year old's sweetie shop of fantasy. Or a sixty year old's. But not mine, just yet, thank Christ. I caught Wollenweider nodding at the patron again. Then a door opened, quite dramatically, in the back wall.

"This is the heavy stuff, Barrett: violence, bestiality, snuff movies."

It was the real stuff, all right. All orifices serviced, all bodily functions catered for. I didn't really need to see people defecating in one another's mouths though. But it was the selection over on the right hand side that Wollenweider had brought me to see: the snuff movies and the serious sado-masochist material. I glanced back at Wollenweider.

"Why do you allow this stuff to be sold here?"

Wollenweider pointed at one of the corners of the ceiling. Did I not see the lens? Of course I didn't, because it was one of those new-fangled fibre optic things that specialists use for looking up your arse or down your throat.

"We record all the crazies who come in here, especially the ones that look like they have an interest in violence. In what the Americans call rough stuff – real rough stuff. Then we have them on tape and can keep them on file."

"Isn't that like leaving bags of heroin on a junkie's doorstep?"

"Not in our point of view. Do you know how many crazies there are in Ireland?"

"Not officially."

"We know here. And we think we underestimate it by, maybe 20 or 30 per cent. There are even some women on the tapes, some women crazies too."

"Equality is a great thing, they say."

I didn't mind traipsing around the cold streets of Amsterdam for the rest of the evening, but I had had enough of gay bars and porn shops. I got whatever point Jon Wollenweider was trying to make. And the company of a gay cop was better than looking at Sherwin's long face for the night, or hanging around in a Dutch court, watching Dekko Tierney play the oppressed Irishman. We ended up back on the Dam Square. Where, if my peers' seventies memories served me right, the Dutch police used to hose down the hippies every afternoon, on the dot of five, before they would all go slink off to get stoned and sleep in the Vondel Park. Before heroin, Aids and inflation, that was.

"You should have seen the seventies here, Thomas! I was very young then, of course."

"We're all paying for it now."

"Oh, don't be so negative, Thomas. I'm sure they said the same thing many years ago."

"Yeah, in Babylon and Rome."

Wollenweider raised his hand and a taxi pulled up beside us. I assumed I was being dropped back to the hotel, but then the taxi headed off in the opposite direction. Wollenweider didn't say a dicky bird until we were both out on the pavement and the taxi had gone whooshing off in the rain. He nodded up at the apartment building in front of us as he took out a set of keys. This was the apartment some of the Irish latchicos – including Dumb Dekko – had once used as a *pied-à-terre* in Amsterdam. Lots of through traffic. As we entered the building, an old lady leaving out a trash can looked at us quizzically but carried on. The apartment, two bedrooms with a large sitting room, was on the fourth floor. Everything had been removed, of course, right down to the amateur chemistry lab in the second bedroom – the site of the little ecstasy operation. Wollenweider reached into the inside pocket of his leather jacket.

"Present for you, Thomas. You remember you asked me to see if there was some connection with that computer you seized in Dublin?"

It was a flash disk that contained all the relevant stuff found on the laptop in the apartment. A laptop which, officially, was still in the hands of the Dutch police.

"We found a couple of connections between this computer and the Dublin computer with the rent boy material."

"A definite connection? You can establish this in court?"

"If necessary."

"It's all off the record, right?"

"Like the best police work."

I slipped the flash drive into my jacket. Now I had a connection between McMenamin, Tommy Ellis's computer, Brian Toomey, through Alannah Harris, and now Amsterdam – and the possible killer of McMenamin. It wasn't beyond the bounds of possibility that McMenamin's killer – the northern one – and his southern accomplice were simply birds of passage from the Netherlands, part of the criminal fraternity who had popped home to do a nixer. In that case, it might not be all that difficult to track them down. We could start with Wollenweider's Irish watch list, work back through travel and transit records – the ones the Americans let us look in on as we pretended we weren't looking, just following the standard EU protocols – and then do a little more checking on both sides of the North Sea. Things were looking up. We took another taxi, and I was dropped at the hotel in time to see Sherwin appear, brolly unfurled, fresh from the midnight court.

"How did it go?"

"No problem. Mr Tierney will be joining us tomorrow. See you down in the lobby at eight for breakfast."

Myself and Wollenweider watched Sherwin head off to the lift. I could have done with another drink then, but I didn't want my companion to get the wrong idea. Wollenweider reminded me, once again, that the flash drive, officially, didn't exist. Sherwin wouldn't get to hear about the flash drive, that was for sure. I didn't need a legal sermon and turbulence and Dekko Tierney for company, all at the one time.

"I must visit you in Dublin, Thomas."

"Any time, Jon, any time. I'm sure we'll both keep in touch."

"I think this too."

Yes, I could just see the tight little bum strutting around the station and O'Leary giving me the eye. Cyril would be less bothered about it than me, because he was still married and was beyond suspicion. I had a solo drink in the hotel bar and headed for bed. In the morning, after breakfast, we picked Declan Tierney up from his holding cell in Wollenweider's spic-and-span station, signed the papers and flew back to Dublin. The plane's tail didn't scrape off the ground at Schiphol either. There was just V1 and V2 and the G-forces breaking up as the plane banked on take-off. And lowlife between us, slowly realising that his idyll in Amsterdam had come to an end, all because of a drunken night in a Thai restaurant. My heart went out to him. Indeed.

Chapter Eight

O VER THE NEXT couple of days, I sat in on the preliminary questioning of good old Dekko, watching his snarling mouth and half-closed eyes. That put-upon look that said: the world hates me. Now, Dekko Tierney wasn't the strongest card in anyone's deck. He was more like the wild card, the one the others used as cannon fodder, when it suited them. It didn't take long to work out that Dekko's previous assault on McMenamin was as much the handiwork of others as his. The earlier shooting incident, at McMenamin's girlfriend's house in the south inner city, seemed to be just a contract warning shot to McMenamin to leave the local dealers alone.

McMenamin's exit from the Provos hadn't been a sweet business, of course. After all, he wasn't exactly throwing in the towel with the sea scouts. But, even if he no longer had the active protection of his former comrades-in-arms, the deal with the Provos was that the past was the past. That much I had got from Danny Mulhall when we met in Balbriggan. So Dekko Tierney's earlier assault on McMenamin looked like it was related to his anti-drugs activities. Looked like – and maybe that was the whole point. Neither myself nor Squirrel reckoned that dumb Dekko was running enough RAM upstairs to bear a long-term grudge. But one thing I did feel was that both he and Tommy shit-for-brains, out in the

WOMA house, probably had a line to whatever technical genius ran the rent boy racket. And that line probably went through Holland and connected up with whoever had been contracted to top McMenamin, whatever the real – as opposed to the apparent – reason was. It was for this reason Jon Wollenweider gave me the flash drive.

The day after I got back from Amsterdam, myself and Squirrel paid an unannounced visit to Tommy Ellis. We were over in that direction anyway, about a BMW that had been stolen in Terenure and used in a ram-raid in the early hours of the morning. Tommy Ellis looked like he had just got out of bed. He met us at the door in a grubby T-shirt, maggoty jeans and scruffy runners.

"What do youse want?"

"Just a social call, Tommy. But we can go back and get a warrant, if neccessary."

Squirrel slipped upstairs while I sat into the kitchen with Tommy Ellis. Now our host was a bit jittery. Too much of something or other the night before. I was standing, just staring into what passed for a back garden – there were breeze blocks and plastic bags thrown everywhere – when I heard a woman screaming upstairs. I nipped up the stairs in time to see a young, blonde-haired woman beating Squirrel's barrel chest with her little fists. Squirrel had obviously had a look around the box room to see if the tenant had been back, then peeped into the room with the sleeping princess. He retreated down the stairs, smiling, as a shoe flew past his head.

"Tommo! Get them fuckin' pigs out of here!"

"That's very unladylike language."

"And don't come fuckin' back, youse bastards!"

The little bristly moustache of Tommy Ellis looked out at me from the kitchen. He knew what was what. I spoke in a whisper, telling him to remember the computer.

"If your computer friend running the rent boy racket comes back, Tommy, give us a bell. Until then, we'll consider that the machine and the files are yours."

There was a brief case conference that afternoon. Just myself, Squirrel and O'Leary. Word from the Police Service of Northern Ireland in Belfast was still that the McMenamin operation was a contract killing, possibly by someone who had gone all commercial after the ceasefire. In all probability, the killer had been brought in from the north, with one or two people in Dublin in on the act. Myself and Squirrel had decided to play down the WOMA connection. It seemed too important to be letting people take notes about it. We both had a gut feeling that the computer wizard might know a bit more about the McMenamin business. O'Leary drew spiders' webs of connections on a scrap of photocopying paper. It was all very logical. Only myself and Squirrel didn't want to put him on overload, so we just nodded along, watching him trace out the names we had already eliminated from the case. Needless to say, we said nothing about the Alannah Harris connection either. O'Leary bit into his pencil.

"So it looks like the crowd in Belfast have it about right. They have a list of possible players they're going to send us. Maybe you two should have a word with that witness again."

"Catherine James?"

"But don't overdo things and get people upset."

"We understand."

I dropped out to the nursing home to see my mother later that day. It was a warm summer's evening, and some of the old ladies were sitting out in the garden, chatting to one another. It was hard to talk with the crowd around, but I was like a dog with a bone. The same sort of conversation I had avoided for over twenty years, I was now courting. I wheeled my mother back into the sitting room, and we sat in the corner while some of the others played whist or read books. Mercifully, the television was kept to a little room further down the hall. It was all very civilised.

"You know the Arland case is up and running now."

"And why wouldn't I know, Thomas? Do you think I never read a paper or watch the television?"

I knew well that my mother could only manage a few lines in the paper now. The headlines. The big picture. I let her lead me down the path then. Get herself into a tizzy, for the thousandth time, about my father's foolishness. It was starting to make a bit more sense now. Finally, "What foolishness?"

"Ah, you know what I mean. Toomey was behind that Arland business all the time, and the other skullduggery."

"What other skullduggery?"

"It's so long ago now."

And that meant the files were still closed. I suppose, up to that point, it wasn't so much that I thought Brian Toomey was innocent, but that I considered him more as a glorified gofer than a Machiavelli. Anyway, I told myself, everything will come out with Arland. And then my mother was off on her hobby-horse again, but this time she seemed a little more sympathetic towards my father. Strangely so, in fact.

"There was the north and all to that. No one wanted to know, Thomas, and then, when your father did wise up, the legal crowd shut him up sharp, him and the paper."

I winced at the mention of my father's gullibility; at how the great Jack Barrett, an investigative journalist when they were very thin on the ground in Dublin, had been shafted. She rambled on with the whole story again: about how my father had helped Brian Toomey out then found he had been gulled by him over the Arland affair; and the half dozen writs lying around the city, just in case any publisher did find the balls to publish things, then my father's slow decline in a puddle of whiskey and beer. Slow, self-pitying decline. And suicide. Why couldn't he have borne up to it, like the hundred and one other snake-eyed journalists who had shut their eyes over embezzlement and child abuse and planning corruption over the years? Why did my father have to be the soft-ie who went under with his glorious conscience? He could have resurfaced, as an old man, and made a mint out of tut-tutting about what he had covered up with all the other journalists, in the fifties and sixties and seventies. What had made my father so special? But my poor mother had no answer for that.

There were three key memories I had of my father: barrowloads of books, a red pack of Carrolls No. 1 on the desk and a blue notepad. I left mother with a CD I had picked up a couple of days before called *Faith of Our Fathers*. It was a collection of hymns that no one under thirty now recognised much. Even the cover had an air of 1932 and the Eucharistic Congress in Dublin about it, when the papal envoy had commanded the hundreds of thousands of pilgrims in the Phoenix Park: men in soutanes and surplices whose very word was law. Another Ireland altogether. And welcome to it they were.

The following morning, I had to put in a brief appearance at Arland, in connection with some picky detail of the raid on Merrigan's, the solicitor's, that backed up the physical evidence Larry McMenamin had given me. Details of transactions, ancient bank accounts and hidden beneficiaries. I was in and out in ten minutes, and Brian Toomey wasn't in court, thank Christ. I was finding it harder and harder to cope with the idea of standing there watching those little eyes read my thoughts, especially as my own distrust of Brian Toomey was growing deeper with the days. What was it that had driven my father to distraction about Brian Toomey? Was it just Arland or was there more, as my mother had hinted? It was at times like this that gossip was badly needed, but the sort of gossip I needed was gossip from the seventies, and that didn't appear in the book of evidence.

Outside the courtroom, I was waylaid by Tom Hunt, with his blotchy skin and tired eyes. He rested his hand on my shoulder. He seemed out of breath, though we hadn't walked very far. All that damp air down in Kerry. If his body was weak though, his mind wasn't.

"We'll get him this time, won't we, Thomas?"

"Be sure of it. Be sure of it."

As he turned to go, he stopped. It was all a bit theatrical, as though he was letting on to be having an afterthought. Only Tom Hunt didn't seem like the sort of person who ever had afterthoughts; they were all forethoughts.

"How are things going with the McMenamin case?"

I muttered something vague then, knocked about slightly that he knew about my involvement in the McMenamin case. But, of course, that really didn't mean much. Ex-guards, like serving guards, especially at senior level, gossiped like ould wans. He would have heard a few things here and there. I didn't pursue the matter further with Hunt though. I watched him make his weary way off to where he had parked his car, illegally of course, outside the Bridewell.

Squirrel didn't put much pass on it when I told him about it. However, when I let it out, gently, that I had met with Danny Mulhall in Balbriggan, he got a bit hot under the collar.

"You should have told me what you were doing, Barrett."

"So you could have talked me out of it?"

"So I could have . . . kept an eyes on things."

"I don't need a surrogate father, Squirrel."

I had borrowed a drive from Squirrel's son and gone through Wollenweider's flash disk on my own computer, making notes on the contents. Most of it was mundane stuff, but I took down all the addresses and so on, to have them cross-checked. I didn't expect to find Alannah Harris's address again. I knew there was a connection with the Clondalkin computer – Wollenweider had told me so, in Amsterdam – but not one as blatant as that. I wasn't looking for it, but there it was, staring me in the face. Now, what were we to do? Reference upwards and speak to O'Leary and then Daly? Squirrel took a sip from his pint.

"You can bug an e-mail line, Barrett. Did you know that?"

"Look, this is getting dodgy, Squirrel."

"Is right, and you go meeting with Mr Mulhall, in the middle of Arland? Are you in your right mind, Barrett?"

"It was just a hunch."

"Hunches are for amateur journalists, Barrett."

"Like my father?"

The truth is, I was beginning to sound like my father: scared. Squirrel got the gen on all the computer stuff from the son, of course. It was all a bit technical for me, but I got the gist of it.

"Look, we know the number that account is downloaded from; it's a floating account, like hotmail, and it's only being accessed from Alannah Harris's home address, in Rathgar. It could be that she has been soliciting for her brother, at arm's length."

I looked into Squirrel's eyes. "Is this all legal, what we're thinking about doing, Squirrel?"

"Well, it's not illegal, yet. It's just a phone tap, after all. The rest . . . the rest is sort of nebulous."

"Nebulous. What a great bullshit word."

Now, there were many questions floating around in my head. Like, who was the mystery man or woman behind the WOMA computer? Was he/she the one who had mediated the contract on McMenamin? All that speculation was standard stuff. A few queries here and there among co-operating parties would throw up odd sightings of northerners, who were as welcome in Dublin working-class areas as rain in July: tolerated, but not welcome. I had a strong feeling that finding out the rent boy runner's identity and whereabouts would give us great inroads into the McMenamin thing. We both agreed that we shouldn't put too much faith in the PSNI list from Belfast, but not say as much. That we should drop in on a few prominent northerners around town. Be seen to be seen. But the Alannah Harris business was a few notches above the regular level of investigation. We couldn't be seen to be seen there. This was really getting too close to Arland for comfort now. Even if we did show valid cause on the premise of a connection with the McMenamin case, we should steer the whole thing well away from Arland. Or the whole case would sink in a week.

"What do you think, Squirrel . . . seriously?"

My compadre downed the last of his pint. His eyes were clear. Cyril clear.

"Let's sleep on it, Barrett."

But there still seemed to be something he wasn't telling me. Was he getting his own back on me for doing a solo run on Mulhall? Hardly. But I somehow knew that Squirrel was holding out.

I had hoped to sleep on something else the following night – namely Ms Deirdre Dunne, schoolteacher. I flattered myself too much though. The end-of-year school concert with the chirpy little school choir, the tin whistle group and the pantomime had given me an opportunity to approach her. When most of the children and parents had left, I made a great show of helping stack the chairs and disconnect the PA system. Then I offered teacher a lift home. I was a bit too gung-ho, but so what. Ms Dunne didn't exactly blow me out that night, but she didn't accept my offer of a drink on the way home either. I dropped her back at her apartment on the quays around midnight, happy, at least, that things were warming up again. When I got home, Angelina was standing on the doorstep.

"I forgot the keys, Thomas! What a big stookawn, I am!"

"Stookawn? That was one of my father's words. I haven't heard it in years."

I let Angelina in and we had a nightcap together. We laid a large map of Dublin out across the kitchen table and, over the second whiskey, went over the salient points, like The Ormond, the National Library and the Martello Tower in Sandycove.

I fell to sleep in a nice whiskey haze that night. I woke the next morning with the 1970s owl-faced image of Alannah Harris in my mind though, a still from the black-and-white footage of her running from the Dáil, behind her brother and the solicitor, that day back in 1973, when all seemed right with the world. Brian Toomey had leaped out of the closet, my father had defended an innocent man, and our little liberal hearts beat stronger. I had the bit between my teeth now, because my mother was right – my father had been a fool. And it had cost him his life, in the end. I wasn't going to stop now, no matter where the Alannah Harris thread led. If it all blew up in my face, I could always go down and live in Kerry, in the rain. Tom Hunt's bitter words were still in my mind, sealed there with just the tiniest touch of vanity.

"We'll get them this time, won't we, Thomas?"

"Be sure of it. Be sure of it."

But I wasn't really that sure of it at all. Playing chess was bad enough, but playing with a blindfold was dynamite altogether. At least I had some training in that department, even if I had never won a game against my father. The problem with blindfold chess was that you had to know which pieces were left and where they were. I didn't even know that much, and I didn't realise that Squirrel was behind me, goading me on silently and watching my every move.

Chapter Nine

I SUPPOSE IT'S a sort of unwritten rule: thou shalt not have it off with thy child's class teacher, but lonely is as lonely does. And, to put it bluntly, the dog in my pants was beginning to take me for a walk at this stage. So when myself and Deirdre Dunne met up the next time, it was all hands on deck. I had signalled earlier to Angelina that I was bringing back someone for dinner that night. The reaction was quizzical, if not downright frosty. (*What's up with her*, I thought. *What does she care?*) I visited my mother earlier on that evening. She was sitting out on the veranda facing the sea, in her little blue cardigan with the red flowers. Making what passed for conversation with another old lady.

"Do you see that little boat out there, Eveline?"

"I don't go to the sea much any more."

"That big red boat."

"It's too crowded, anyway."

She perked up when she saw me. I thought, for just one moment, that I saw a tear in the corner of her eye, as though there was something she wanted to say but couldn't quite articulate. A couple of minutes later, Anna appeared out on the verandah in a yellow top and jeans. I hadn't being expecting her and I was thrown off balance.

"How are things, Mrs Barrett?"

"Grand . . . grand . . . and . . . you . . ."

We sat on either side of my mother, awkwardly. When a nurse took the other old lady off, myself and Anna made an effort to swap civilised sentences with one another. A plane was bearing in over the sea for Dublin Airport. My mother shielded her eyes as she looked out to sea.

"Is that big plane coming from America, Thomas?"

"Europe, England, somewhere like that."

"I hope it lands safely."

"I'm sure it will. I'm sure it will."

After chatting with the matron in the front office, I walked with Anna to the car park. Now, there was no need for her to wait for me. I thought, maybe she just wants to soften the blow of the court business, which had been slated for October. At least it wasn't going to be one of those wife-beating, drunken husband affairs. None of the usual sort of stuff that clogged up the courts. I wanted to reach out to Anna, there and then; to run my hand through her blonde hair and say, "What about the El Molino for dinner?"

With all due respects, I would have dropped Deirdre Dunne like hot snot if Anna had been willing. My ex-wife-to-be turned towards me. The little frown had been replaced by a half-smile. She called me Thomas, which set my teeth on edge straightaway. It sounded very much like breaking-the-ties strategy.

"Look, Thomas, my solicitor is dead against it, but why don't we try and sort it out before we go into court."

"And what's in it for me, Anna?"

"Peace?"

"I'll think about it."

I waited until she was well gone down the driveway before

letting the whole thing well up in me. *Fuck! Fuck! Fuck!* I banged the steering-wheel. Gritting my teeth. I had thrown away gold, and I knew it.

I was getting very tired of courts. Arland was running that morning, and I had been in the box again. The smarmy solicitors swanned around the courtroom taking little pecks at me.

"So, the initiative and authority for the raid on Mr Merrigan's office came from where exactly?"

"Haven't we been through this already?"

"Please answer the question, Detective Barrett."

After my less than glittering performance, I killed a half-hour in the Wig and Pen before heading back to the station. There was a message from Jon Wollenweider in my e-mail. It had only been there a day. It read:

Hello, Thomas!

Good to make contact with you. Phone me as soon as you can.

Jon

Although the tone was a bit palsy-walsy for an inter-force message, I phoned right away. Anyway, I wanted to clear it with Wollenweider that I could say the Alannah Harris e-mail address-es came from him, if the shit hit the fan later on down the line. An ass that wasn't covered was an exposed ass. I didn't want to end up, in twenty years time, in the middle of a retrospective court case myself. Allanah Harris's connection had to be looked into though, because, besides the fact that we now had a connection between the WOMA computer and the Dutch one, there was the more specific question of why Alannah Harris's e-mail address was on both. Surely you didn't need to go through a Dutch comput-er to hire a bum boy for the night? Myself and Squirrel had decid-ed that we should camouflage the surveillance with a couple of other requests for taps. We discussed it on the way to look at a burned-out car in Ranelagh that had been used in a petrol station hold-up, earlier in the morning.

As we walked around the blackened wreck, I said to Squirrel, "This Alannah Harris connection is probably important, I'm afraid."

"That's what I was afraid of too."

Before heading back to the station, we dropped into technical in Harcourt Street to have a word with the boys in the white coats and the grown-up look. A young techno from Gorey with a funny lisp dealt with us. I just wanted some help in getting my head around a few facts. Almost all of the e-mail addresses in the WOMA computer and on the Dutch disk were dead drops. Some of them were redundant. Others had recently received encrypted messages collected from them. Most of the servers, according to Whizzo in Harcourt Street, could be a daisy chain of laptops, in any country you liked. Or any collection of countries. A sort of mathematical progression that couldn't be figured out with a simple formula. You could trace the senders the pick-ups and drops had originated from, but that didn't mean much. The hotmail.com stuff and all the other free mail accounts could be accesssed from umpteen sites. Encrypted messages could be left to post the location of the next open site. Equally, laptop servers could be opened and shut at will. Cyberspace was everywhere and nowhere. Squirrel got to the point.

"Is it possible to trace where these contacts are?"

"With the help of the service provider, yes."

"And without?"

"You would have to put a trace on the line and see where the stuff is coming from."

"Can we read it?"

The little garda geek in the jeans grinned at us shyly, like a baby who had just broken wind.

"You can, actually."

"What does actually mean, in that sentence?"

"If it's not encrypted. You can tap it digitally and reconstruct it digitally, roughly speaking."

"And that's all legal, of course?"

"It's still, technically, just tapping the line, as long as you don't interfere with the service provider."

"We're back to nebulous, Squirrel?"

"I'm sorry, Detective Barrett?"

Squirrel clapped him on the back. We were in. Or, rather, we were not. The Alannah Harris tap was slipped in with another couple of taps. It looked, among the others, drug-related, which was what we wanted. It should look to the outsider as though we were looking for an overlap between the McMenamin case and the Mulhuddart heroin case, a few months before. Although it still seemed to us, even at this late stage, that it was just a drugs and murder case, it was getting more and more like sex would have some role to play in things. Syringe, gun, knife, penis. But I had the location all wrong, as it happened, because neither Amsterdam nor cyberspace was where things would eventually end up. I didn't honestly know this when I suggested to Deirdre Dunne, when I woke beside her the next morning, that we take a weekend away before she headed off to America at the end of July. I didn't know it at all. At least, I didn't know it with the front of my brain. Sometimes you know, but you don't know, if you know what I mean. Gut feelings seemed to me located somewhere in the back of the brain, in the monkey department.

Chapter Ten

THE ARLAND TRIAL was becoming a solid wall of newsprint, courtesy of *The Irish Times* and the *Irish Independent*. The minor figures were dispensed with first, naturally enough: gunslingers like myself and Squirrel, revenue inspectors and a couple of look-the-other-way accountants. The real star of the circus made his first lengthy appearance about a week after I finished my spiel. Brian Toomey looked hale and hearty on the TV screens that evening. He was gone to fat a little, as we nearly all must in our late fifties. As I watched the footage of him leaving the Four Courts, I thought back again to the old black-and-white pictures of Toomey, his solicitor and Alannah Harris, making their way through the crowds outside the Dáil. I remembered sitting with my father that evening in the late autumn of 1973, watching the nine o'clock news, the sharp smell of a smouldering Woodbine in the ashtray beside him.

"The British thought they could make a fool of us but it backfired on them!"

I went along with my father's celebration of Toomey for a while. After all, what did I know? The liberal thinking was that, however ulterior Toomey's motives were, they helped, in a roundabout way, to get a sympathetic hearing for the gay brigade. Not that Toomey wanted any connection with that lobby. If they wanted to wash their dirty jocks in public, he wasn't going to be part of it. Over the next year or so, it became clear to most that Brian Toomey's coming out had more to do with self-interest than it had at first seemed. The sinking of Arland investigation Mark 1, in the seventies, was followed by Tom Hunt's exile to Kerry and the silencing of several newspaper editors.

Myself and Squirrel met up with Catherine James, who had overheard Larry McMenamin's northern executioner as she cowered behind the skip. Now Catherine James wasn't too eager to see us again. Her long dark hair looked more unkempt than usual. The thought of someone – even a northerner – being topped like that had upset her greatly. She didn't want us anywhere near the flat and her child, so we met in the Carlton instead. Myself and Squirrel sat into a quiet corner with her, but took no notes. Through bitter lips, she told us she was sorry she had even reported the killing in the first place. That her family down in Limerick had given out to her about it. She wasn't going to testify either. Myself and Squirrel let that pass. We would deal with that when the time came. No point getting into dirty talk about subpoenas. I ordered Catherine James another bottle of Carlsberg. She bit her finger nails.

"I mean, it's not like I'm out on the town every night."

"We all have to get out now and then, Catherine."

Squirrel did the family man routine. Everything works out in the end, sort of caper. Catherine James's story was much the same as the first time. Through weepy sniffles, she told us that she had definitely heard a northern accent. Along with the local one. She hadn't made much of the Dublin accent first time, maybe because a northern accent, of instinct, spelt no good to her.

"So, a Dublin accent and a northern one?"

"That's right."

Now, short-term memory, as the mongrel in the street knows, is sometimes affected by stress. That's why a second or third interview is often more important than the first. We reckoned we would get a little more from Catherine James than we had at the first two interviews, and we were right. She was more comfortable with Squirrel than with me. She had got it out of me that I was separated. A potential cat out on the tiles. I took a quiet mental note of everything she said though. And the way that she said it.

"Do you think McMenamin knew both men, Catherine?"

"That's what I think now."

"Why is that?"

"Well, he called one of them by a sort of nickname . . . Brownie . . . no, Bruno . . . Bruno."

"Bruno, was that it, Catherine?"

"That's what I think it was: Bruno."

I looked away from Squirrel and called for another Black Bush. I stole a sideways glance at our star witness. Catherine James wasn't making this up. And no such name had been mentioned in the papers, or by us, for that matter. When we had finished our little parley, I dropped Catherine James back to the corner of Belgrave Square. I suddenly felt a little uneasy about her safety now. Uneasy enough to want to put her on her guard, but not frighten her.

"Look, just keep our conversation quiet, Catherine."

"Why?"

"That's what we tell everyone. It can prejudice the investigation."

I gave her my card again, telling her to give me a buzz if any fresh details came to mind. Squirrel was idling over a second whiskey when I got back to the Carlton. He read my thoughts.

"Are you thinking what I'm thinking, Barrett?"

"Maybe she heard wrong."

"My eye, Barrett."

"I suppose you're right. A man with a gun pointed at his head is probably going to shout out the right name."

"Where is the little bollox now, anyway? No, don't tell me, Barrett."

"The Netherlands. Bruno Downes's name was on Wollenweider's Irish watch list."

I didn't tell Squirrel, just then, that I had arranged with Deirdre Dunne to have a dirty weekend break in the Dutch capital. That I had already made up my mind to have a second, entirely unofficial, meeting with Wollenweider. Pass a little info his way about wayward Paddies in return for any more info he might have dug up. I hadn't expected Bruno Downes's name to crop up. Maybe this would lead us nearer to the phantom rent boy impressario in WOMA. Maybe McMenamin's northern nemesis was somewhere in the loop. I just didn't want to have to get there by way of Alannah Harris, if at all possible. Anyway, the Amsterdam link seemed like it might be enough to get the McMenamin case rolling. We could then roll with that, do the business at the Arland trial and pass on the Alannah Harris information at a later date. If at all. Alannah Harris's involvement in things had to be peripheral. Didn't it? In a way, I just didn't want to know. Like my father before me. I didn't want to know because it might upset everything. I still had an awful feeling that, because it might not be possible to circumnavigate the well-rounded personage of Alannah Harris, there might be no choice but to go through her. I asked my creator, silently, to let the chalice pass from me, knowing full well that life never works like that.

Aoife's eighth birthday was a couple of days later. I brought her and a gaggle of her little squeaky friends out to a Disney film in town. We had a party back in the house. Angelina waded in, making little cakes and a tart that they all wolfed down. There were curious faces when the parents arrived to pick up their progeny and found Angelina dancing around the sitting room with streamers in her hair. I thought to myself again, *Of course, we're all in Europe now*. And now we had our very own Euroscumbags. Dekko Tierney, Bruno Downes and the detritus of the northern barney.

Myself and Aoife sat up late that night, drawing cartoons together. I did a picture of a Papa Bear and a Baby Bear and she insisted on drawing in a Mama Bear. We moved on to less sensitive pictures then. Wolves and rhinoceroses and a child in a wheelchair flying through the air, from a story I had once told her, years before. She was colouring in the armrests of the wheelchair when she said, without looking up at me, "Why did you leave me, Dad?"

I tried to keep my composure. After all, I was talking to an eight year old. I must be reasonable and sensible and adult. But my daughter's eyes bored into me. So I just hugged her and told her how much I loved her.

"I'm sorry it worked out like this, Aoife."

"But why did you leave me? Why don't the two of you go back and live together?"

Which was the same question I wanted to ask Anna. Myself and Aoife never got to the end of the explanation, of course. I ended up falling asleep beside her and not waking until the next morning, which was Saturday and, for once, a day off. I woke to Angelina thumping the bedroom door. Aoife was downstairs watching TV.

"A phone call for you, Thomas."

I looked like shit warmed up in the bathroom mirror. I was glad I didn't remember my dreams. They must have been awful. The Gorey techno was on the line. I waded gingerly through his lisps.

"I thought you might want to hear what's going on with that new surveillance, Sergeant Barrett. I wasn't able to reach you yesterday."

"Is it important, do you think?"

"Well, it's your call, like. No way can I go into it on the phone."

So it was another jaunt into Harcourt Street, past the security gates and the young guards on duty. I had never been in the surveillance room before, just read whatever transcripts came through for us. There was the expected array of computers and magic boxes. A couple of guys were sitting huddled over screens. I heard one say to the other, "There's the Kilkenny line. Log on."

No one actually had to plug anything in any more. No one had to climb up telegraph poles. Maybe they never really did. My own personal techno stood up to shake hands, brought me out into the office and handed me over a couple of pages of transcripts. I glanced through them. They were e-mails that contained nothing but numbers.

"It's code. They're not using words, and they're shutting down and opening up servers, to confuse anyone who's trying to break into their ring."

"Like pass-the-parcel?"

"More like musical chairs."

"So, we haven't a bull's what's going on, in other words?"

"Not yet we don't. We've started the decryption work though."

He pointed to the couple of pages of transcripts. The thing was, first of all, to decipher a few of the messages, to build up a profile of the connections and then push on from there.

"But, if it's just guys with laptops, driving all over the place – Ireland, England, Holland, anywhere – what can you do?"

"Have faith, Sergeant Barrett. We've just started here."

He handed me over a fresh page with a dozen or so phone numbers. There was one number I recognised, but I just couldn't put my finger on whose it was. When I got home to Aoife and Angelina, I dug out my phone book from the secret drawer under the desk and sat into the sitting room with it. Keeping a little notebook with numbers related to old and current cases was against protocol. Any info like that should have stayed in the station or on someone's database. Fuck that for a game of cowboys. I discovered the familiar phone number belonged to a transvestite club I had once had occasion to visit a couple of years before, in connection with the murder of one Charles Begadan, a cross-dressing business-man, in the Phoenix Park. Miss Katie, the lady at the other end of the line, who had been a lady almost as long as she had been a man, was most helpful then. Miss Katie, who dressed more to maim than to kill, ran a TV club called Les Charmettes, tucked away discreetly down a laneway near the city centre. It was a relaxed, low-light, high-life sort of place, where a tired business-man could slip into an evening dress and unwind. Tall and well-proportioned, Miss Katie had been in the business long enough to have serviced clientele in the seventies and eighties. She went easy on the mascara but had a tendency to overdo it in the cleavage department. She was a dear old contact of mine. Her information had helped me on more than one occasion, and her help, if you could call it that, had bought her out of involvement in a dodgy suicide, a few years before. She had also agreed to stick to what she knew best: dressing the flesh of Dublin's bankers and wankers. But Miss Katie's number had come up where it shouldn't have. I would have to have a word with her, pursed lips and pout and all. She would tighten her stays when she saw me coming.

I dropped Aoife back at six that evening, weighed down with birthday presents. When I got home, I didn't quite know what to do with myself. I was always like that after I dropped her back to Anna. I wasn't bothered enough to phone Deirdre Dunne or fraught enough to need to phone Squirrel, so I brought Angelina out to a film instead. Afterwards we caught a late drink in the Earl Mooney, where I was sniffed out for a cop at fifty yards. I promised Angelina grandly that I would do a dozen walks around Dublin with her before she headed back home. It was the end of a very pleasant evening. Harmless. And I went to bed happy as a pig in shit. And a very naïve pig at that.

Chapter Eleven

Bʀᴜɴᴏ Dᴏᴡɴᴇs's ᴄʜɪʟᴅʜᴏᴏᴅ and adolescence followed a trajectory I was very familiar with, having worked as a plodder in the south inner city when I first started off. With two parents and a couple of uncles and aunts around, he had grown up in a flat complex near the quays, waking to the screech of stolen cars at three in the morning and passing glass-eyed junkies in the communal stairwells. Then came decentralisation, when the inner city working classes were shifted out to the reservations in places like WOMA. Whereupon, more joy-riding, tea-leaving and drug deaths. But Bruno Downes wasn't Dumb Dekko. No, sir. Bruno Downes was more like one of the smart-but-tough Christian Brothers' boys I learned to survive during my own schooldays. I could see where he was coming from, and I knew where he was going. Wollenweider wanted a picture of Bruno, so I sent him on one with a choice caricature as well, emphasising Bruno's haircut, his hawkish nose and the high forehead. Whether in photo or in caricature, you could recognise Bruno Downes easily enough. Brains and brawn. Whoops!

The word from the technos was encouraging. It appeared that all sorts of things were now possible in cyberspace. Sniffers — packet filters they were officially called — were being used to monitor material intercepted on-line. Although encryption was being used in some of the messages received, I was assured once more that this would be sorted out soon enough. Then the sorting and sifting could take place. But the geeks in Harcourt Street sounded one less encouraging note.

"What's the problem?"

"This special line of yours hasn't sent or received any e-mail in a week. All the others have."

"Maybe it's not being used."

"Maybe. I think it's just being used infrequently. And we have no server we can raid to check on earlier messages."

"So, we just sit and wait, then?"

"Sort of."

It seemed that nobody could put their hand on your leg in cyberspace without your permission though. Myself and Squirrel decided to leave it to the computer boys. I got back to the real world and what I was best at – sticking my nose up other people's holes to see what they had for breakfast.

I hadn't visited Les Charmettes in almost two years, not since the close of the investigation into the murder of poor Sadie – or the businessman formerly known as Charles Begadan – in the Phoenix Park. Miss Katie, in a turquoise off-the-shoulder number, was still open for business in Les Charmettes though. The businessmen, bankers and wankers who slipped into the tacky boudoir to be dressed like their mammies were still fetching up. Fridays and Saturdays were the busy nights. I pictured the suits slipping away from home and hearth for a few drinks with the lads. Then, an hour or so later, sitting at the bar in Les Charmettes, adjusting their stays as they eyed the man in the skirt next to them. When I phoned her, Miss Katie was less than welcoming.

"This is Eveline Q, Miss Katie . . ."

There was an annoyed silence on the other end of the line, which was one female trick that Miss Katie could really pull with conviction.

"Our business is finished, Barrett."

"You could be of great assistance to me."

"I was the last time, and you said that was the finish of it."

In the end, I just showed up on her doorstep. It was Wednesday night, early closing night. Only Miss Katie and her new sidekick, a crabby little real female lesbian called Maeve, were on the premises. I looked around me on the laneway as I buzzed the intercom.

"Are you going to let me in, or am I going to have to come back with a warrant?"

Maeve opened the door. She was in a tizzy, on behalf of her mistress. I was being an unhelpful person. Miss Katie had had a day of it too. In the bar, I found my gal draped over the counter, sipping on a gin. There was a certain charm to the whole scene, with the low lights and the red cushions strewn around the room. There was a distinct smell of poppers about the place: that stinking, bowels-of-the-earth smell you got in gay clubs. The private booths were all empty now. The correction room was closed. All the boys had uncross-dressed and gone home. I sat up at the bar beside Miss Katie, who was more jittery than I thought she needed to be. That was a good sign. In the glare of the bar lights, her mascara looked uncharacteristically smudged and her eyes looked a little goofy. Her general demeanour was unfeminine, to say the least. Still, she was, after all, Richard Gleeson, from Ballyhaunis. I couldn't bear to see a woman cry though, so I took it easy with her. Maeve poured me a Black Bush and disappeared backstage. I had Miss Katie all to myself now.

"How is business, my dear?"

"Up and down. Get to the point, Barrett."

But I would have to warm Miss Katie up. Win her heart. Threaten her, that is.

"No trouble from my crowd lately, Miss Katie?"

"No thanks to you!"

"Plenty of thanks to me. I've kept the pack from your door for almost two years now."

Which was true. Miss Katie bit her lip. There had been a rugby international a few months before. Ructions. Broken glasses, broken furniture and some of the girls in tears. The guards had been called, but when Miss Katie mentioned my name, I got everything sorted out, from a discreet distance. Now, I was calling in the chips. Give and take.

"What do you want this time?"

"A little technical help. I found your phone number on a tap. I was surprised to see it there."

Miss Katie took another sip of her drink. Her number was probably coded into a lot of mobile phones. Angry the wife who punched in a number by accident and got in touch with Miss Katie and her cohorts. Unhappy differences would surely arise.

"The person's name happened to be one Alannah Harris."

Miss Katie twitched. She would have known Alannah Harris from of old. When I casually dropped details of Larry McMenamin's murder, Miss Katie twitched again. I decided to leave it at that for the moment. The lady with the blue dress and the husky voice was clearly getting distressed. When I told her I would be in touch again, Miss Katie didn't even look up. It was all rather melodramatic. She called her little companion, who appeared from one of the far rooms.

"See Detective Barrett out, will you, Maeve."

Myself and Deirdre Dunne hit Amsterdam the following Friday night. A cheap weekend deal. I seemed to be getting into my stride with the little Dutch country now. I even recognised one of the dippers on the Schiphol train, from the Dekko trip. We did a little late evening tour of the city centre, then spent the rest of the night doing what I hadn't done in some time. A refresher course in real-time riding. We woke to a bright, warm Amsterdam morning and, after breakfasting, set off to do the tourist bit. The Reijk museum, the Anne Frank house and all the little places around the Dam Square. Dublin would never be like this, no matter how much we pretended we were in Europe. Amsterdam was too ordered, too upbeat and too optimistic. Dublin was far too American to ever be Europe. We didn't even have a decent public transport system. I let it slip softly to Deirdre Dunne, as we sat drinking coffee at a pavement café, that I had to keep an appointment in Rotterdam later on that evening. She brushed back her long dark hair from her shoulders and smiled. The eyes showed no surprise. I told her I would be back in plenty of time to go back on the town, later that night.

"Do you lot never go off duty, Barrett?"

When Wollenweider appeared, he winked at Deirdre and gave her a peck on the cheek in a fussy, gay sort of way. All very New York City. I saw a stray thought flash across Deirdre Dunne's eyes. Had she missed something obvious here?

"When will you be back, Barrett?"

I turned to Wollenweider.

"Eleven . . . eleven, at the latest."

"If I'm asleep, wake me and we'll head out then."

I was wondering why no one ever seemed to call me much by my first name, when we turned on to the motorway. We had hardly left Amsterdam when we were in Rotterdam. Good roads. Of course, there wasn't much space in Holland that didn't have some sort of structure on it. Our destination was a club on the outskirts of the city where some of the Irish mob went to mix and match and discuss common defence policy. There were three clubbing possibilities that particular night. Wollenweider was only given the definite location of our boy Bruno while we were coming in off the motorway. The purpose of the expedition was to ID Bruno and try and give Wollenweider a little gen on his companions. I asked whether the same technology used in the porn shops couldn't be used in the clubs.

"Civil rights problem. Anyway, an Irish like you can ID these guys personally."

"Right."

"Give us some background. Tell us who we should watch."

Betty Grable's was off the beaten track, in an old warehouse district of the docks. Lots of high buildings, ancient gantries and rail tracks running along the streets. I slipped on my slightly tinted glasses, then put on the super-cool woolly I had picked up in Amsterdam that morning.

"I feel naked, Jon."

"You're with me. Don't worry. I'm armed."

There were a couple of local thugs on the warehouse entrance, boys who didn't look as though they had fully mastered joined-up writing yet. Just slightly above Dutch football hooligan types. They glanced at Wollenweider's little leather jacket then nodded us in. Wollenweider chatted to me in Dutch as we made for the bar. The place was dark as hell. Over in one corner, a raised section had been set aside for a dance floor. Strobes and coloured lights and boom-boom-boom music. We stayed over at the first of the two bars, relatively inconspicuous. This was a place that had a lot of through traffic. Regulars probably made up no more than 50 per cent of the clientele. We managed to get a little table in an alcove.

"If we talk lowly, we can talk in English, Barrett."

"I can't talk in anything else, as it happens."

"You know what I mean."

From time to time, Wollenweider would look into my eyes and touch my shoulder. I tried not to flinch when he did so, but old hetero habits die hard. The dance floor was filling up fairly quickly, and it was only ten or so. I thought I spotted a familiar face across the crowded room, but let it pass. It was Bruno and the boys we wanted, after all. And then, suddenly, they were there. It was a classy entrance. Five of them appeared together, with big Bruno Downes and his bullet head in the lead. I turned, like most of the clientele, when I heard his voice booming across the room in the direction of the chap I had spotted earlier, a guy called Hynes, from the North Strand.

"Hey, fuckface! We're here!"

The little Celtic mob strode across the floor to their companion. I named four of them straight away: Bruno Downes, Terry Hogan, Carlo Jones and Robbie Nelligan. All lads of distinction. The good, the bad, the congenitally ugly and the educationally subnormal. Wollenweider and myself went back to our beers and to eyeing one another up. I ran through the list for my boozing buddy. He already had a little something on Bruno – bringing in money to the country. A taped conversation in the files. The others seemed like minor players, though Carlo Jones was thought to be a rising star in the heroin world. There was enough to get an extradition warrant for Bruno though. But was I sure I wanted him delivered that early in the investigation? I wasn't. For a start, Bruno mightn't have been the actual triggerman. For two, we should really find out who his associates were.

It was sometime around eleven, when we were getting round to leave, that a figure approached the Dublin headbangers' collective. This was a different sort, a smoothly dressed creature who looked like he showered frequently and was well-groomed into the bargain. Myself and Wollenweider headed for the bar, and I stood to one side, playing the princess, while my buddy ordered a couple of beers. I stared ahead of me, taking in the voices all around. The new arrival spoke little, but when he did, his snappy little northern Irish accent cut a swathe through the loud, mushy expanse of the southerners' soft, slurred vowels.

"I'm away, Bruno. Catch ye later, boy."

"Cheers, Gerry!"

We managed to get ahead of Gerry, the dapper little northerner, just as he stepped out of Betty Grable's to where his snazzy black Toyota Celica was parked. I caught the number as it pulled away into the night. I suppose now that I overlooked the little northerner's possible importance because he looked so peripheral to the group of lowlife southerners. And I wasn't really that used to seeing southerners and northerners co-operate on the criminal front. I should have sussed wee Gerry straightaway, recognised that he was player number two in the Catherine James story, because wee Gerry was clearly a graduate of Her Majesty's prison service. There was self-discipline in his bearing, the ability to defer gratification like a Jesuit, that would have helped him survive three decades of conflict until the Brits were ready to deal. Such training cost dear and was not to be ignored. I had done duty in Portlaoise prison the time of the 1981 hunger strikes, and I still had nightmares about those self-righteous northern bastards. But I couldn't see the wood for the trees that night. I was too much into the northern paramilitary mode of thought. The reality was, now that peace was breaking out everywhere up north, there were more guns for hire down here.

Miss Katie slipped in among my thoughts as we scooted back to Amsterdam. I was sure now that she stood somewhere at the crossroads between killers and killee. Her demeanour in Les Charmettes told me she was some way involved, unwittingly or otherwise. Miss Katie also had a track record as a procurer of young men. We had marked her cards before for that. Maybe she had decided to take up her side-line again – this time in cyberspace. It was too far-fetched to believe that she was involved in Larry McMenamin's murder. What was in it for her? The last time I had crossed swords with Miss Katie was in the Charles Begadan case. Although Miss Katie was a smart bitch, she was not quite as smart as she thought. If she wanted to play hard ball, I could still pull something out of my own garter to wake her up.

Perhaps things did start and end in Dublin after all. Maybe the hand that had blown away Laurence McMenamin was still in Dublin. Maybe lots of things. Though I was playing devil's advocate with myself now, I wasn't really doing a very convincing job. Our boy could be in Dublin, Belfast or Amsterdam.

Myself and Wollenweider agreed to stay in touch, and Wollenweider offered to monitor Bruno's contacts and movements and see what else he could come up with. Northerners tended to stick out in southern groups or keep to their own little cabals, so when the northern paramilitary lot started doing business with the southern gouger lot, you know things were serious. It was, in a way, a sort of United Ireland approach.

Chapter Twelve

IT SEEMED THAT everything was going to come out of the wood-work during the course of Arland; that the rotten beauty board wood of the early seventies would finally be peeled away from the walls. Gun-runners, crooked politicians, bombers and whoremas-ters: once we pulled away the board, we would see all the vermin behind. Some were less verminous than others. Some were more reptilian than verminous. The first paramilitary out of the pack had been part of the local defence committees during the '69 troubles in Belfast. He was a solid-looking, avuncular figure, a working-class hero, I was half-prepared to believe, who sided with the newly founded Provisional IRA after the famous split in December 1969.

Malachy Goran had a special hatred in his heart for the south-ern opportunists who made a financial killing from the misery of the north. I didn't like what Malachy Goran and his colleagues had gotten up to, but I could understand his disdain for Toomey and his fellow-travellers. In his tweed jacket and cavalry twill trousers, he was every bit the well-scrubbed working man of ear-lier generations. My sympathy went out to him as he faced the silver-tongued southern barristers who tried to ensnare him with their silken snares. Malachy Goran's answers were clear and to the point. There was no equivocation.

"June 1971. The Castle Arms Hotel in Monaghan town."

"And the source of this information, Mr Goran?"

"I was there."

"In what capacity?"

"I was riding shotgun."

"Which means?"

"I was looking after one of the members who was to meet up with this Dublin politician."

"For what purpose?"

"I was told it had to do with funding for defence."

"You were misled?"

"Conned, more like it."

The Castle Arms Hotel was one of the meeting points for the bombing-on-contract crowd. That and a bar in Clones and a couple of bungalow blisses scattered around Cavan, Monaghan and Louth that hadn't yet attracted the attention of the security forces down here. It was all very gentlemanly. Goran told of a large bomb in Newry and the purchase of the bombed-out property within a week. Mr Cummins, barrister-at-law, glanced around the courtroom to make sure he had an audience.

"There aren't any documents to support these claims, of course?"

Malachy Goran shifted uncomfortably in the witness box. You could see he loathed southern smartass talk.

"We didn't employ secretarial staff in the active service units of the republican movement, at that particular time."

"Indeed, Mr Goran."

The material – cheque book stubs, receipts, account numbers and names Larry McMenamin had given me – were all being trawled up now. Malachy Goran's testimony would be corroborated by this material, but I still found it impossible to believe that Brian Toomey had arranged to have Larry McMenamin topped over Arland. After all, this was the Republic of Ireland. Not GB. The most Toomey would get in jail would be a couple of years. It was the principle of doing him down that was the thing. Nevertheless, Larry McMenamin had definitely been on edge when he made that last phone call to me with Tommy Ellis's name. And he wasn't splitting on Ellis, as such. Someone behind Ellis. Could it be Miss Katie? But why?

The Arland trial would have to wait for another couple of days before getting to the crux of the matter. Although it might have been unethical to buy up bombed-out property and profit from other people's misfortunes, paying to have the property bombed before buying it up was another matter. The newspapers put a little pepper up Arland's ass.

Goran to Tell All – Names, Dates and Figures

Squirrel was on a week's leave just then. He had headed off to some Ballymun-in-the-sun Spanish resort with his wife and eldest son. I was obliged to share the car with a much lesser, leaner figure, seconded from Kevin Street. Mind you, it took the pressure off me to tell Squirrel what I was getting up to. No point in having Squirrel fretting too much. I had glossed over the Amsterdam weekend with Deirdre, although I knew, by Squirrel's selective silence, that he knew he was in information defecit.

"Don't lose the run of yourself now, Barrett."

Which was what my father used to regularly counsel me. But it was Papa who seemed to be driving me, like a kidney stone that couldn't be ignored. Persistent, painful and impossible to ignore. If Papa had been made look a gobshite, I wasn't going to be.

I took Mother out for a meal with Angelina that week, in a small restaurant in Dalkey. Angelina was kindness itself and gave me the nod to leave the two of them on their own for a while. Mother, or what was left of her thoughts, was a smart woman. It upset her no end to have nothing but the company of chattering ould ones, fawning nurses and the yakky ephemera of television. Sometimes I read to her when I visited, a piece from the paper or even, on a couple of occasions, a story by a favourite author. And Mother knew her Joyce, a strange thing, for a woman of her vintage. She put Angelina right on a few points, corrected her on a few dates and characters, and then, just like that, as though something had snapped, her wandering started all over again. Angelina picked up the change immediately, noticing Mother's anger with herself and her distress. Dignity undone.

"Thomas, I must get back into the town. I have an appointment."

"Mother, Angelina has to go."

I took the first walk with Angelina the next morning. I hadn't swum or gone for a run in a week and needed the blow out. We started right at the front door and headed down towards the Tolka and up Milbourne Terrace, where the downsizing Joyces had once lived. Then it was a roundabout path through Glasnevin to Phibsboro. I walked the legs off my Italian guest that morning. Even though the rain came and went, we ploughed on, down Manor Street and over through Smithfield, that vista of damp brick and narrow streets that said it all for me. After passing through the fruit markets at the back of the Four Courts – where Arland and Malachy Goran were chugging away – we made for Capel Street and had a one-and-one in an Italian chipper. Angelina laid out her map on the table.

"Maybe a little more walking, Thomas. Just a little."

We ended up heading back up towards the Black Church and the little streets around it, streets like Fontenoy Street, where it seemed as though the front walls were about to fall into the street with age and infirmity. I did the decent thing when we reached Dorset Street – stopped a taxi and headed home to Drumcondra. Angelina spent the afternoon with her feet in a basin of water, a cup of tea at her side, peering over her glases at her heavily marked map of Dublin. I left her to it.

The walk with Angelina had helped me put off what I really had to do – contact Danny Mulhall again. I wasn't foolish enough to phone from home or the station, so I got in touch with our go-between from a public phone box in Phibsboro. I confidentially expected to be contacted back by Mulhall within a couple of days, but no call came. I was puzzled at what was going on. News came through around that time too that a fairly full file was being prepared on good old Dekko Tierney, as he languished in Mountjoy, on remand. But Dekko didn't really have anything to add to the sum of things, and it was far too early to go chasing Wollenweider up about the possibilities of extraditing Bruno Downes, who was a more likely suspect altogether. When I contacted the technos in Harcourt Street, I found that the traffic into the Clondalkin house was either harmless or too random to be of any importance. There was the odd indiscretion on the line, a few comments on shifting the pirated designer goods and a few miscellaneous phone calls from the semi-live-in lover. Alannah Harris's line hadn't stirred in weeks. Someone had sussed they were being watched or information had been passed on from higher up. People like Alannah Harris still had low friends in high places. I asked one of the technos –

the one with the doctorate and the west of Ireland accent – what his general take on it was.

"They're gone off-line, Detective Barrett. This one is probably using another line to get access to the servers."

"Musical chairs."

"So, now, we have them making contact with anonymous servers, from God-knows where."

"That's a great help."

"You asked me, Detective."

So the story seemed to be that, for the moment, the lines weren't going to give anything away. Since I felt I had reached a near dead-end, I decided to contact, off my own bat, retired Superintendent Hunt, down in the Kingdom of Kerry. I set up the meeting with him a couple of days before driving south. That day, as I drove out from Dublin, with Aoife chattering away in the back seat, for a father-and-daughter holiday breakaway, the news gushed out of the radio: "Fresh Revelations at the Arland Trial as Malachy Goran Goes into His Seventh Day of Evidence."

I pointed the car for the Naas Road towards Glenshane and the Kingdom of Kerry.

Chapter Thirteen

THERE WERE SHEETS of rain beating off the Audi as we rode over the Conor Pass. A VW, of the type favoured by the older German hippie, met us on a crooked bend and almost took us out. Fortunately, Aoife was snoozing in the back seat and saw nothing. I hadn't booked ahead anywhere, just decided to play it by ear, after I met up with Hunt. I could take the rest of my holidays in the autumn, when things quietened down in Dublin. Maybe get Deirdre Dunne – if we were still an item – to take the October week with me somewhere bright and warm. Despite the rain, everything seemed good that morning. Everything seemed possible once more. Gobshite.

Glenshane, Hunt's bolthole, was a little biteen of a place not too far from Dingle. Two pubs and a scatter of houses. Hunt's bungalow was near a beach, where a foreign personage, of Teutonic tendency, had fenced off part of the foreshore against all appeals to reason. The bungalow was much as he had described it: a stark white run-of-the-mill affair with a great satellite dish on the roof and a vintage Ford Prefect parked beside a spanking new Nissan Primera.

"Where are we, Daddy?"

"I'm dropping in on an old friend, for a few minutes."

"Just a few minutes, now, Dad."

Hunt was in the parlour reading, with his broad ex-police-man's back to the brooding Atlantic. His wife, Julia, a well-padded woman with a wary eye, was sitting in the kitchen chatting with a local woman. She led me into the parlour as Hunt made a great show of leaving aside the book he was reading. *Profiles in Courage.* Right.

"Mr Barrett . . ."

"Thomas, you can call me Thomas."

"Would the little girl like something to eat?"

Julia Hunt brought Aoife off into the kitchen and left us with a large pot of tea and a plate of arrowroot biscuits. It took a while for Hunt's sarkiness to break through as we diced around the subject of Arland 2 and the ramifications of recent evidence. Hunt put me right on a few details he felt I had fluffed. He didn't have much to say on Brian Toomey, oddly enough, as though Toomey had nothing at all to do with his being exiled to Kerry more than twenty years earlier.

"You don't bear a grudge against him, then?"

"You can't blame a cat for landing on all fours."

When Hunt's wife appeared again and offered to take Aoife off into town for an hour or so, I relented without too much fuss. I wanted to get Hunt out of his lair, on his own, with no wife to monitor his mouth. We settled on a walk down by the German's stretch of strand. Even though the sky promised trouble, we headed out. There was a lot of wood and seaweed on the beach, testimony to the storm which had hit the area the week before. That was Kerry – love it or leave it. Even Dublin weather seemed stable in comparison to the weather down here. Hunt leaned heavily on his walking stick as we strolled along the sand. At first, I thought it was just an old man's affectation – Hunt playing to the gallery – but I slowly realised he wasn't too well in himself. We stopped not far from where the beach was fenced off with razor wire and sat down on some rocks.

"Your German friend must think he owns the place."

"These effers would fence off the whole beach if they could."

"I suppose."

"But wait till he needs us some night in an emergency; then he won't be so shaggin' smart. Barbed wire!"

"Must be in the blood."

But the real bitterness in Hunt's heart was for his former colleagues and the spineless journalists of the Dublin press. For the quislings who ran for the bunker and the safety of their pensions. Though nobody likes hearing their father spoken ill of, I held my tongue as Hunt said his bit.

"I don't exactly hold your father's behaviour in high esteem either."

"I can understand that."

The whole putrid mess of Arland 1 spewed out then. From Hunt's original tip-off to my father – way back in the early seventies – about the bombs-for-money deal, from a republican source. (Who was the actual source? But this wasn't the time to ask.) Then the photocopies of bank statements and cheques and lists of phone numbers handed over to Hunt at a secret meeting in a house in Meath. Enough evidence, in other words, to sink ten governments. However, it wasn't in the interests of either the Brits or the Irish to add to the instability already around. The Sunningdale power-sharing circus was the main show in town, and, like the peace process, nothing was going to be allowed to interfere with that. All political cats were intent on landing on all fours.

"So the British conspired with our lot in scuppering Arland 1?"

"That's self-evident, isn't it?"

Dublin newspaper editors had their cards marked for them, and Hunt and a couple of other guards were pushed aside. Hunt dug his walking stick into the sand. He turned to face me. The wrinkled forehead. The tired eyes.

"So where were all the brave journalists then, Thomas?"

"I know what you mean."

"They weren't too keen to find out the real story."

"How do you mean?"

I stared ahead of me at the grey Atlantic. Hunt's smile was bittersweet. He had me on a hook. He stood up and spat on to the sand. It was a very showy sort of thing to do. He turned back to face the sea as he spoke. He was only going to say this once. I knew that much.

"Look, Thomas, there was every kind of divilment going on in Belfast in the early seventies. In times of war, that's what happens. Things that would be sorted out in more normal times get . . . overlooked. Abnormal things."

"Abnormal things?"

He turned around slowly to eye me then, but I knew there would be no more. We made back slowly over the strand, past the German's redoubt. The clouds over the bay had turned suddenly nasty now. The Atlantic was about to have its wicked way with us, and the next hour would be a real Kerry summer. Back in the parlour, we batted a little on the subject of Arland 2 and how things might go. It was harmless talk, talk to take the sting out of the revelation on the beach. I traded a little info on the McMenamin case. Guards' gossip. I even mentioned, against my better judgement, that I had met up with Danny Mulhall. I knew Hunt had had a hand in arresting Mulhall for membership of an illegal organisation, back at the beginning of the troubles. Hunt took a deep breath.

"Watch your step there, Thomas."

"How so?"

"You could be compromised. The centres of power might use it as an excuse to crush the Arland trial."

The centres of power. I loved the term. It had a faintly Byzantine ring to it. Hunt was beginning to sound like O'Leary now, screaming six bells and see no evil, hear no evil.

"Do you mind my asking: was it Danny Mulhall who first blew the whistle on the bombs-for-property scandal?"

"What does it matter, Thomas, who blew what whistle?"

"Just wondering."

"It's the message that's important, not the messenger."

When Julia Hunt arrived back with Aoife, I decided to hit the tar road. I had resisted the urge to apologise for my father's behaviour. Just about. I had traded a little scandal with Hunt. And Hunt had, quite carefully, let a cat out of the bag. A cat of a different colour. Abnormal things. Like what? Bestiality? Sodomy? Or even a rent boy ring? Hunt didn't come to the door with me, and it was left for Julia Hunt to see us off. Julia Hunt glanced at the parlour window.

"You know he's not well."

"I thought that."

"It's ca . . . the liver . . ."

"I'm sorry to hear that."

"That's not what's driving him though. He just wants the truth to come out at last."

I tossed the notion of truth about in my mind as Aoife fell asleep in the back, the rain started up again, and the cheerful weatherwoman on the car radio spoofed on about scattered showers with sunny intervals. Making it up as she went along. One thing was sure now: I was going back to see Miss Katie again, as soon as the couple of days with Aoife were over. Yes, I was going back to Miss Katie again, and I would put in another call to Danny Mulhall's contacts. As the car pulled us back over the Conor Pass, I let on it was myself in the back seat sleeping soundly, on the way to the little b. & b. outside Limerick, safe in the belief that my father, at the wheel, was a paragon of truth and light in a world gone wonky. A world of abnormal things. Whatever that meant, back in 1973.

Chapter Fourteen

JULY CLOSED WITH a wet whine. There were floods in the west and the deep south of bogland. And Dublin wasn't much better. Some pointed the finger at the ozone layer. I, myself, thought it was just the usual bout of poxy Irish summer weather, but it didn't last long enough, as in the miserable mid-eighties, for people to start seeing moving statues. Deirdre Dunne was heading off on holiday to New England for the rest of the summer, but there was still one woman left in my life: Angelina Marcusi, my Italian guest, decided to extend her stay until the end of August. I liked having her around the place. Her Latin bubbliness was a counterpoint to the uncertain skies outside. I could delude myself into thinking that good weather, somehow or other, was on the way. Squirrel came back from Spain without the slightest hint of having been in the sun, of course. He had gamely resisted all demands from his wife to linger on the beach with the other lobster red Irish tourists.

"I don't go for that beach caper, Barrett. It's unnatural."

It was time to take him into my confidence, so, the night after his return, I had him over to the house after we knocked off. Angelina had put together a pasta dish with mushrooms and cream, served with a side salad. It was well done and healthy and so on, but Squirrel wasn't convinced.

"No offence to Angelina there, but that didn't rate as much of a dinner, Barrett."

I told Squirrel the lot. I gave him the details about the meetings with Danny Mulhall and Tom Hunt, down in Kerry, my second trip to Amsterdam and my conversation with Miss Katie in Les Charmettes. He listened carefully, throwing his long legs up on the bockety coffee table as he turned the whole thing over in his mind. He wondered whether we shouldn't speak with O'Leary now. I went against him on this, as gently as possible, because I wasn't going to lose Squirrel. The whole thing just wasn't doable on my own, of course, especially as I wanted to contact Mulhall again and return to Miss Katie.

"Why are you so anxious to look up her skirt, Barrett?"

"Miss Katie was in touch with Tommy Ellis's line. She seems to be involved in some new rent boy racket. And Alannah Harris's name was on Tommy Ellis's computer. Let's say, I just have a feeling that it's all connected."

"Spare me the feelings."

To be fair to Squirrel, he didn't push me too much. We opened a couple of cans of beer then and sat out in the garden. The place was in a mess. I hadn't mowed the lawn in weeks. There were big pookey snails coming out of the old brick walls, and Aoife had already lost schoolteacher Barbie in the maze of weeds and grass. So nothing would do Squirrel but to drag out the Flymo and set to. He didn't make a big song-and-dance out of doing it. Just got on with it, while he thought about Arland, Alannah Harris, Larry McMenamin and the spaces in between. When he had finished, he bagged the grass methodically and sat back with me to go over the new separation documents – affidavits of means and all that bullshit – I had received in the post the day before.

"Nothing odd in them. Nothing you haven't already arranged with Anna."

"She wants to meet with me over it."

"Then meet her, Barrett. It can't hurt – legally, I mean."

I put the finishing touches to the cartoon I was drawing: a large, moustachioed cop pushing a lawnmower on a beach in Spain. Squirrel grinned. It passed. If I kept on like this, I might soon start to smile again. Regularly.

On the Wednesday night, myself and Squirrel dropped in to see Miss Katie. I had phoned just before we arrived, to check that Maeve, the snappy little sidekick, was out. Miss Katie was alone and the premises was officially closed for business.

"Open up, dear. I have another detective with me too."

Squirrel hadn't been in the club before, though he knew all about it. We had been on different teams during the Charles Begadan murder investigation. But he was up to speed on everything else. He knew all he needed to know about Miss Katie and some of her close associates. I had prepped Squirrel to butt in at the appropriate time.

Miss Katie was a real pouting witch that evening. I sat beside her at the bar as she snarled staccato answers to my questions. Squirrel prowled about club, turning up cushions, glancing at TV magazines and checking videos. I could hear doors opening and closing at the back of the club.

"What's that lanky bollox up to?"

"Why don't you ask him?"

Miss Katie was even nervier than the last time. I insisted again that I was only here to help. She listened silently, staring straight over her gin at the images in the mirror behind the bar. When I had done, she turned to face me, a sly smirk on her lips.

"Aren't you afraid you might mess up the Arland case Barrett, if this harassment gets into the papers."

At that point, Squirrel appeared in the little bar. Miss Katie froze, realising she had been overheard. Squirrel edged his arse up on to the seat beside her, reached over the counter and poured himelf a glass of water. He sipped slowly, as though savouring the flavour, then spoke to Miss Katie as he stared straight ahead into the mirror.

"We could reopen the Arthur Begadan case."

"What business is that of yours?"

Squirrel just ignored the question, adjusting his spotted tie as he spoke.

"Chicago rules, Miss Katie. You pull a knife, we pull a gun. You pull a gun, we call in a NATO airstrike."

"And your point is, Detective?"

It was pure Squirrel and nicely paced. Sort of thing I could never do. Squirrel emptied his glass and set it down in the sink. That was the best thing about having long limbs.

"You touch one of us, you touch all of us. And now, I'm going to leave you with Detective Barrett. To have a private chat."

And, with that, Squirrel was gone to wait in the Audi, down the lane. I didn't get any real specifics from Miss Katie there and then, but I got a sort of commitment to get me into the bigger picture; to connect me, like she had done, the time of the Begadan case. And the big picture seemed to be on the neighbouring island. We didn't even mention the name of Alannah Harris. Didn't mention the WOMA computer either. But what we were getting into seemed to be the meat of the thing whoever or whatever Alannah Harris and the WOMA computer were connected to and, by implication, those connected with the

Larry McMenamin case. At this stage, myself and Squirrel were still happy enough to let on to one another that this was all about McMenamin. We both knew that Miss Katie had procured trannies and rent boys for people over the years. Maybe Alannah Harris was doing a little procuring for her brother, through Miss Katie. I had a feeling this game wouldn't last much longer.

I watched Miss Katie sniffle a little as she balanced up the situation in her mind again. Help Barrett and take the risks associated with that or be difficult and face the re-opening of the Arthur Begadan case and possible detention in Mountjoy. A fussy TV slopping out her own cell, on remand for an accomplice-to-murder charge. Heap bad medicine.

It was Squirrel who took the phone-call from Wollenweider in the station. It seemed that the Netherlands police had managed, with the help of certain supportive elements in the British police, to tie down a few of the internet merchants in London and Manchester. A cross-check of the Amsterdam Irish computer threw up at least one fresh link: Manchester. Now I was wary of having the Brits in on any of this, at least at this stage in the game. For one, I was acting outside my own brief. For two, they had helped the Irish "centres of power", as Tom Hunt charmingly called them, in the seventies. The Brits would blow with the wind, in the general interest of good Anglo-Irish relations. If it was expedient for them to sink the Arland bombs-for-property trial, as it had been with the earlier failed investigation in the 1970s, then that's what they would do. Old empires die hard.

When I spoke to Wollenweider myself, the following day, I made a personal plea to keep a distance between ourselves and the Brits. It had nothing to do with 1169 and all of that. I was just afraid that the interests of the elites in Dublin and London might overlap again. That the price of fiddling with the peace process might just be too high. It was becoming vaguely clear, if that's possible, that what Wollenweider and myself were coming up against, in the nebulous interface between reality and fantasy that was cyberspace, was the outer fringes of a rent boy ring. It would soon be time to make another decision: whether to cross out of the misty wastes of cyberspace and come to earth or stay put for the moment. And where was where, when it was at home? Amsterdam? London? Dublin? Manchester?

I tried not to worry too much about how long I could keep officialdom out of the ever-expanding McMenamin investigation, but the whole thing was really developing into a game of four-level chess. Game one was Miss Katie's lead into the ring and game two was the Amsterdam game. Game three would be Arland itself. And game four would be the riddle of Larry McMenamin's murder. Sooner or later, the games would merge into one game.

Malachy Goran's evidence at the Arland bombs-for-property tribunal had come to a close. The past few days had been spent ploughing through material not shredded in the seventies. It was time for the star turn to return to the dock, now that the ground had been carefully laid by the prosecution. Brian Toomey took the witness stand on a fine August day. The Europeans were back with the TV cameras. It was all very exciting. I would have liked to squeeze into the public gallery that day, to cast an eye on the proceedings, but a crime-busting copper enjoying a free day in court wouldn't have been par for the course at all. Instead, I was obliged to get my vicarious thrills from the papers, the radio and the TV. I was sitting in the Shady Nook with Squirrel when the nine o'clock news came on that night. The sermonisers at the bar fell quiet. Over the intro music, we heard the voiceover say:

Brian Toomey Admits His Involvement in 1970s Bombs-for-Property Deals.

The silence fell even more silent. I turned to Squirrel. What the fuck was Toomey doing, throwing in the towel like that? Surely there should have been some attempt at obfuscation and throwing the hounds off the scent. But Squirrel said nothing, just strained his pint through the red hedge of his moustache. The camera cut to Toomey outside the Four Courts. Now he was opening his arms out, speaking to us directly. But this wasn't America! The case wasn't even over yet. My jaw dropped.

"He can't do that! It's *sub judice*!"

"That's his game, Barrett. He's sinking the case."

"But don't RTÉ know that?"

"What do you think, Thomas?"

The plummy, chummy face of Mr Brian Toomey, TD, looked out from the television into the lounge of the Shady Nook. That swarthy complexion burnished by regular jaunts to Spain and France. Generations of good grubbing. Hundreds of years of privilege. The high ground above the bog. I barely heard my own words. They seemed to be coming from somewhere else.

"The clever little bollox!"

Squirrel slowly poured the remainder of the pint into him. I saw something in Brian Toomey's eyes at that moment, something I hadn't wanted to see before. That my father hadn't wanted to see. Not the shrewdness of the elder statesman at all, or the stance of a public figure who had gone against the trend in the seventies and stood up for the right to poke one's peers in the butthole as a pretext for escaping criminal charges or protecting others. No, this was a smarmier creature altogether, one who had quite calculatedly used our own vanity against us. This was the side of Mr Brian Toomey that had finally embittered my father. As the camera cut back to the studio, I couldn't help feeling that I, Barrett junior, had been gulled. Just like the da.

Now I really began to wonder what my father had found out, all those years ago, but the nearest person to me, who just might throw some light on things, was in a nursing home in Killiney, suffering from cerebral ataxia. And Mummy just couldn't knit things together on demand any more. Maybe she didn't know the full extent of things of course, but what was clear to me was that things went back much further than Arland. They must do, if Brian Toomey was willing to risk everything on the throw of a dice. I wondered to myself, as I dropped Squirrel back at his well-appointed housing estate at the foot of the Dublin mountains, just what Brian Toomey was not admitting to. But there were no newspaper files to go back to, and no garda files in the Department of Justice central archives. The events of 1971–1973 had been airbrushed out, as surely as Leon Trotsky had been airbrushed out of the official Soviet photographs. So I would have to rely on other people's shaky memories. Which didn't give me a lot of hope.

Dalkey seemed like just the place to have dinner with an ex-wife-to-be. Or maybe the meal there with mother and Angelina had lulled me into a false sense of reality. Its little winding streets seemed reassuring. It had the smell of money lost and found. When Anna first made the suggestion of meeting up before the "trial", I was less than warm. Sub-zero, in fact. The chill had gone out of my attitude as the days went by. Maybe it was Angelina. Maybe it was Squirrel. Or maybe it was the old foolishness rearing its blow-dried head again – the notion that a few cartoons and an exchange of witty repartee over a bottle of red wine would get things on the road again. I was still fourteen, even now. Still full of Papa's hankering for perfection and simplicity in all things. The trouble was, Anna was a grown-up now.

Cabrillo's, in Dalkey, was one of those fake Italian joints where they made a song-and-dance out of coming to the table with a phallic-looking pepper mill after they had served the main course. It all looked quite silly. I took the Dart out to Dalkey, thinking to myself that I should leave my options open. Which meant, I would get a few under my belt first to embolden myself. To see what might be seen. But this strategy left me a slobbering stew after a couple of glasses of wine. We had just finished the polenta – yet another jazzed up Italian peasants' dish that had gotten uppity when it went north of the Alps – when Anna took the serious-looking documents from a serious-looking plastic folder.

"This is the draft agreement our solictors have worked out."

"I've looked at it."

"So, let's just go over it and try and agree between us."

"OK."

"Get it out of the way."

Anna slipped her reading glasses on. I felt a little like my father must have felt when the penny dropped about Brian Toomey: shafted, gulled, done for. A stookawn, as my Italian lodger might say, in her wonderful Hiberno-English. I could feel my thoughts slowly sinking in the wine as we spoke. And, underneath the thoughts, feelings gurgling up. If I hadn't felt so put upon that day, I might have sensed that Anna was throwing me a line, calling my bluff, to see if I had woken up yet. But my father's old bitterness got hold of me again. That deep sense of being hard-done-by. I began to lash the booze into me like a lager lout on a two-week splurge in Spain. Slowly, the legal documents were put away. I could see Anna's eyes cloud over. She wasn't going to risk anything here, not in public. She excused herself for a moment. When she returned, Anna was composed and resolute, as though she had snorted a deal of get-up-and-go in the bathroom. She sat on the edge of the chair. She was being kind now, which killed me altogether. And then she started to use my first name. Worse still.

"Look, let's leave it for the moment, Thomas."

"Why, Anna?"

"Another time maybe . . . when you're ready."

Anna's softly-softly counselling voice trailed away. So I was left with the bill, an empty chair and the resounding echo of my own adolescent angst deep within. There was nothing for it but to finish my drink and head home. As the taxi sped back towards town and Drumcondra, I tried denial. When I tiptoed back into my own house, I tried indifference. In the end though, the only thing that got me to sleep that night was the drunken caricature I drew of myself on the living room table as I cast an eye over the late Sky news. (Hostage taking in Washington, suicide bombers foiled in Israel, kick in the bollox for the Dow Jones.) The caricature showed a little boy sitting in a second-rate Italian restaurant, opposite a smart looking lady. He is licking a lollipop. She is sipping a glass of champagne. The caption has the lady saying, "I'll Wait for You to Catch Up with Me."

And that was as close as I got to self-knowledge before I tumbled into bed for the night, if not drunk as a lord then drunk as a dim-witted detective.

Chapter Fifteen

THE FOLLOWING MONDAY, the roof fell in on everything. I arrived in the station late, having just dropped Aoife back to her mother. A couple of odd bits and pieces – a district court appearance and a few summonses to sort out – were waiting for me in the station. I was standing over by the window, going through some files, with Squirrel talking to me between grunts, when Teevin, a new boy from the west, popped his head in.

"O'Leary wants to see you upstairs, Detective Barrett."

Squirrel lifted his head. This was a solo call. I hadn't even noticed O'Leary's car pull into the car park. I slipped the files back into the drawer.

"Watch your step there, Barrett."

To tell you the truth, I got a bit of a land when I saw Inspector Daly there, in his buttons and braces, with the tight-fitting hat and the beefy smile. It felt too sweet to be wholesome from the start. O'Leary averted his eyes from me. This wasn't his call. Daly was all 1950s gardaspeak. He left the hat and gloves down on the desk. Daly, sweating in the stuffy air of the station, stood awkwardly, leaning on the desk as O'Leary sat staring into space. I tried to read O'Leary's silence, but it was as inscrutable as Charlie Haughey's face at election time.

"We feel the McMenamin case should be left aside until . . ."

"Until after Arland?"

"We must fold our tents for the moment, Detective Barrett."

"Do you mind my asking why?"

"Well, a lot of the material on which the Arland trial is based came from Larry McMenamin, originally . . . true?"

"True."

"And now that he has been killed violently, it could cast a cloud over the value of the evidence, or the defence could do it. Do you see what I'm driving at?"

"Right, right."

More bullshit, and we all knew it. O'Leary scarcely spoke during the whole encounter. It was hard to get a straight answer from his eyes either. I wondered just where the smoking gun lay. It was a reasonable enough request, mind you, to lay off a touchy investigation like the McMenamin case until Arland was over, but why did I feel so odd about it? And who had snitched on me and my over-zealousness? It could have been someone close to the McMenamin murder. Perhaps even Tommy Ellis, out in WOMA. Someone, somewhere, was feeling the heat. Perhaps the elites were more worried about what myself and Squirrel might turn up on the McMenamin investigation than what Arland might turn up. I was beginning to see the whole McMenamin thing as one long trail of bailer twine, leading back through so many caves.

I scanned Daly's sullen face. He was only doing what he was told, until the pension came winging through the door in a few years. Daly had probably been given a sort of blanket order: back-pedal on McMenamin so as not to sink Arland. I felt Papa's paranoia creep up on me again. At this point, my father would have reached for the pack of Woodbine and muttered under his breath, "They're all in it together, Thomas."

I don't know why, but at that moment, in my mind's eye, I suddenly saw Brian Toomey's dark eyes, framed by the podgy face. The silk tie and the fawn suit. That strangulated little neo-Brit Dublin accent. If I was near him, I would have wrung his fucking neck, there and then. Now even Brian Toomey was getting to me.

O'Leary stood up and turned to stare out of the window, as though he wasn't part of the whole set-up at all. But this was a ready-up all right, a little something they had cooked up before the show.

"Myself and Sergeant O'Leary feel that you might benefit from a few week's . . . break."

"I'm sorry?"

"Compassionate leave, if you like."

My jaw dropped. O'Leary, the creeping Jesus, turned back from the window. He didn't want to over-personalise things, he said, but he too felt that a break might help everyone. There was the strain of the impending separation case, my mother's illness and the personal ramifications of Arland. Not to mention resurrecting the memory of my late father. It was a lot for one man to bear, all at the one time. I floundered about for an answer.

"I appreciate your concern, Inspector Daly . . ."

"Actually, it has all been pretty much decided, Detective Barrett."

"Without consulting me?"

"We are consulting you. And it's very simple: either you take the recommended break or I will be obliged to put you on temporary leave, with full pay, of course."

"On what grounds?"

"On the grounds of inability to discharge your duties due to temporary circumstances. Of course, there'll be nothing on your record."

I couldn't believe what I was hearing. *Et tu, O'Leary*, I thought, in my own mind. But O'Leary just carried on scanning the walls like an altar boy trying to dodge a clatter. Daly slowly ground to a halt. I don't remember much of what was said after that. There was mention of twenty-four hours' notice and of doctor's certs. Something like post-viral fatigue would do on the cert. I left the office speechless with anger. I had to plank my arse down on the bog for five minutes to regain my composure. My leave, for two weeks, and longer, if necessary, was to start as soon as I went off shift. Daly and O'Leary were still talking in the office half an hour later when I finally faced Squirrel in the back room. My paranoia was fuelled by too much coffee now, of course.

"OK, Judas, what's going on here? Are you in on this caper?"

"You've been told to take a break, Barrrett. O'Leary told me earlier."

"And the McMenamin investigation? And Amsterdam? And Miss Katie?"

"Listen, Barrett, the graveyards are full of indispensable people."

"That has a nice rehearsed ring to it, Squirrel. Who wrote your script?"

When I clocked off that evening, I called out to see my mother in Killiney, still reeling with the shock of being out on compassionate leave. Maybe they were all right. Maybe I was losing the run of myself. And I had no one to discuss it with. No Anna to turn to. And I couldn't bring myself to speak to Angelina about it. I brought my mother out a couple of audio tapes of novels. Although she couldn't follow the narrative of a written story any more, she seemed to be able to manage tapes. A cartoon passed through my mind as I sat watching her fumble with the cassette boxes. The three monkeys. "See no Arland! Hear no Arland! Speak no Arland!"

I stopped into Cooney's for a few scoops on the way back from the nursing home to dumb down. Sky television was giving breaking news on Arland, straight from jolly old Éire. There was talk of Toomey and his co-accused preparing a submission for the court the following morning, demanding that a mistrial be declared. I looked into the creamy face of my pint. *Plus ça shaggin' change. Plus c'est le meme shaggin' chose.* The chap next to me, a top-heavy office worker type in an ill-fitting toupee, ran his finger under his nose.

"They were never going to let it go to a penalty shoot-out anyway."

"Really?"

"Too much dirty washing to come out."

There was a hoarse message from Squirrel on the answering machine when I got home. No particulars. He wished me well on my temporary retirement and suggested a nightcap in The Schooner. I felt like phoning him back and telling him to go fuck himself, then I thought to myself: *The Schooner?* Because The Schooner was, strictly speaking, a place we usually didn't frequent. Strictly speaking, an ould lads' pub. Gutty little fellows with caps and overcoats, reading what they referred to as the *Evening Herdeld.* Something Angelina would have loved. I headed on up there anyway, rather than die wondering. There was Squirrel, perched on a solitary stool at the bar. We retired to the snug – it was a dead Monday night – and I sat back to wait for the communication. Instead, Squirrel clapped me on the back.

"You're a free man, for the next few weeks, Barrett."

"Is that a fact now?"

"You're free to run with the ball now."

"Really?"

Squirrel was vague on specifics, but the gist of it was that I could follow up all the leads now: WOMA, Manchester, Amsterdam and wherever.

"What has Manchester got to do with anything?"

"Don't know, Barrett, but it's in the loop."

"So, you're going to tell me that the gun that killed McMenamin came from Mosside?"

"Nobody knows yet what the connection is. But we do know that Miss Katie acts as a portal for a lot of through traffic."

"What sort of traffic?"

"Sex, drugs and rock and roll . . . a bit of everything, we think."

"And who is *we*, when *we're* at home, Squirrel?"

But Squirrel played dumb from there on. He seemed to be saying three things: you're off the leash to follow the McMenamin contract through Miss Katie; we're keeping our distance from you for the moment; and we're behind you, just in case. Very touching.

"And does Alannah Harris have anything to do with this?"

"We don't know yet."

"But you think so, right?"

"Put it this way, Barrett, if Alannah Harris has friends in high places, so do you."

"So did my very late father."

"Who hasn't been forgotten."

"Aye, fucked but not forgotten, just like Tom Hunt."

Squirrel twitched a bit at the mention of old Hunt's name. Christ knows how many of them were in it now, playing little Thomas Barrett like a video game. Squirrel got all dark and conspiratorial. I blew a little froth from my pint.

"Speak up, Squirrel, you're getting me edgy."

It got a bit woolly at that point. There should be proper procedures in the days and weeks ahead, Squirrel said. Even though I was alone; however, he, Detective Cyril Murray, was still there. Like a guardian angel. But guardian angels never counted for much when I was in school, when the brainless ones were beating shit out of you in the playground or Brother Declan was leathering you in the classroom over Irish irregular verbs.

"So, what you're telling me is I'm off duty but I'm still on duty."

"Look, Barrett, if you feel uneasy about it, just take your compassionate leave with grace and . . ."

"Sit scratching the high hole of my arse?"

One of the old men looked up from his pint and smirked. Of course, there was no point in wondering what my dear father would have done in this situation. He would just have run for cover. Duck and dive. What was the worst that could happen to me? I could be nobbled and dismissed for insubordination. I would then take an action, with a couple of shrinks in tow, be compensated and earn my beer money as a badly dressed bouncer on the door of a Leeson Street night club. No, wait a minute. The worst was Aoife or Anna being targeted. I saw the flash of the .38 as Laurence McMenamin's head splattered against the yellow skip. Another cartoon reared up in my mind's eye. A chap with a balaclava, begging on a street corner. "Please Spare a Shilling! Out-of-Work Provo!" Yes, that was the worst thing that could happen.

Squirrel stood up slowly. He had promised Ruth an early night.

"Keep records, Barrett."

"In case I'm tapped by my own crowd?"

"It's just good office practice."

I lay a long while in bed before I slept that night, floating on a haze of stout and watching the ceiling revolve slowly. My father's face was before me, my mother's voice in my ears: "Wasn't your father an awful fool, Thomas?"

Tomorrow I was on leave. Compassionate leave or sick leave or holiday leave. I would enter the loop. Get Miss Katie to hook me up with whatever nasties were next in the sequence that would lead me to the murderers of Larry McMenamin. Or, at the very least, Alannah Harris's contacts. I suppose it crossed my drunken mind to wonder why McMenamin was suddenly so important now. An ex-Provo turned anti-drugs campaigner: very sad, I mean, but so what? Surely there were better causes to stake my career on? But my tipsy nose told me this was all heading back in the direction of Arland and Brian Toomey, somehow or other, even if the connection was, to say the least, tenuous. So what if, at the worst, Alannah Harris was procuring rent boys for her brother, Brian Toomey, through Miss Katie? He wouldn't be the first Dáil darling to have gone that road. I had a foreboding that I was crossing into Injun territory.

I was more afraid for Aoife and Anna than I was for myself now. Squirrel promised to have the odd unmarked car seen in the vicinity of Anna's house, to send the message out to anyone who was watching that the force, as company policy, was on the watch. As I turned for sleep and began planning my next step, my head filled up with a thousand and one sideshows. Dekko Tierney and

Bruno Downes and the little northerner called Gerry, in Betty Grable's, in Rotterdam. I pictured Alannah Harris, sunglasses and beehive hair, her brother's smarmy Cheshire cat smile in the foreground. Maybe it was Alannah Harris, with one simple coded message on a computer, who had set up Larry McMenamin for execution, without having to leave her well-got lair in Rathgar for the lower echelons in WOMA. Maybe Larry McMenamin had threatened to go state's witness because of his own knowledge of Arland in the seventies. Or, maybe, McMenamin had something else on Toomey and Arland was just the start. Now that was more like it.

I began to wonder whether Squirrel and Redmond in the CAB office weren't singing from the same hymn sheet. Great. It was one thing going into war. It was quite another thing going off to fight in a fog surrounded by companions you couldn't see. Tomorrow I would cross Miss Katie's portal. As I fell asleep, I saw myself sitting across the desk from my father as he stubbed out a smouldering Woodbine. A little pile of pawns in the box beside the chess board.

"Six pawns down, Thomas. You know what that means."

My hand reached out for the black velvet blindfold nervously, and I tried frantically to memorise the board as I slipped it on. My queen was in a rut, cornered by a bishop and a rook. The king was cowering in the back row. And then the blindfold was on, and I heard my father's voice through the darkness.

"Your move, I think, Thomas."

Chapter Sixteen

I DID A LOT of checking out of old contacts in the flesh trade. And old republicans – the early 1970s lot, before they went all Baader Meinhoff and morphed into a cell structure. Mulhall's heyday, that is, when they liked to use military terms like "brigade" and "battalion" for cadres who couldn't spell either. I tried to steer well clear of the whirlpool of Arland.

It became clear to me, through my contacts in the flesh trade, that Miss Katie had embraced the new technology all right. She was running some high-class rent boy network on the net. Very discreet though. And I wondered where Miss Katie would guide me, if she was given another push. Militarily speaking, to the junction of four map segments. Which was where?

I had a few conversations with Wollenweider in the meantime. He sent some files with numbers and traces. I had to have some idea of the sea I was heading into. The illusion of control is always important, of course, even if you don't quite believe it yourself. Wollenweider had made inroads on some of the nodes that formed the components of the ring Miss Katie was introducing me to. Servers shutting down and opening up like glands in a body that had more heads than an Irish semi-state company. A couple of the nodes were English based: London and Manchester, or the fringes thereof. Amsterdam, with its own stable of servers, had its own ring members. Amsterdam seemed to be used as a sort of clearing house, an electronic forwarding and fox-the-enemy service. All that was needed was one push to enter the circle, to suss out the overlap with Alannah Harris and, by extension, Brian Toomey, which no one was telling me about yet. Squirrel had obviously been tasked with lending me a hand — from a distance. But Miss Katie still needed to be persuaded to go all the way, to drop her drawers, so I called in Squirrel to tie things down.

Squirrel tracked Miss Katie down in a small pub, not far from the club, where she had her tipple before opening up for business. It was late afternoon, just about the time when the solicitors and bankers and businessmen were working out the dresses they would slip into for the night in Miss Katie's. It was that lovely Dublin pub hour, when the bar-staff leave you to yourself and you can sink into a corner without one of them wiping your table and saying, "Are you all right there?"

Miss Katie, a lady who liked to keep up with things, was seated by the door, sipping a sherry and reading *The Irish Times*. Squirrel leaned across the bar to order his snifter, then he turned around to the target. From my position in the snug, I could hear Miss Katie fooster with her things, but she wasn't quick enough. Squirrel was beside her in a flash. And then he did a most ungentlemanly thing: dropped the hand on Miss Katie and grabbed her firmly by her first sex. I couldn't hear a word of what they said, but I did hear the thunk of an envelope on the table as Squirrel threw down the gauntlet. It was a file containing tape transcripts, photos and statements relating to Miss Katie's role in the Arthur Begadan murder. Myself and Squirrel had gone scout's honour on this one. The deal with Miss Katie would be that if she helped us with the McMenamin case, the Begadan file would be closed for ever. I saw the barman glance over his shoulder and turn back to Sky news on the TV above his head. More suicide bombings in Iraq. A new disease of sheep. The next cure for cancer, somewhere in the Brazilian rain forest. I pulled myself back further into the shadows, trying to catch the conversation downstream. But why should Miss Katie accept our promises though? I was pondering this point, which Squirrel had avoided discussing in the car, when I saw him stand up suddenly, cross to the bar and rap his glass on the counter to call the barman back. He turned to face Miss Katie. This was obviously for my consumption as well.

"And, by the way, we know that computer is your baby. You could be sent down for this rent boy racket alone, while we're revisiting the Begadan business."

The silence told all. Sealed the deal. Squirrel turned back to the bar to let the message sink in and called for a couple of drinks. By the time the glasses were on the counter, the guest in the grey suit had arrived in the bar. Squirrel hadn't let me in on the fact that O'Leary was coming, but this was the imprimatur on the whole deal, as far as Miss Katie was concerned. O'Leary stayed at the bar until Squirrel had finished his spake with Miss Katie, then he took a seat, a little up from them as though he wasn't really with them. The barman knocked off the TV and vanished again. I caught the last of O'Leary's words.

"And that's the deal, my dear."

"But what do I really get?"

"You get protection and immunity from prosecution."

Miss Katie's voice jumped a couple of octaves. Now she was whining like a girl.

"You didn't do much of a job protecting Larry McMenamin."

"Do you want to go down that road then? We can discuss McMenamin here too, if you like."

"I'm only saying . . ."

I kept exactly where I was told to sit until Miss Katie had dried her tears and gone back to her lair, to open up shop. Squirrel coughed. The coast was clear. I stood up and crossed to the bar. O'Leary threw back the last of his scotch. He reminded me that I was still on leave; that, technically speaking, it was he and Squirrel who were at the coalface here. It crossed my mind, at that point, that maybe Hunt down in Kerry had more friends left on the force than he advertised. The guards had long memories. My father had always said that to me.

"Don't get on the wrong side of that lot, whatever you do."

"How do you mean?"

"They're like a bunch of bad-tempered parish priests. Never forget a face."

Which I thought was just old Civil War talk or his memories of internment in the Curragh. But maybe there was a collective will working here. The dirt done on a couple of their members in the seventies was going to be paid for. It was on the tip of my tongue to ask about Daly and O'Leary and Hunt then, but I knew the answer well enough. I was like the guy they sent ahead to scout for Indians before calling in an air strike. I said nothing much to O'Leary, and then O'Leary and his grey, anonymous suit were out the door, into the late afternoon sunshine. It was just me and my buddy, who didn't really want to be seen in public with me either. Squirrel passed me a piece of paper.

"This is Missie's mobile."

"So, what happens from here?"

"We've given her until seven o'clock to give an answer."

"And if she backs down?"

"Just keep her hot. Unless we get her now, she may bolt."

"This is all McMenamin, right? And Alannah Harris . . . ?"

At seven, on the dot, I gave Miss Katie a bell from Drumcondra. The phone rang for some time before our lady friend answered. I knew by the resigned tone that she had seen the light. Better co-operate with us now and wipe the slate clean on Begadan than risk going down for both Begadan and whatever McMenamin and Arland threw up. Bit like remortgaging your house to clear old debts, once and for all. In the current investigation, Miss Katie was accused of nothing, as yet, though she was probably guilty of being a conduit for criminal activity. Of aiding and abetting. A go-between, between high and low, as in the Arthur Begadan case. And possibly the McMenamin case too. A sort of facilitator, who didn't get her own hands dirty at all. We arranged to meet in her apartment at ten that night. Just the two of us.

"Shall I bring a bottle of wine or flowers?"

"Fuck you, Barrett!"

"That's nice talk for a lady."

It was important now to walk the walk with Miss Katie.

Her apartment was in Donnybrook, not far from the river. I settled on bringing her copies of incriminating statements made against her during the Begadan investigation, statements which we had never used, largely because we thought they couldn't stand up in court. But they had been made by some of Miss Katie's former associates. I sat sipping a beer from the well-stocked bar as Miss Katie flicked through the pages in a dismissive manner, but her shaking hands told the truth. She knew she was even further in the net now.

"Is that it, Barrett?"

"We've got tapes too."

I watched her face drain of the little colour it had. Miss Katie went into the bedroom then, and I heard the whirr of a hard drive kicking in. I let her at if for a few minutes, trusting to her common sense. Miss Katie wasn't going to do anything that wasn't in her own interest. Her greed for spondulicks had brought her to this. She was a girl who liked to dress well and knew style, but whose tastes were expensive: Brown Thomas and all the pricey little boutiques around Grafton Street, not to mention trips abroad. Making TV contacts and arranging trysts for people here with Britain and the Continent was the second string to her bow. She was a sort of matchmaker. Which must be where Brian Toomey came in. But what we were interested in, for the moment, was the McMenamin murder link – whether murder had been negotiated or ordered on the net, and by whom. Anything else would be a bonus. I still believed, at that stage, that Miss Katie was merely a conduit; that her hard disk and her hard neck were just the meeting points of so many lines of criminal activity. I left down my glass and leaned against the door jamb for effect. It was a very Squirrel moment.

"That computer really was yours, wasn't it, Miss Katie?"

But there was no reply. Not that it bothered me. The agreement with Miss Katie had been sealed by O'Leary's lips. I watched the heavy hands beat away on the laptop keyboard. In all likelihood, this laptop was probably one of Wollenweider's musical chairs. One of the laptops that went on and off as the ring demanded.

"You're quite the computer buff, Miss Katie."

The mascara-ed man turned around to me. Quite an elegant calf too.

"Do you really know where you're going here, Barrett?"

"Wherever you take me, dear."

"Haven't they told you yet, Barrett?"

I frowned, suddenly uncertain. Was there more Arland stuff to be dug out? I realised, as in many an investigation in the past, that I hadn't a breeze what I was actually after. One thing was sure: touch one lead, you got twenty others. Miss Katie was just fulfilling her part of the deal: putting me in touch with the criminal ring. The Alannah Harris connection I would have to work out for myself. Miss Katie was simply a bouncer and procurer, but, more importantly, she could rig up the entrée that would show I was the real thing. To whoever. The laptop screen suddenly cut to a series of what looked like coded files. Miss Katie was typing furiously now, chasing the internet rabbit down a thousand cyber burrows. Her fingers finally stopped and she turned back to me.

"Give me a name I can convert into code, Barrett."

I thought for a moment. Suddenly I was stuck. Something from a television programme came to me then, a children's programme that Aoife loved.

"Mugwump."

"Spell it."

The fingers beat away on the computer. We were in. I was accredited or whatever you'd like to call it, and Miss Katie was setting up the introduction. Her hands rose from the keyboard. I glanced around the room.

"That's it?"

"We have to wait for a reply. It will be back in an hour. Everything has to be checked out, just in case."

"Just in case we're tapping the line?"

The next hour was the oddest I had spent in a long time. As

though we had just met for a drink, myself and Miss Katie sat in the living room watching *Newsnight*. It was all about how the Chinese economy was on the up and up and how New York yuppies were hiring Mandarin-speaking nannies for their children. Miss Katie chatted away about stocks and shares. She told me she had been intending to get out of business soon anyway. Out of all of her business interests. This line was intended for me and my buddies.

"The matchmaker business too?"

"Barrett, I have names in this book here, and copies of these names . . ." She tapped her lacquered head three times, ". . . that would shock you. Irish men and teenage boys."

My eyes widened. Was this what Hunt meant by abnormal things, on the beach in Kerry that day?

"There must be a price on your head, Miss Katie."

"There will be, if you let me down."

We weren't talking high moral ground here, or even the middle moral ground. Miss Katie was thinking of weighing anchor for practical reasons. I realised, as I watched her from the corner of my eye, what a clever chap Miss Katie was. In another time, another space, she might have been something else, not sitting beside me in a patterned dress. So, how did she end up like this: potty-trained too early, perhaps? Father fond of spanking her bottom in public? It didn't matter a flying fuck at this stage. She was what she was. Exactly an hour after she had logged off, Miss Katie went back into the bedroom and made her way back through the internet to hook up with central command. I sat on a chair beside the door, watching her type in more commands and codes.

"You're there, Barrett."

"I'm where?"

"Manchester, next Wednesday. The exact location will come through in a few days."

"Which means what?"

"This is your handshake meeting."

"What? Handshake meeting for what?"

Miss Katie allowed herself a little laugh then. I took note of the crows' feet on her face.

"You're going to be vetted, Barrett. Hasn't that lanky bollox of a sidekick of yours put you in the picture yet?"

"Right, right. I didn't think it was done with computers, that's all."

I couldn't keep the surprise out of my features, although I tried to bluff my way out of it. I had a queasy feeling that I had drifted back into Brian Toomey territory again. That this wasn't part of the McMenamin thing at all, or only vaguely so.

In the car, I phoned said lanky bollox with the red moustache. His mobile was powered off, of course, and he was unavailable. Squirrel's son took a message, and I was unconscious in bed when the phone rang about twelve.

"Barrett, is there a problem?"

"Right, Squirrel, what am I getting into here?"

"Can't go into it over the phone."

"Then we're going into it tomorrow. You could have warned me."

"Look, Barrett, we're not sure about it ourselves."

"And you want to let me go it alone, just in case there's a booby-trap."

"Just to get into the circle."

"You're only following orders. Right?"

I booked my ticket for Manchester the following morning, after I had met Squirrel for a pre-briefing in Cooney's, that is. This was Arland all right. Or, more to the point, latter-day Toomey. So putting two and two together, I figured out that they were all trying, once more, to tie the seventies Toomey up by using the current Toomey to ensnare him with the rent boy racket. Just as we had done with Miss Katie. I wasn't sure which Venn diagram I was getting into. Was it the one marked guns, the one marked sex or the one marked drugs? Or an overlap of all three? Squirrel's tone was less than convincing.

"They just want to make a connection, that's all."

"They?"

"A solid connection with Alannah Harris that will stand up alongside Miss Katie's evidence, so we can join up the past and the present."

I pulled out into the dark drizzle of a Dublin summer's evening, wondering just what was ahead of me in grim old Manchester. And who was behind me, if I looked about.

Chapter Seventeen

THOUGH I THOUGHT I had never been to Manchester before, I realised when I got there that I had: Belfast. Manchester had the same basic stock of stout nineteenth-century red-brick Victorian buildings. Cotton, steel, coal and the remnants thereof. It had soul-numbing Belfast skies too. I took a bus in from the airport, rather than miss all the action in a taxi. The city centre seemed to have lots of shops and bits of shopping centres and not much else. And, surprise, surprise, the main square looked like Donegal Square in Belfast. I took a taxi from there to The Hamptons, the hotel Miss Katie had settled on for me, one of many, I assumed, used by the ring. I had a Black Bush to settle my stomach after the flight, then headed up to my room to take a nap. Images wove in and out of my head as I snoozed: that first night behind the barracks in Rathmines, with Larry McMenamin at my feet and me leaning on the wall as I brought up Mario's pizza on the ground; the edgy face of our main witness, Catherine James, who had gotten much edgier.

"I'm going back down home to Limerick for a while."

"Maybe that's a good idea, Catherine."

"No one can touch me there."

Home. No one can touch me there. Right? Maybe Larry McMenamin had once thought the same. Safe in the south.

Squirrel had advised me to leave a trail as a basis for any case that might arise from my adventures, but leaving an electronic trail, at this point, could throw everything into chaos. Miss Kate must have figured in my dreams too somewhere, because her mannish voice was still in my ears as the phone woke me from my catnap.

"I'm only the gatekeeper, Barrett."

"I sure hope so, darling."

I shook myself awake as I reached for the phone, running my tongue around my mouth and pursing my lips as though preparing for a face-to-camera shot in a studio. I lifted the receiver. An Avon Lady type voice filled the vacuum.

"Is that room 23?"

"Yes. Room 23 here."

"Excellent. Pick you up in half an hour, say?"

"Half an hour is fine."

I didn't know what to expect in half an hour, but my sense of the thing convinced me to play uncertain and afraid. I wasn't wired and I wasn't carrying a gun.

I had half-intended tracking down John Reed, the *Guardian* journalist who had interviewed Toomey in 1973, but when I heard he was ill in a hospital in Surrey, I put it on the back-boiler. I made a mental post-it note to take up the lead when I got back to Dublin.

Dorothy, the woman who called for me, was in her mid-thirties: twin-set, chiffon scarf and a complexion that was pure peaches-and-Ponds. She was full of illuminating chat about the awful bout of weather recently. I began to wonder whether I had stumbled, by mistake, on some sort of Tupperware underground. She made sure the girl on the reception desk overheard all the harmless talk. I replied in kind. No, it had been no trouble finding the hotel. And yes, the room was fine. We pulled away from the hotel in a sensible little family saloon. I assumed we were quite a distance from our rendezvous. Dorothy gave a running commentary as we drove through the different areas, obviously going the long way round to somewhere. My eyes glazed over as I let her draw all the talk from me that she needed. I saw her join the dots together as I put on a show of being edgy and ill-at-ease, settling easily into my role as a single, hypersensitive man with a string of broken relationships and no children. Parents dead. Not sure I should be getting into this business in Manchester at all. Full of misgivings. Dorothy's voice was tender. She understood.

"As long as you don't hurt the boys, it's all right. Isn't it, Richard?"

"I suppose so."

"As long as no one gets hurt. They're just young men, after all."

My back story had to be coherent but not so seamless that it seemed concocted. I should be forthcoming but not forward. We swung into the car park of a suburban pub. Dorothy turned off the ignition and stared straight ahead of her as she spoke. She might have been an intimate friend recommending an enema or a skin lotion, but her words were considerate and as cold as cold could be.

"This is only a first meeting, after all. You can make your mind up after that. Good luck."

She leaned over and gave me a peck on the cheek. As I made my way into the lounge and took up a position near the door, I realised that Dorothy was probably on the phone at that moment to the next link in the chain. I ordered a Bloody Mary and sat back in the corner with the *Daily Mail*. It was the sort of pub the

British do so well. The Pig and Whistle. The Fish and Tit. No sharp edges. I was reading an article about alien abductors in the US when I realised I was being watched. Another housewifey woman had come to pick me up. I wondered to myself at the provenance of these women. Had they all been conned or compromised into this? Or was there some strange kick they got out of it? It was beyond my comprehension that they could be as screwy as their male counterparts. The woman in the fawn trouser suit crossed the floor and stretched out her hand.

"Mr Martin?"

"Yes, that's me."

"I'm Sandra."

"Wonderful."

There was more of the vetting going on now. This one was sharper than the last though, a little closer to the centre of the action. It was like speaking into a polygraph with a two-way mirror in front of me. It was important, I reminded myself again, not to be too smooth. And then we were off through the anonymous estates again.

In no time at all, with darkness falling, I had lost all sense of where I was. We were clearly still in the general area of Manchester though – Salford, perhaps – but more than that, I couldn't say. The car drew up outside a bungalow set in from the road, in an estate of retiree-looking bungalows. Sandra's Jolly Polly voice was back again.

"Here we are!"

It was all very upbeat. The bungalow had all the appearance of somewhere that was well kept but not actually lived in. Andrew and Marge, who met me in the living room, were in their forties and seemed strangely un-at-home in their house. Had I had a good flight? Wonderful! How was the hotel? Sometimes people from Éire, they confided in me, chose to fly through Belfast, for discretion. To muddy their tracks a little more. Brian Toomey slipped in among my thoughts at that point. What was the purpose of my visit? Linking the present with the past. That was it. To nab Toomey for the sins of the present rather than the sins of the past? Especially now that Arland 2 was on the rocks, he had to be made pay for something. My second escort disappeared almost as soon as we arrived, and I was left with Andrew and Marge in the lounge, among the porcelain ornaments, the Dali prints and the spotless pink carpet.

"A drink to loosen up?"

I was poured a stiff scotch and left on my tod, in order to rise to room temperature. I heard Andrew and Marge pottering about in the adjoining room. It would all have been quite comical if it hadn't been so serious. Working on the principle that I was being observed-through a two-way mirror or a lens, I played up the nervous routine, crossing and uncrossing my legs like a secretary at a board meeting.

Out of the blue, Marge slipped back in and, almost as an afterthought, said, "We'll just be a moment. You might like to watch one of the videos while you wait."

In the distance, just before the videotape clicked home, I heard the clacketty-clack of a computer keyboard. Andrew, or whatever his real name was, must have been up on the net, checking my credentials. I didn't really sweat about it. After all, they were hardly likely to take out an Irish copper. It did cross my mind, as the video kicked in, that I could be set up though. A detective on compassionate leave who had developed an unhealthy obsession with teenage boys. The screen cleared. The camera showed a young boy of about fifteen or sixteen going into a nondescript room where a middle-aged man lay fully clothed on a bed. There was mood music in the background, dolphin-hugging new age stuff. Like most hard porn films, this master-piece was wordless, save for the odd grunt. I made sure to appear engrossed, going as far, to add a bit of realism, as to touch myself through my trousers. There was a great saving on scriptwriting all right. At the point where the hero slipped off his jocks to contin-ue the encounter, Marge arrived back in. Her face was beaming, in a motherly, prizewinning ceremony sort of way.

"Of course, you're used to seeing that sort of thing."

"Well, not in real life."

"Real life is better . . . much better, Richard."

I wondered again whether the women I had met that evening weren't getting off on the whole show. I had once come across a real off-the-wall scenario in Crumlin: a woman, in her late thir-ties, who used her teenage, dope-eyed son as a paramour. Yick. But, beyond that, I had never really come across women at the forefront of the really heavy stuff. Maybe they tended to be more behind the scenes. The hand that rents the cradle, sort of thing. Andrew appeared with a second Scotch. He seemed pleased with himself, as though someone had given him a complimentary blowjob backstage. He had a sort of photo album with him. The type of thing that would usually be stuffed full of pictures of wed-dings, christenings, alcoholic uncles and snuffed-out grandpar-ents. He passed it to Marge. His tone was gentle and understanding. We were all friends here. Helping one another. We might have been sorting out a knotty marital problem.

"You haven't made any commitment, as yet. You understand that?"

"Yes, of course."

"So, when you go home, you can think things over. If you want to go on to the next stage and so on. Anyway, here's our little display of playmates. I'm sure you'll find something there to interest you."

I took another sip of the Scotch. I didn't even have to fake the jitteriness now. My heart raced as I flicked through the album. There were a lot of photos but most seemed to revolve around the capers of about half a dozen well hung young men, mostly with blond hair. Most of the photos were cropped, to cut out the features of the adult accomplice, but a small few were a little more lax. Hadn't they heard of digital photography in Manchester? I was left for a while in the lounge while the pair of them got on with their own business behind the scenes. I had worked myself up into a reasonable imitation of a bag of nerves when one of the photos caught my eye. There was a vaguely familiar face in the shadows here. The photo seemed to have been taken, from hip level, at a party. A lot of nude male torsos could be seen, with just one female fluff box in focus. In the background, however, full clothed, was a face that rang a bell: a woman in a tight dress and the plastered-on makeup of a transvestite, a face I seemed to recognise from the past. Maybe from the Arthur Begadan investigation? But there was no way I could lift the photograph. Or was there? I called out to Marge, in the next room. She appeared through the double doors, all sweetness and light. I had to use the bathroom. There was a knowing look in her eyes. She had been here before. Sir, obviously, wanted to spank the monkey in the privacy of the bathroom. Take the photos out for a manual test drive. The odds were against there being a camera in the bathroom, I hoped. And anyway, if I lifted a photo and they noticed it the same day, so what? I wasn't coming back anyway, just getting evidence of the Dublin-Manchester link.

"May I take the album in with me?"

"Of course. Take your time."

I took my time in the bog. Let out a couple of suitable grunts and groans as I slipped the photo from under the cellophane cover, rearranged the other photos and tucked it away under my shirt. I might have been fourteen again and whacking away goodo in the family bathroom. Some training stands to you for ever, of course. I made sure to overdo it to the point where there was a knock on the door.

"Are you all right in there?"

"Yes, yes. Just a moment."

I suppose they were worried that Sir might take a turn, with the excitement of the whole thing. I heard a subdued giggle from the far room. When I was ready, I flushed the jacks a few times and made for the lounge again. The two were all smiles now. I slipped a little hesitation into my voice though, a little post-wanking pause for thought. Marge and Andrew were very understanding.

"Give it a few days, and if you want to go ahead, you can make arrangements through your contact in Ireland."

She pronounced Ireland like Arland. I felt myself twitch. I didn't see Marge as I was leaving. She was probably in the kitchen setting up a shagfest for another middle-aged gent. These two weren't slag street though. There would be legal people, doctors and educators on their books, not that I would ever meet any of them or wanted to. I had my mits on the keeper of the Dublin portal now: Miss Katie. All I needed now was to find the point where all the circles overlapped. And who might the woman in the photograph be? This was all clearly Toomey territory and had nothing at all to do with McMenamin. I had a sinking suspicion that neither Squirrel nor Daly really knew what *they* were looking for in Manchester, that they themselves were being guided from above.

Marge dropped me near a shopping centre with a pub at its centre. From there, I took a taxi back to the city centre. My driver sounded like her mouth was full of thumb tacks.

"The Hamptons? Cost you, my friend."

"Cost my company, you mean."

I was quite a way from the centre of Manchester, after all. I resisted the urge to take out the photo and try and ID the Dublin transvestite in the cab. You never knew with taxi drivers. I thought of some of the cutting-edge transvestites I had met during the Arthur Begadan investigation. Lolly and Erika and Phyllis. But fashions and faces changed as much as mascara. One woman's man was another man's TV. It wasn't that easy to penetrate under the foundation cream, after all.

I went for a dander later on that night around the centre of Manchester. I tried to be fair to the city as I walked along. I told myself of its great university, its industrial past and so on, but none of it worked, because Manchester was really Belfast by any other name. And I loathed Belfast. When I slept that night, under a well-earned blanket of three Black Bushes, I imagined someone whispering the name of the Dublin TV in the photograph in my ear. But, if they did, the name was long gone when I woke. It would have to wait until Dublin and the eyes of O'Leary and Squirrel and Miss Katie and others. I had made the connection, at any rate. Now it was time to start listing the elements of the various Venn diagrams. Time to find their common elements too.

Chapter Eighteen

ARLAND WAS ALL over the shop when I arrived back in Dublin. Everywhere you looked, Brian Toomey's plummy face beamed back at you, but there were no further interviews with RTÉ – a stop had been put to that from on high – and the papers kept out of the legal firestorm. Toomey's counsel, of course, had already called for the whole case to be dismissed. That meant the ball was back in the High Court. In Cooney's, I overheard one old boy say to the next, "It's all a ready-up to get him off the hook anyway."

There was a message on the answering machine when I got back from Manchester that night. Mulhall had finally seen fit to get his sidekick to contact me again. I didn't see the point in jumping in too quickly though. Watching Arland sink slowly beneath the waves was excitement enough for me. The McMenamin case looked like it was in the doldrums too, for the moment. Though we knew we were on the right track, there was nothing yet to link Bruno Downes and his buddy to the murder of McMenamin. Squirrel called to the house the night after I came back. The word was put around the station that everything had got too much for me. As if anyone bought that.

Squirrel was edgy that night, knowing that it was time to sit down and face the music. Angelina knew well enough to keep away from us. I closed over the sitting room door and sat Squirrel down in my father's old armchair.

"Now, Detective Murray, let's start from the beginning. What else haven't I been told here?"

"How do you mean, Barrett?"

"Let's say you misled me, Squirrel."

I tried to keep a lid on it as best I could. I drew deep breaths as I paced the floor. Squirrel dug his hands into his jacket pockets. I looked across at him.

"This is all to find something current on Toomey, right?"

"Yes."

"But you don't know what, exactly?"

"Miss Katie is only the portal, Barrett."

"I want to speak to that fucking bitch again!"

"No can do, Barrett."

"Say what?"

"She's gone AWOL."

Angelina called us from the kitchen. Supper was ready. Squirrel smiled. And I smiled back.

"Well I'm going down to see that shrew Maeve, then."

I wasn't in any form for pasta that night. My stomach was already in knots. The only solution, if I didn't want to hurt Angelina's feelings or lie awake all night with the *carbonara* pushing its way through my gut like a football, was to drink copious amounts of red wine. When Angelina disappeared upstairs for a moment, Squirrel smiled at me and said, "You're a free agent, Barrett, on compassionate leave."

Something inside me was turning sourer by the hour now. I had no great problem with accepting the "coming out" scam Toomey had pulled in order to get out of Arland in the seventies, even if he had caused my father alcoholic depression. But I failed to see why my father should have taken it so badly. Many a journalist had to keep his trap shut about politicians and priests over the last fifty years. Why had it driven my father to drink and death? Was it that he was especially weak? Or something else? Toomey was simply a cat landing on all fours, like Tom Hunt said. But this was the new millenium and my pig's snout was out for whatever else lay underneath Arland. Everywhere I came across Toomey's close-set eyes, on the television or in the papers, something told me there was even more to this than I imagined. But it was Toomey's cream-fed voice that really got to me.

"We really should be careful about what we say here."

The pursed lips, the precious smile. Squirrel's words cut through my thoughts.

"Just go for the facts, Barrett. The facts. Past and present."

"Is that what O'Leary told you to tell me?"

It was early Wednesday evening when I arrived outside Les Charmettes. There were a couple of early birds at the bar, perched modestly on silver sixties-style stools. I was adamant when I spoke to Maeve through the intercom.

"Let me in, dear, or I'll be back with all my mates. And they won't be wearing dresses."

The door clicked open. As soon as I appeared, the ladies at the bar counter got the smell of pig and were away to the changing rooms post-haste. In a flash, they were out the door and off home to their loved ones, especially the one who, through the make-up, bore more than passing resemblance to a local bank manager of my acquaintance. Maeve busied herself stacking the bar. Giving me the silent treatment. Picture, no sound. All very ho-hum and what can I do for you, Sergeant Barrett?

"OK, where's Miss Katie?"

"No idea. Next question."

"Didn't she leave a telephone number? E-mail address?"

"I said, I've no idea."

Maeve's head popped up from beneath the shelves. The ring in the nose glinted under the bar lights.

"Didn't I hear you were on the sick, Detective Barrett?"

"Now, where would you hear a thing like that?"

Where, indeed. When I got my breath back, the table-tennis continued. The gist of the message seemed to be that Miss Katie was all right. No one had taken her out. That her nerves had gotten to her and she had decided to lie low for a few days. But I didn't buy it. It sounded too much like the sort of story that had been put around the station about me. If I wanted to take up the Manchester thread again, I couldn't let things go cold like that. And anyway, I had a deep down feeling that Miss Katie was playing a double game, keeping sweet with both sides, to see which way the dice would fall.

Aoife was ill with a stomach bug that weekend. Angelina appeared during the second bout and made a big fuss of us both. There was a lot of mammying and cuddling of Aoife, though Angelina had no children of her own. Pre-loaded software – you can't bate it. While Angelina took care of Aoife, I brewed up tea and made toast. Anna made a big fuss of me not phoning her to say Aoife was sick, when I left her back, but what was the point? The child was all right. I told her Angelina had kept an eye on her too. Bad move. Mammy bear smells other potential mammy bear.

"Look, I'm just saying, you should have let me know. We're joint parenting her, you know."

"OK. Point taken . . . joint parenting . . . right."

Angelina's Dublin summer was drawing to a close, though I got the impression she could live without Milan in the summer anyway. I secretly hoped she would stay on a little longer. I would miss her garrulousness around the house. This great revelation came over breakfast, during her telling me about some bit of Joyceana she had mined the day before, or perhaps on that last walk we had taken down around Richmond Street and into Bally-bough. But there was something else Angelina was doing to me that I wouldn't really admit until she was well back home. She was warming me up again, emotionally speaking. I realised slowly, and admitted it to myself even more slowly, that I was the type of man who would never really be happy with just a six-pack and a furtive shag in the car, even if it was freely available, seven days a week. I wanted to be back in love. For keeps. Whatever keeps meant these days. I was vaguely aware that, if love was ever to enter my life again, that I would have to do a little work on my own pre-loaded software. But I wasn't about to go saying that to Squirrel Murray. Or Anna Barrett, for that matter.

It was Jon Wollenweider who put me wise on certain devel-opments up in the political stratosphere a few days later. Now maybe O'Leary and some of the others knew, but if they did, they didn't pass it on to me. There wasn't a whisper about it in the papers either. Reading about Arland in *The Irish Times* was like watching a sick horse keel over and die. It was not a matter of if, but when. At first, I didn't understand what Wollenweider was on about, but then the picture cleared. Toomey, it seemed, was try-ing to do a reprise of his seventies interview in my father's house.

This time though, it would be with the *Independent*. The London one, that is. He was trying to add to the RTÉ *sub judice* trick and compound it by further prejudicing his own trial.

"Where did you find this out, Jon?"

"We're all in Europe now, Thomas."

"We are, when it suits us."

But it didn't work out that handy for Toomey. Even though Arland was a dead duck now, things had changed sufficiently across the water for them not to want to screw with internal affairs in Dublin. The Brits didn't even need to put a D-notice on the London *Independent*, like they had been fond of doing with the *Guardian* in the seventies, when fishy stories of special ops in Northern Ireland were being touted about. The truth was, you could pinch Her Royal Highness's bottom with impunity if it could be shown, beyond reasonable doubt, that busting you would *damage the peace process*. And we were all trying of course, to *move the process forward*. ShinnerSpeak. Right. Not even Brian Toomey's erstwhile political cronies could bypass the new boys on the block. The great and the good, in Britain and Ireland, had flexed their muscles. Our man was not going to be let off the hook a second time running, but it would still be too little, too late. I began to envy Angelina's passion for times dead and gone. There was a lot to be said for living in the past, in a Dublin of trams and bicycles and dairy shops. As long as you weren't exposed to the TB, malnutrition, diphtheria etc. that living in the past would really demand.

In the heel of the reel, it wasn't Mulhall I met the next week, but a younger acolyte of the republican cause, a fellow in his late twenties in a suit and tie, who looked like he was going to offer me a good deal on an Axminster. We met in a coffee shop in a shopping centre on the northside. Among the trollies and the plastic bags, I told him that I needed to meet Mulhall again. Then I threw in a few bits and pieces about Miss Katie and the business Wollenweider had spoken to me about. I didn't expect Danny Mulhall to get back to me for a few days, but the mobile rang that evening. And the wily schoolmasterish tone was very clear.

"Detective Barrett?"

I didn't carp at being phoned on my personal number because I realised that there must be a good reason for Mulhall doing it. To be heard by those who counted. Needless to say, he knew more than I had told his sidekick. Because Danny Mulhall still had ins, within many overlapping circles of power.

"I hear you've been ill, Thomas?"

"News travels fast."

We arranged to meet on the Saturday. Just me and two-shot Danny. Only I didn't mention I was bringing someone else along with me, so as not to *damage the peace process*. So as to *move the process forward*.

Chapter Nineteen

THERE WAS A real end-of-summer feeling about the last weeks of August, the sense that the odd evening swilling beer at the garden table was over for another year. It was an Indian summer of sorts. Podgy men in undersized T-shirts roamed the streets of Dublin. Women with cellulite-rich thighs were everywhere to be seen. Squirrel seemed to be the only one in the whole city who didn't lose the run of himself altogether. He stayed in sensible shirt, tie and pressed trousers, someone who wouldn't be easily swayed by a few days' decent weather. He arrived over at the house a day or two before the arse fell out of Arland altogether. We sat out in the back garden, sipping cans of Heineken as Angelina prepared a final feast in the kitchen before her imminent departure, a couple of days later. Squirrel frowned.

"Do you think we should give her a hand in there, Barrett?"

"Spoil her for the next man, Squirrel."

We talked in our own code: snippets and tidbits that even a nosy neighbour would have found hard to string together. I heard Angelina open a bottle of wine as the smell of pizza wafted out to us. I slipped the Manchester photo back into the folder when she appeared at the table. Maeve, Miss Katie's shadow-on-earth, had been unable or unwilling to ID the photo. Squirrel was, truth to tell, as puzzled as I was by the thing. He had copied the photo and shown it about, but no one had been able to hang a handle on the face. Angelina clapped her hands.

"Last supper, Thomas! Very sad!"

"Sadder for me, Angelina. I've got to go back to my own cooking."

When we were halfway through the meal, the phone rang in the sitting room. Before I even lifted the receiver, I knew this was going to be an unusual phone call. The muffled voice on the other end was one I remembered from my father's time: Dick Keegan, a sub-editor who had stood by my father during the early days of Arland 1, in 1973. Another one, like my father, who had come up the hard way, reporting on district court cases, hurling matches and cattle marts.

"As you know, Mr Barrett, the Arland trial won't last the week, but some of us feel, however, that justice must be done."

"I don't understand."

There was an intake of breath, as though the caller was dealing with a slow child. I wasn't comfortable being called Mr Barrett. It felt too much like being invited to a dinner party. Or faking it. Maybe that was because I still hadn't buried the real Mr Barrett.

"You will receive an envelope in the post, in the next few days."

"I'm sorry?"

"The rest you will be able to sort out yourself. Right back to 1973."

"Hello? Hello?"

The line, no doubt from a public phone box, went dead then.

I was out of sorts when I rejoined Squirrel and Angelina. Squirrel's red moustache was covered in pizza crumbs, and

Angelina was rambling on about how much she would miss Dublino. I didn't get a chance to tell Squirrel about the phone call or the message, but it didn't matter that much. If the mysterious letter did arrive, I would be on the blower to him ASAP.

The morning Arland finally sank under the waves, the buff-coloured envelope arrived in Drumcondra. I was on my way over to visit mother and I just threw it in the glove compartment to read later. Whatever was in it could keep until I had done my filial duty. I really wasn't expecting much anyway. It was bucketting as I pulled into the nursing home. The Indian summer had suddenly come to grief over the Atlantic, and a grey sky covered the whole of Dublin. Mother was sitting near a bay window, looking out on the whole mess when I arrived. Without turning to me, as though she recognised my footsteps, she said, "Will it ever stop, Thomas?"

"Maybe next summer."

"I won't be here then, next summer."

"You shouldn't talk like that, Mam."

She seemed strangely lucid all of a sudden. We chatted for a while about one thing and another. Although it might have seemed an odd, disjointed conversation to an outsider, there was a logic to the conversation that bothered me. It was as though my mother was coming up for one last glimpse of reality before going under for the last time. An Indian summer in the midwinter of cerebral ataxia. It was the sound of the television clicking on and the magic word Arland on the one o'clock news that really started the roll. Her eyes seemed suddenly sharper. I told myself to shut up, that there mightn't be another chance.

"It was this Arland business that really broke your father, you know."

"I suppose so."

"He put so much . . . so much faith in that . . . in that whore-master Toomey."

I was shocked by my mother's tone, but I ignored the faces that turned towards us, resolving silently to strangle the nurse in the corner, if she tried to put a stop to my mother's gallop. With the concentration of someone trying to thread a needle by candle-light, my mother screwed up her tired eyes and pushed on. It was the seventies again. My father was at the height of his career, a cub reporter on a bog paper who had risen through the ranks to be trusted by the barflies of the nation for the column he wrote under the rubric of *Draper's Letter*. How many bar conversations in the fifties and sixties had started with "What does your man *Draper* make of it all?"

Now our house in Drumcondra was a busy one, with com-ings and goings and phone calls at all hours of the night and a little too much attention from the gardaí after the interview my father did with one of Danny Mulhall's lieutenants in the mid-seventies. Before that particular volunteer blew himself up on a road in County Down. I suppose that's the main sense I had of my father, in other people's minds: he was trusted and respected until the first aborted Arland investigation undid all that. Moth-er was flicking back through the catalogue of events now. Her whole life floating before her as she drowned in her own thoughts. Family celebrations, the death of her sister in an acci-dent and my father's unexpected death. She rhymed off the names of the high and low who had crossed the threshold of our house in Drumcondra. I knew where it was all leading, of course. But I thought, at first, that it was going to be the usual diatribe about what a fool my father was. When the face of Brian Toomey leared out of the TV screen at us, she whispered to me, "Let's go over by the window."

My mother eased herself into the bay window seat, and I drew up a high-backed chair and arranged myself so as to frighten away any potential intruder. Her lips were trembling now. The frailness in the eyes and the shallow breathing told me that there would be no more ascendance. I took her hand in mine. She drew in her breath slowly, almost as an afterthought.

"The whole crux of the thing is still back in Belfast, you know, Thomas."

"What do you mean?"

"Toomey's carry-on. One of those chaps who thinks from the waist down."

"You mean the bombs and the Belvue bar and all that?"

When my mother tried to look me in the eye, I flinched, suddenly realising that the woman knew something else, something she hadn't told me before. That she had, in police parlance, withheld information. I was suddenly in interrogation mode, ready to squeeze the story out of her if I had to.

"Not the Belvue, you gom, you."

"Where, then?"

"The Willington Lodge . . . the Willington Lodge."

"The where?"

"That's where Toomey's little game went on."

"The Willington Lodge."

"And it all ended in tragedy for that poor young chap."

What happened next was even more distressing. I thought mother was sliding into one of those turns of hers, so I asked her whether I should get someone, but she was adamant. She wanted no help. No help at all. I took my eye off her then, just in case it would rattle her and make her lose the thread of things. This was about part of my past and a lot of my present: Arland, the seventies and my father. This was the last line my mother might ever throw me. Her old face looked up at me, age-freckled and puzzled. It was as though what she had to say had been loaded just a few minutes before, the fag-end of a half-forgotten file. That she was only the embassy of her own words now. On autoplay.

"That poor young chap had to die because of them . . . he had to die."

"McMenamin, you mean?"

"Who, Thomas?"

I cleared my throat and looked into the eyes that were starting to cloud over already.

"Who do you mean, Mother?"

"Your father only mentioned the murder once, in my hearing."

I could see my mother's thoughts stumbling now. She was losing the run of them. I tried another tack, a gentler one.

"The Willington Lodge . . . that was the name of the place, Thomas, wasn't it?"

I boxed clever. Let on I knew what she was talking about.

"Yes, that's right. The Willington Lodge."

"That poor . . . Phillip . . ."

"Phillip?"

And then there was just silence. I became aware of a young nurse standing in front of me, smiling, like I had just beaten my mother into signing a dodgy will. But the coin had dropped through the slot, and my mother's memory machine clicked off.

I hung around until it was time for dinner, then made my farewells and headed back for town and over the East Link bridge for Drumcondra. I could catch the sawbones at his evening surgery to boost up my sick cert for another week. Keep everything sweet and legal. I could have given Squirrel a bell then, but I felt like just lying low. The encounter with Mother had drained me a bit. The really lucid episodes were going to get rarer and rarer now. Soon the sentences would give way to phrases and the phrases to single words. And then silence would set in. I made the Cat and Cage just in time to catch the lunchtime news. The crowd in the bar were all eyeing the screen.

A voice called out, "Would you ever turn that up, Pat, like a good man."

The camera's eye swept along the Liffey. Sky Television. An outside eye. Then up the river to the Four Courts. It was all very dramatic. A voiceover said, "Irish Bombs-for-Property Trial Collapses".

There was silence all along the bar. The Irish, apparently, had made a balls of things again. Chortle, chortle. The camera cut back to Belfast in the seventies. The troubles boiling over. Greedy southerners making money out of the north's misery. Bombs and more bombs. Then cut to shots taken, scarcely an hour before, of Mr Brian Toomey and his entourage on the steps of the Four Courts. The grey suit and the upbeat tie. The hair brushed high across the forehead like everyone's favourite head boy. And now Toomey was doing a to-camera piece. He might have been talking to me personally, the PC Plod who had just been shafted.

"I have been vindicated. My accusers have been silenced!"

And then Mr Toomey was off in a waiting car with his little flank of retainers, but there was no sign of Alannah Harris, that seventies spectre, this time. Just the suave, seamless men of the new millennium: the spin doctors, the lawyers and the political acolytes. The barman set down the neat Bushmills.

"That crowd always escapes in the last reel."

"Is that a fact, now?"

I took the whole thing personally, of course. Toomey's supercilious grin in the tube seemed to be for me and me alone. Got you, Barrett! You and Daddy! Two for the price of one. I grunted as I ripped open the brown envelope that had arrived that morning. It contained photocopies of old hotel bills from Belfast, the sort of stuff we had rooted out from dusty boxes during the raid on Merrigan's, the solicitors. More McMenamin material. It was déjà bleeding vu, all over again. Bit late in the day for this sort of stuff. And then the letterhead caught my eye. There was no Belvue Hotel there. The photocopies said clearly "The Willington Lodge".

I could feel a piece of mustard-covered sandwich stick in my throat. I couldn't find the mobile quickly enough as I headed for the bog. A yuppie type was shaking the last drops from Charlie Brown as I entered the toilet, smiled at him and disappeared into the cubicle. The phone in the nursing home rang. No, Mrs Barrett couldn't come to the phone. She was asleep after her dinner. Was there a message?

I could hardly say, "Ask her about The Willington Lodge. Who was the killee?"

I knew well that whatever Mother had said to me was about all she was going to say on the subject, whether she wanted to say more or not. I left a message to say I would drop back out in the evening and headed back for the bar. I realised that my mother must have been more than a little uneasy about exploring Arland again. Arland, after all, had made a lot of mischief between herself and my father, as it had done between me and Anna, twenty years later. I glanced at the envelope in my hand. I wasn't convinced that father's old friend was acting on his own here; I smelled the hand of Danny Mulhall in the thing, among others.

There were lots of ideas in my head now, each as odd as the other, and behind all these ideas was the notion that I was being watched. If I was to proceed any further, it was time to put the hounds off the trail – to set a dead trail, a trail that the great and the not-so-good could follow while I carried on elsewhere. Manchester would be the trail. They could follow me to Manchester, through Miss Katie. From there, I would give them the slip. It was time to start using my opponents' methods: dead letter drops on the internet and anonymous landlines. In the meantime, I would get in touch with Mulhall and Hunt and my father's old buddy, Dick Keegan, the man who had sent the photocopies in the first place. This was the real lead. This was the real game. And everyone seemed to know what the real show was, except muggins here.

Brian Toomey was very much in my mind as I headed back through the lunchtime traffic for hearth and home that day. It was time to turn my attention to a new board now, one that I hadn't known existed before: the one that my mother and Dick Keegan had just opened play on. With the figure of Brian Toomey on the far side, five o'clock shadow and all.

Chapter Twenty

DUNEVIN LODGE WAS snuggled into a ferny gap in the Wicklow Mountains, not far from Glendalough. It was the sort of nook where the Wicklow tribes had gathered, a couple of hundreds years earlier, on their way to harassing the poor English on the military roads. I suspected that the walls of the Dunevin Lodge had seen plenty of interesting comings and goings over recent years too: illicit affairs between Dublin worthies; senior civic functionaries playing pass-the-parcel with public funds. It was far enough off the road to be slightly awkward to get to, but near enough to both Dublin and the south to be, well, near enough to both. I sat in the lounge alone, looking out on to the long, gravel driveway that lead down to the main road. I chose the gunslinger seat – back to the wall, one hundred and eight degree plus vision – but I didn't leave it all to chance. Squirrel was sitting in the dining room, keeping lookout just in case some renegade republican with a long memory decided to mix it with me.

Mulhall, in a fetching fawn three-piece suit and matching tie, was in the room before I knew he was there at all. I hadn't even noticed the car draw up, which meant he had arrived before us and had kept out of the way. The snappy northern accent ensured just the right amount of deference from the barman.

"Ice with your whiskey, sir?"

"Do you want to drown the poor thing?"

"Sorry, sir."

Danny Mulhall pulled up a chair. We both agreed that it was a chilly night, for August. The evening had just closed in, and though there were a few foreign voices around the lounge, we knew the Dunevin Lodge wouldn't get too crowded. I hadn't known who would arrive first. Mulhall, as it happened, had beaten his opponent to the draw.

Top Provo Insists on Good Timekeeping

When his eyes met Tom Hunt's across the carpeted floor a few minutes later, Danny Mulhall stiffened in his seat like a tabby cat spotting a Doberman.

"Is this some sort of joke, Detective Barrett?"

"No joke at all, Mr Mulhall."

I set down the envelope with the Willington Lodge photocopies on the table between us and went to get Hunt a drink. Hunt was standing at the side of the bar, leaning awkwardly on a walking stick. He didn't seem overly worried about meeting a Provo in a public place. He was going down the chute fast with the big C. I handed Hunt his brandy, and he followed me over to the table. All he wanted was a little revenge. Danny Mulhall was all sweetness and light at first.

"And how are you today, Mr Hunt?"

"Sound as a trout."

"Glad to hear it."

Where do you begin, with an ex-superintendent and a semi-retired Provo? Little chinwag about the virtues of semtex versus co-op mix? In the end, I didn't have to worry. Mulhall weighed in first.

"Let's get to the point, boys. Why are we all here?"

"That's what I'd like to know, Detective Barrett."

Hunt's voice was frail and tetchy. I took up the envelope on the table and pulled out the photocopies. My own voice didn't sound too certain.

"Willington Lodge. I thought you gentlemen might be able to help me here."

Hunt's rheumy eyes looked across the table at his counterpart. Danny Mulhall took a sip of his orange juice.

"Ah, yes . . . the Willington Lodge."

"Which Mr Mulhall's acquaintances bombed to the ground in the mid-seventies."

"With no loss of life, Mr Hunt."

"Operation go wrong, did it, Mr Mulhall?"

Danny Mulhall gave a weary sigh, like a vexed Christian Brother groaning at some childish joke.

"I think we're straying from the point here, Mr Hunt. It's not the seventies; there's no need to play sheriff any more."

"Once an outlaw, always an outlaw."

"Ah well, now, if you're going to take that sort of an attitude . . ."

I grasped Mulhall's elbow as he started to rise. A few well-got heads turned towards us as I pleaded softly with Danny Mulhall to stay. This was the new millennium, I assured him. Peace in our time. And why should a few dead bodies come between us? My words were silky smooth.

"Look, lads, we all have a vested interest here. I think I can help you, if you help me, that is."

Danny Mulhall sat down slowly, but there was a palpable air of menace between both men. I asked about the McMenamin business then, by way of warming up with a more recent corpse. While Hunt sat and huffed, Danny Mulhall gave a standard spiel about a good man done down for "defending his community from drugs". I didn't bother asking which community, but moved right on to the Arland case. Hunt thawed out a bit then. Or, at least, he went through the motions of explaining his role in Arland 1, which I knew every detail of, from my father. From the start of the investigation in the early seventies, through the writs lying in half a dozen solicitors' offices, to the hint that rogue republicans, with debts of honour to certain government apparatchiks, might be called in. Not to mention the subtext threat to my father, his family and livelihood. The chirpy Spanish lounge girl arrived with the another orange and a second brandy. I opted for coffee.

"Moving on to the Willington Lodge . . ."

"Ah, yes. The Willington Lodge."

I poured myself a coffee from the little silver pot, my eyes fixed on Danny Mulhall."

"Why did your people bomb it?"

"That was a long time ago, Thomas – could have been any number of reasons."

Hunt swished the whiskey about in the tumbler.

"Oh, now, Mr Mulhall, I'm sure you, of all people, must know the answer to that."

Danny Mulhall stared across the table at Hunt, but Hunt didn't flinch. He was clearly afraid of nobody any more.

"Look, like I said, it could have been any one of a number of things. Most of the units had autonomy, in those days. Could have been used as a loyalist meeting place."

"A little guest house like the Willington Lodge?"

"Maybe even a personal vendetta . . ."

Danny Mulhall's eyes met mine. This was more like it now. A personal vendetta. A debt squared. This made sense now. I passed the photocopies to the two men. We smiled at the quaint-looking billheads with the profile of Queen Victoria and the tacky typeface. The bills had been typed only a couple of months before the Willington Lodge was bombed to the ground. The name on the bills was the same name that had incriminated Brian Toomey on the Arland material: Mr Neal Downey, a name Toomey used for a string of hidden bank accounts.

It was clear enough, at this stage, that the fox and the wolf in front of me knew what I needed to know and what they knew was pretty much the same thing that was locked away in my mother's head in the nursing home. All I needed was a nod in the right direction. I could do the rest. It was clear, too, that both the fox and the wolf wanted me to sniff out the truth. Hunt's motive was clear enough: revenge on Brian Toomey. Mulhall's motivation was still a puzzle. I suspected there was a personal note there somewhere, but Danny Mulhall didn't do personal, at least not in front of me. All I really had to go on was my mother's mutterings. There was nothing more to add to the picture, or nothing that wasn't the product of my own imagination. I had ransacked my father's old files and gone back through old newspaper clippings, but I didn't find anything about the Willington Lodge except for the fact that it had been bombed. Either additional notes had been consigned to the fire – by my mother? – or my father had been prudent enough not to make any notes at all. When Hunt toddled off to drain the lizard, I knew it was time to show my hand. Poker had never come easily to me. Mulhall gazed nonchalantly over his glass.

"Was there something else, Detective Barrett? I've come a long way."

"We all have, Danny. As a matter of fact . . ."

"Yes?"

I looked up into Danny Mulhall's charming blue eyes, the killer-clear eyes that had sent dozens of volunteers out on hundreds of missions, some never to come back. Minstrel boys, gone to the war. I knew now that Mulhall wanted to play ball with me because there was something in it for him. Whatever it was, I would worry about that later. But he couldn't be seen to be the one who sold the pass to the gardaí. There were enough non-peaceniks who might jump at the chance to take him out. Who did not want to *move the process forward,* so to speak.

"The Willington Lodge: was there someone killed there in the bombing that no one knew about?"

"Almost right. Someone was murdered there: my nephew, Phillip Keane . . . only a young fellow."

"And this has some connection with our friend Toomey?"

"Right again, Thomas. Now you've got the picture."

"Are you telling me that Brian Toomey was involved in the . . ."

"Murder."

"In the murder of your nephew?"

"That's exactly what I'm telling you."

"How? Why? And why, if you don't mind my asking . . ."

"Yes?"

"Why are you bothering to let this go to court?"

Mulhall sat back and smiled.

"It's peace and flowers time now, Detective Barrett. Don't you follow the newspapers? Anyway, I believe in people being tried and convicted first before . . ."

"Before what? Before what?"

Mulhall glanced over his shoulder as Hunt made his way back towards us. Pissing was a permanent pastime for Hunt now, I suspected. Pissing, punctuated by eating and sleeping. The long dribble before death. Mulhall looked at me with a look that said: *Keep mum, now.* I was so dead set on reading his eyes that I hadn't even noticed Mulhall palming the piece of paper. Before I realised it, the piece of paper had been placed in my hand.

"There you go now, Thomas. Wee tip on the 3.15, at Epsom."

The tannoy was playing Phil Coulter's glissando version of that awful dirge, "The Fields of Athenry". I excused myself as Hunt sat down and made for the bathroom to read the slip of paper Mulhall had slipped me: "d'Alton".

Now I didn't have to rummage around much in my memory banks to sort out who d'Alton was. It had to be Martin d'Alton, a well-got British liberal QC who had defended many an Irish case in the seventies and eighties, at a time when the sniff of an Irish accent in a pub or a café could send a frisson of fear and loathing along the whole counter. And that charmingly naïve British query: "Why can't you Irish just live together?"

My father had had some dealings with d'Alton, but I hadn't known there was any Arland connection. Martin d'Alton was still practising. He just didn't get into the papers as much any more. I tore up the piece of paper and, burying it under a mound of toilet paper, flushed it away to kingdom come.

Hunt was standing up to leave when I arrived back. It seemed as though he and Mulhall had been sniping at one another again, but if they couldn't stand the sight of one another that much, they would have turned heel as soon as they met. Their need was greater than their loathing. Hunt insisted on making his way out to the car on his own, so I left him to it. He told me he was to stay with a sister in Dalkey that night. I glanced at the sunken eyes once more. It was amazing how revenge could keep one alive, just that little bit longer. Another few months – or weeks – and Hunt would be at the brow of the hill. Like my mother. Then it would be all downhill, as he hurtled for the abyss. When Hunt left, I turned back to Danny Mulhall who was putting on a big show of being in a hurry himself now. I kept my voice low.

"Mr McMenamin was killed over Arland, not drugs. Right?"

"More or less. Arland and the rest. You have the ball now, Thomas. Don't drop it."

I swallowed hard. It didn't come easy to me, accepting a pat on the back from a Provo, a crowd my father hated as much as the crowd who had screwed him. I left it for about ten minutes or so, until Mulhall's car had pulled away, then I headed for Squirrel, in the dining room. He was well-placed to watch all the entrances and exits. He wiped his moustache with a monogrammed napkin.

"They're both in bed together all right, Barrett."

"You're sure?"

"There was traffic between Hunt's sister in Dalkey and one of Mulhall's boys, about an hour ago."

"Q.E.D., then."

"Kind of odd though, one of them ringing her."

I took out the envelope with the Manchester photograph. The restaurant was practically empty now. No eyes to see or ears to hear. I bit my lip and looked across the table at Squirrel. The Manchester photograph had been taken with a good camera. What was meant to be in focus was in focus. The naked teenage boy sat on the knee of the man in the party mask. My eyes closed in on the TV standing, out-of-focus, to the left of the boy. Only she wasn't a TV at all. The gawky wig and the tight skirt had thrown me. This was a real woman, but an inelegant, ugly one.

"That's who I think it is, isn't it, Squirrel?"

"It's Alannah Harris all right. We didn't realise that earlier. That's why we think you're being set up, Barrett."

"By Miss Katie?"

"We think her hand is being forced. She owes someone and she's the jailbait, but it's your call. You don't have to go any further."

"And walk away from the wreckage, like my father?"

"I didn't say that, Barrett."

I threw a quick whiskey into me, then myself and Squirrel piled into the car pool Primera and headed off down the gravel drive. I was feeling uneasy, even at that stage, wondering just who was doing the watching and waiting. I didn't think we were in any immediate danger though. I thought that would come in Manchester, maybe, when Ms Slut, from Les Charmettes, had lead me a bit further up the path. I reckon now that we must have been tagged from point one. Now, I'm wary enough about pulling out on to mountain roads, especially after dark, but Squirrel was that bit warier. I didn't hear the big black Pajero hurtling round the bend until it was almost on top of us. Squirrel, in a split second decision, put the metal to the floor and sent us shooting across the road into the ditch as the Pajero flew by us, skimming the rear bumper.

"What the fuck was that all about?"

Squirrel knocked off the ignition and turned on the hazard lights in one go, then we were both out of the Primera like shit off a shovel and into the ditch, guns drawn. There was a smell of oil and petrol all around us.

"That was deliberate, Barrett!"

"You don't say?"

There was an even heavier smell of oil now. Squirrel must have torn the bollox out of the sump when we hit the ditch. I called in a request for assistance while Squirrel sniffed about in the car. An Emergency Response Unit team arrived like hot snot. They had been cruising around Rathfarnham, waiting to be asked to party. I had cooled down by the time they had arrived though. But if someone was coming back for a second stab at the rasher, I wasn't going to walk out like a soft idiot saying, "Excuse me! Armed gardaí – drop your weapons, pretty please!" I would shoot first. Then arrest them, dead or alive.

As we rode down off the mountain in the ERU car, I signalled to Squirrel to keep things simple. Tell 'em nothing. In the morning, I would start setting up the contact with Mr d'Alton, through Dick Keegan, my father's old colleague. I would make sure to leave an electronic trail when I headed back to England, but one that would lead in the opposite direction. I still needed Miss Katie for that, because something else might turn up in Manchester that would tie up 1973 with 2005. I felt more and more like a little boy, in a circle of elders now: a circle of manipulative elders that included Hunt and Mulhall, a couple of my father's old buddies and some high-ranking insiders who still wanted a shot at Toomey. It wasn't so much that I minded being the minstrel boy. After all, I was really only out to get the man who killed my pa. However, it would have been nice to know who was behind me and who wasn't, because it's hard enough playing one-level chess. But four-level chess, with a blindfold . . .

Chapter Twenty-One

THE NEXT DAY was a late summer's day all right. The warm rain beat down steadily on the perspex roof of the extension a friend of my father's had jerry-built in the sixties. I sat in the kitchen, sipping a cold cup of coffee and trying to get a handle on things. I had almost been killed outside the Dunevin Lodge. A nice jam sandwich myself and Squirrel would have made if he hadn't got us out of the way pronto. We hadn't been quite quick enough to ID the black Pajero, but we both reckoned it was a hired-hand job. I knew I would have to get in touch with Anna and put her on her guard, once more. Just in case. There was a frosty response from the receptionist in the Land Registry Office where she worked. I had obviously been nominated as bad bastard ex-husband of the year.

"Just a moment and I'll put you through to Ms Barrett."

I asked Anna to meet me as soon as possible. She agreed to meet me for lunch, but not without a struggle.

"This is not about us, Anna."

"Then, what's it about?"

"Can't talk on the phone."

"Unless you've had a few drinks, that is."

"*Touché*."

The Handy Andy was full of smart skirts and pressed shirts all grabbing a sandwich and a cup of coffee before heading back to the nine-to-whenever. When Anna appeared in the doorway, I caught my breath. How could I ever forget those blue eyes? Or that wild smile. Anna joined me in the alcove by the back door.

"Can we get this over with quickly?"

"Sure. What are you having?"

She put on her Lois Lane glasses to read the menu. I tried to keep my mind on matters, to be very subject-verb-object about it all, but I just couldn't help asking myself, what if I hadn't been such a self-engrossed asshole and it was just the two of us again? What if this was a normal husband-and-wife lunch. Only we hadn't had such a thing in years. My eyes caught hers. The buzz of conversation in the background fell away.

"Look, you said you had something important to tell me, Thomas."

I knuckled down to going over the whole business of the McMenamin investigation. About how things were suddenly hotting up, the nearer we got to a resolution.

"I thought the Arland case had been thrown out of court?"

"Yes, the case, but the investigation is still ongoing . . . and more recent matters."

I glanced over my shoulder.

"I'm technically on sick leave."

"I get the picture. If you blow it, they disown you."

"That's not very fair of you, Anna."

"Look, whatever is between us, I don't want you ending up like your father."

The image of Brian Toomey was flickering away inside my head again: the fuzzy smile, a baby blue ball in a golf sweater straining at the seams.

"I won't end up like him, no matter what happens."

I didn't mention the near-miss at the Dunevin Lodge, and I didn't mention the Manchester-Amsterdam connection either. It was all on a need-to-know basis. And all that Anna needed to know, for the moment, was that the next couple of weeks could be complicated.

"Are you saying myself and Aoife are in danger?"

"I just think it's better to be prudent in the coming weeks."

I got Anna to agree to break her routine for the next few weeks, to come and go at odd times.

We parted as the mob scurried back to their offices. At the corner of the street, something took me and I leaned forward and gave Anna a farewell kiss on the cheek. I expected a slap on the face or at least a few swear words, but the cold, angry look Anna gave me was worse than either, because it meant hurt. Hurt and look what we're missing, you gobdaw.

I took Aoife that weekend, despite Anna's misgivings. We took in a film and visited the zoo with herself and Angelina, who had decided to stay a few more weeks. I was beginning to feel like some sort of sugar daddy to my own daughter now, the guy that bought the books and the sweets at the weekend but wasn't connected to the real week of work and school at all. It was still better than nothing. When I put Aoife to bed that Saturday night, I wasn't ready for what she came out with though. Not by a long shot.

"Mammy is meeting her friend again this weekend."

"Oh."

I shut up and let it roll.

"We bumped into him in Superquinn, the other day."

"Really?"

"But he's not as nice as you."

I was snappy with Angelina that evening. I had had quite enough of Joyce and Dublin and all that bolloxology. She knew something had triggered my bad humour though and kept out of my way until after the late news, when I found a glass of wine on the coffee table and a little note that said, "Faint heart never won fair lady."

Before I went to sleep that night, I put together a little cartoon: Barrett and Anna sitting in the Handy Andy, each with one eye looking at the other, the other eye looking at the menu. But I still hadn't worked out a caption. In short, I was lost for words. When I woke, I stuffed the drawing in my pocket, in case Aoife saw it and made up her own story. I wasn't even sure that my eight year old wasn't making up the story about Anna and her friend anyway. Moving the pieces on the board. Chess game level five.

There was still no sign of Miss Katie around Dublin. Venus in blue dress had gone to ground. At first, myself and Squirrel thought that someone might have got to her. But Maeve's composure in Les Charmettes told me that Miss Katie was probably lying low. At any rate, I wanted Miss Katie back to help me get back to the mob in Manchester, to be seen to be following my nose and playing the wrong chess game, which was the gig myself and Squirrel had agreed on at the Dunevin, when Squirrel finally came clean on a few details. Not that we didn't turn a dozen apartments upside down. We left no scumbag unturned in our search for Miss Katie, but she had disappeared into cyberspace, and it was only in cyberspace that we would find her. At kissmyass.com. Where everybody ended up, at some stage or other. Now Miss Katie had to log on to her virtual bordello at some stage, wherever she was billeted, to keep her rent boy routine going. It wouldn't be so much a matter of finding the end of the cable she was attached to. But it sort of made sense to me, and I ran with it. Ignorance is great sauce.

Because I was still technically off duty, I had to arrange my contact with the Gorey techno through Squirrel. If I really was being "handled" from afar, everyone would be authorised to be nice to me, up to a point, but I still couldn't be seen anywhere near official business. So the techno paid me a visit in Drumcondra. Angelina let him in, raising a quizzical eyebrow, and we went straight to work. We chatted about nothing much as he went about his job. Born in the early seventies. Missing a lot of the references I took for granted. The Beatles, Bob Marley and Bloody Sunday. He had a heavy-duty laptop with him in his briefcase and the CDs with the sound files he had made from the phone taps of the late Charles Begadan and Miss Katie from three years earlier. It wasn't so much a case of finding Miss Katie on the net as a case of finding the post she might piss on at any given time. But there were lots of posts and all of them had to be booby-trapped with the sound files. All the contact nodes even vaguely connected to the Clondalkin computer had been sifted and sorted.

"I'm spiking around fifty of them. She's bound to run into one sooner or later."

"I'm very impressed."

"Well, let's just see if it works."

It took a couple of minutes to hook up to the line and upload the stuff. A nice surprise it would be for Miss Katie: a voice from the grave; tapes we hadn't actually let her hear before, that we had saved for a rainy day. Like today.

"That's it, Detective Barrett."

"I'm on leave, you know."

"You're still a detective though."

I didn't get to sleep until late that night, waiting, like a jilted lover, for the phone to ring. It didn't ring at twelve or one or two, but it did ring eventually, sometime around 4 a.m., which says something about the irregular hours fashionable ladies keep. A dream of flying fish and a deep, dark sea was blown away by the sound of the phone. I scarcely recognised the voice on the phone. It didn't sound in the least bit ladylike.

"You bastard, Barrett!"

"And how are you today, Miss Katie?"

"Just tell me what you want."

"I want you back in Dublin, darling. By 6 p.m. tomorrow. Latest."

The phone went dead. I didn't really need to know where Miss Katie was phoning from, but, in the heel of the reel, it turned out to be a British mobile. I pictured Miss Katie sitting in an anonymous apartment, working her way through the internet, sucking up codes, exchanging more codes, clicking on tricky icons. Her eyes narrowing, as she came across an odd icon that kept reappearing, at various locations. Finally giving into curiosity and clicking on it. Then that terrible feeling you might get, the millisecond before you touched the booby-trapped door handle. A glimpse of eternity. The sound file opening. The voice of the very late and very frightened Arthur Begadan, terrrified of Miss Katie's wrath.

"Look, tell them I'll pay all the money by next Friday."

"By next Friday, Arthur, is that right?"

"By next Friday I swear!"

"That may not be good enough for them, Arthur."

I imagined the colour draining from Miss Katie's face, the eyes narrowing, the eyelids closing over. Barrett rides again. Then I lay back in the bed, plotting out how I would speak with Miss Katie the following evening, while she made the arrangements for my very public return visit to Manchester. When I would help her set me up. Get me in to get me out.

Chapter Twenty-Two

THE BAD BITCH in the bright blue dress roared back into town the following day. A call came through from Miss Katie as I was standing in a telephone shop in Tallaght, picking up a second, anonymous mobile. It was my stealth line – a little red Motorola. The young woman serving me looked away shyly, thinking, I suppose, that it was a simple case of a man two-timing a wife or girlfriend. I could hardly tell her I was two-timing the TV queen of Les Charmettes, who had put more men through her frocks than she had had hot dinners. I was brief with Miss Katie on the phone. I would see her later on in the day. No tricks, no touts. I had been phoned at home, an hour earlier, to say that my mother had taken a little turn out in Eden House. It wasn't an emergency but I was asked to drop out, just in case.

It was a sunny morning as I drove out to Killiney. Goose-pimpled office girl flesh was back on the streets. White male torsos strutted the scaffolding of the new Dublin. I followed the little line of cars down through Dalkey village, for the seafront. Nice day for visiting your dying mother. Nice day for a visit to a devious, cold-hearted TV too. When I arrived at the nursing home, the doctor had already been and gone. All indications were that nothing serious had happened, that it was just another jolt on the road. But that day, more than any other, marked the point where my mother crested the hill and really started her downward way.

My mother was sitting up in her bed when I arrived. There was a quizzical smile on her dry lips, as though she really didn't know what all the fuss was about. I handed the bunch of flowers over to the nurse.

"I like the colours, Thomas. Are they chrys . . . chrysanthemums?"

I glanced over at the nurse for an answer. Flowers. Colour. Smell. I wasn't sure.

"Yes, they're chrysanthemums, Mrs Barrett."

I could see that a little more damage had been done during the night, that a few more brain cells had been vaporised. As I settled the pillow behind her head, I glanced at my mother's face, at the weak eyes and the weary skin. Yes, she was at the brow of the hill now. She would soon be hurtling downhill to Never-Never Land, from which no one had ever returned intact. Or, at least, I hadn't met them in Lower Drumcondra. My aloofness upset me, but I knew, too, that this was just a way of steeling myself for what was to come. That when the parting finally came, I would crack up like all the other mammy's boys. I reached out my hand to touch hers.

"Is there anything I can get you, Mam?"

My mother seemed suddenly tired. It was at times like this that I missed having a sister. Someone female and sensible and family, who would know what to do and how to do it. I didn't mind any amount of running and fetching, of driving here and driving there, but a dying mother needed a daughter. At least, I thought gloomily to myself, she has Anna. An ex-daughter-in-law.

When she had fallen to sleep, I kissed my mother's forehead

and walked back out into the sunshine. I would phone later that evening, just in case they needed to contact me urgently. Outside, you could actually see Dublin Bay, for once. Still, I was like Squirrel. I didn't trust the whole charade. And sure enough, by the time I had reached the East Link Bridge, to cross the river back to the northside, the sky had darkened and doubt filled my mind again.

I phoned my father's old pal Dick Keegan and arranged to meet him later that evening. It hadn't been hard to track him down. Since being retired early from the now defunct *Irish Press*, he spent most of his mornings in the National Library – living in the past, wallowing in old newspapers, doing something he referred to vaguely as "research". Keegan would set up the meeting with John Reed, the retired *Guardian* journalist. It was necessary to go back to primary sources all right, to lose myself in the black-and-white frame of the seventies again. I could see the glitter and the platform heels and the fur-lined parka jackets already. The picture was becoming very clear to me now, especially after my words with Danny Mulhall. At least now I knew what I was looking for, but I needed to point up the picture for everyone else. And that meant evidence. Pieces of paper. There would be no more talking with my mother on the subject either. She had told me all she could, and Danny Mulhall had joined up a lot of dots. Now, I needed to see John Reed, in his hospital bed in Surrey. However, I must be careful to lay down an electronic path for myself, to make sure anyone snooping thought I was playing chess game number one. I have to say, at this point, that I wasn't fooled by Miss Katie either. She had still one throw of the dice left. She could still try and turn things on their head, when the time was right, and leave Thomas Barrett in the shit, like dear old dad. I didn't trust her as far as I'd throw her, but I had to play along with her for the moment and let her be seen to set me up. By whomsoever.

I contacted Jon Wollenweider from home, assuming that I would be bugged. I told him about my proposed visit to Manchester, playing to the hidden gallery. Quite a lot had happened in the station over the past week. Although I was officially off the McMenamin case, Squirrel had kept me abreast of everything. Circuits had opened and closed. Connections had been made. Because a gun with a history had been used, it seemed that it was now possible to place Bruno Downes in Dublin, on the night of the McMenamin murder, even though Brainless probably wasn't clear about the big picture. I sat into Squirrel's car outside the Skylon with the engine running and the windows all steamed up, drawing a cartoon on a scrap of paper. Squirrel stared through the window as he spoke.

"It's like the Arland outing, a cover for the real thing."

"Which is?"

"The same story it was in 1973."

"So, McMenamin was topped because he was going to talk, Squirrel?"

"About more than Arland."

Squirrel coughed politely.

"They probably got Bruno Downes to top him, letting on it was because of the anti-drugs thing."

"And the northerner knew? The one at the skip?"

"He must have walked Brainless Bruno into it. We think the northerner is your friend from Amsterdam, Gerry McGuckian. So does Wollenweider."

"Evidence?"

"He'll get it. Are you ready for Manchester, Barrett?"

I rubbed the steamed up window of the car. Thoughts of my mother were in my mind again. I saw her weak face in the bed, in the great house out in Killiney.

"Am I covered?"

"O'Leary is having some of the new blood in Britland cover you. He's afraid the old stock might leak it to Toomey's mates but . . ."

"But?"

"But you might still meet up with a Manchester Bruno Downes over there. Maybe you should carry."

"I'll think about it."

So Bruno Downes had been tasked with taking out Mr Bigmouth McMenamin after all. It was just a question of tying the northern individual into the picture. It must have seemed like a regular hit to Bruno Downes, all the same. A contract killing, after which himself and Gerry McGuckian could slip out of the country and lie low in the Lowlands. I nodded at Squirrel.

"Wish me luck. I'm going to head off to Miss Katie's, meet up with Keegan and get ready for the trip."

"Take it easy, Barrett. We're behind you, but we're not beside you."

"No problem."

There was ritzy, lazy sort of music playing in Les Charmettes that evening. Music to fellate to. It was Thursday night – late night – and a few stragglers were still in the little lounge. They scarcely glanced at me, in my jeans and sweater, as Maeve led me into the inner sanctum. I could hear voices in a closed cubicle further down the corridor. I imagined the scenario behind the door: sensible businessmen in sensible dresses. I passed quickly through the large open room where Miss Katie stored her frills and flounces, past racks and racks of dresses and skirts and tops and rows of shoes of all sorts, from slingback to court shoes. Miss Katie had obviously topped up her stock. A wise business decision. There were a few more clubs on the scene now, and competition was brisk. Unless Miss Katie kept an eye on things, the lads would weigh anchor for a better class of boudoir.

Miss Katie's lair, in the very back of the mews, was away from all the action. It was a spartan little suite, not at all like the rooms down the corridor, with their pink uplighters and red carpets. I knocked softly on the door. Miss Katie looked up from the laptop as I walked in. Her cold, deathray eyes reminded me of Margaret Thatcher at prime minister's question time. Not enough sleep, dear? Stress of high office? I was left alone with Miss Katie then, while her companion pattered off down the corridor to oversee someone who wanted a change of dress.

"We're quits now, Miss Katie."

"We'd fuckinwell better be, Barrett!"

I threw down the photo I had been carrying around all day, the one I had lifted in the bungalow in Manchester during my first visit. Double bluff time. Switch between chess boards.

"That's who I think it is, isn't it, Miss Katie, thirty years on?"

The man in the tight black dress nodded. I heard my voice deepen.

"Alannah Harris . . . am I right?"

There was a Gallic shrug of the shoulders. Something snapped in me then, something like the memory of the real story of the Willington Lodge, that I had drawn out of Mulhall in the Dunevin. I was suddenly shouting and jabbing my finger at Miss Katie's face.

"Don't mess with me, you dirty bitch!"

"Is that why your wife blew you out, Barrett? Do you like beating up women?"

I lowered my hand. It was important to show sincerity, to half-strangle her to death in case she smelt a rat.

In a minute, the little laptop was humming away contentedly to itself. A minute later, the stubby little fingers were charging up and down the keyboard. I saw a couple of fancy icons flash across the screen as Miss Katie crossed the portal into the cyberspace. We were in. I could almost sense the resentment and rage radiating from the manwoman's back. Her reflection in the laptop screen and the viciousness in the hands as they stabbed at the keyboard told it all. Miss Katie didn't turn around when she spoke, but she didn't need to. The tone of her voice was enough for me.

"Manchester's all set up. Thursday night. I'll have the details tomorrow night."

When I stepped out into the little laneway on which Les Charmettes stood, my step was light. I was heading back to 1973. For a moment, as I stood there buttoning up my jacket, I tried to imagine that night in Belfast: the squeal of sirens, the sound of a bomb going off near the city centre, gunfire being exchanged off the Ormeau Road. I tried to think of a young man who had pushed the envelope too far and paid the price. Then I shrugged and made my way towards the car. 1973 would appear, in its own good time and its own good place. Danny Mulhall had given me the picture. I just needed to back it up with evidence now.

Chapter Twenty-Three

ITOOK A cramped, early morning flight to grim old Manchester, and in no time at all I was tramping around its sodden streets. In a crowded pub near the shopping centre the Provos took out, during one of the ceasefire hiccups, I made a few calls on my old mobile, just to make absolutely sure I was being tailed by the forces of darkness. In the seclusion of the gents, I took out the bright red Motorola. I sent a text message to the Gorey techno in Dublin, leaving the line open, so that I could be tracked from then on. I arrived at the Elam Arms sometime around three o'clock. It was all very Coronation Street, right down to the glasses hanging over the bar, the top-heavy barmaid and the stained wood. In my cramped little bedroom, I ran through the protocol again before taking a nap to straighten out my nerves after the flight. The phone rang earlier than expected, as though someone couldn't bear the wait. A woman's voice, a sweet northern voice spoke.

"Everything all right, Mr Martin?"

"Fine, thank you."

"We're going to phone you back around teatime. All right?"

"Fine."

I took a stroll to settle the nerves the catnap hadn't dealt with. What if Squirrel was right and some lowlife had been hired to sort me out? On balance though, I thought it fairly unlikely. Video and tape and photographs were more likely. Which meant I would have to leave before anything incriminating happened. Evil had to be punished though, especially wilful, high IQ evil like Brian Toomey's war with his own twisted self, aided and abetted by the chief high procurer – his sister. I was beginning to sound like a health tract from the back of a cornflakes box. I ordered myself to shut up.

The second phone call came around six. This time, it was a man's voice telling me that a car would be outside the door to pick me up in ten minutes. I injected a little uneasiness into my voice. I was also supposed to be a nervous cop, which, hopefully, they would buy. Exactly ten minutes later, a well-got, forty-something couple pulled up in a well-appointed Rover. As I slid into the car, I noticed the man in the fawn overcoat at the wheel, scanning the street.

"Nice to see you, Mr Martin. There's a newspaper in the back, if you want to catch up on things."

I took the hint. Within a minute or two I had lost all sense of bearing. We were heading into deep, anonymous estate land, where one street and one house looked much the same as the next, give or take a gnome or two. The scenario was pretty much as it had been before. I was dropped at a suburban pub, sat in a corner for a few moments and was then picked up by a pleasant-looking gent who introduced himself as Walter. Not an eye turned as we left the bar. People kept their northern noses in their drinks and got on with their own lives.

There was some desultory chat in the car. Wasn't the weather awful, for the time or year? Things seemed to have settled down in Ireland again. Wasn't all that bombing business dreadful?

"Dreadful."

"How can those people do such things?"

I didn't really have to overplay nervous cop because I really was nervous. The whole surreal expedition was suddenly getting to me. Here I was, with ex-wife and child at home, inviting myself to be set up. And, the truth was, I didn't entirely trust the British police either. Nothing personal or political, you understand, just a slight panic, in case the centres of power from the seventies had started cosying up to one another again. Not for the first time, I questioned the burden of carrying Papa's guilt around on my humped back. I looked up as we pulled into the driveway of a pastel-coloured bungalow, just off the main road.

A pleasant-looking woman of about forty, who called herself Doreen, answered the door and led me into the lounge. She seemed fairly bothered by the weather too, though there was no mention of the Irish "situation", thank Christ. There was the same air about this house as the first house. For all the standard lamps and Van Gogh prints and magazines carefully scattered around the place, this was a house that had seen very little normal life. Like the laptop servers, these houses were probably used only a few times a year, then taken off-line.

"Maybe you'd like to loosen up. There's the remote control. Drink?"

"A . . . a whiskey, please."

"Only Scotch, I'm afraid, and?"

"Neat, please."

"Kills the taste, they say, water."

The screen flickered into life. It was the same show as the last time. Blond-haired Adonises and old gentlemen fellating. This was probably part of the set-up. Somewhere in the room, a camera was probably pointing at me. I kept my jacket on, my hands dug deep into my pockets. There had been no mention of money. That, in itself, was suspicious enough. That would probably come next. More video evidence. Then there would be the sting: either Detective Thomas Barrett backed off barking up Brian Toomey's tree, or he himself would be shafted. I felt the open mobile in my pocket and hoped to fuck the cavalry got here in time, before I was pushed too far and compromised. But I needn't have worried, because it was the other side who jumped the gun. Now, in all my years on the force, as tubby sergeants say when they are hauled into the witness box, I have yet to come across a sex session that was paid for after the event. Sex is always paid for pre-coitally, when the customer is hot under the collar and can't think straight and the monkey part of the brain overrides the higher regions. That's why, when I was suddenly called out into the carpeted hallway, to see a middle-aged man leading a teenage boy down the stairs, I decided to go for it rather than risk a bridge too far. The young boy had that special, scrubbed look that children from institutions sometimes have, which was probably where he was sourced from, a hundred miles away. I caught the silly smile of the woman called Doreen at the foot of the stairs. It was a smile that said, "Gotcha, Detective Barrett!"

But the grin was suddenly wiped off her face when I took the young boy's hand and said, "Hello! I'm Detective Thomas Barrett, from Dublin."

It all happened in a flash then. I was most impressed by the Brits. Most impressed. There was a squeal of tyres on the driveway, and a dozen swat squad types burst in through the front and back doors, all armed with shiny black Heckler and Kochs. I grabbed the boy and pulled him into the front room and down on the floor, just in case a shot was fired. When Doreen and her sidekick had been handcuffed, a uniformed policewoman appeared in the living room, with an armed detective. (I loved the new Kevlar jackets and made a mental note to suggest an upgrade to O'Leary, back in Dublin.)

"You're Detective Barrett, I believe?"

"Yes, that's right."

"I'm Detective Inspector Watkins. All the excitement seems to be over for the moment."

We pissed on one another's posts a bit then. Name dropping. That edgy way policemen have of validating one another. All the while I spoke with Watkins, the chap with the gun stood to one side, watching me, just in case I was part of another game of chess. I could see the youth being led away by a tiny little policewoman. He looked dazed and confused, as though he had been woken from one nightmare to another. He half-smiled over his shoulder as he was led away. I remember thinking: will the next institution be any better than his present one? I played it cagey with the Brits though, just in case one of their number was non-right-thinking and leaked news of my real destination to the forces of darkness, back in Dublin. After the formalities had been gotten out of the way in the station – I had to make a preliminary statement and make a video link-up with Dublin – I was driven back to the Elam Arms to gather up my bits and pieces. I slept with a chair against the door all the same. Just in case.

In the Manchester morning rain, I caught a taxi out to the airport and the first shuttle down to London, not Dublin. As we hit V1 and V2 and the G-forces drove me back into the seat, I reminded myself to phone Squirrel on the Motorola, just to make sure that he had paid that all-important visit to our mutual republican friend in Mountjoy. Mr Pat McDonagh, one-time associate of Danny Mulhall's, who was doing time for extortion, was a man who had memories of a night in Belfast in 1973 to sell, and who was now ready to deal. Then I lay back in my seat and went into denial that I was cruising at thirty thousand and odd feet. I ran through what I would say to Jack Reed when I met him that evening down in Surrey. And, most of all, what I would say to Martin d'Alton, as we reeled in the seventies again. Yes, I could smell the platforms and the damp parka jackets all right, even from thirty thousand feet. It was time to go back to the seventies and sort things out once and for all. Chucky our ducky time, Mr Toomey. And Pat McDonagh could work the memory lode my mother had unwittingly opened up for me, with the help of Danny Mulhall.

Chapter Twenty-Four

I HAD A few hours to kill in London before heading down to leafy stockbroker Surrey. I took the tube from Heathrow and did the royal round of Piccadilly and Leicester Square and Trafalgar Square. Pigeon shit, Japanese tourists and the charming tattiness of tourist London. I ended up back in the little streets of Soho, my head and body well stretched after the events of the night before in the Athens of the north. I felt suddenly lost for company though. Woman company. No Deirdre Dunne, no Angelina and, most of all, no Anna, the one who really counted. It would have been nice to scrap and squabble with someone as I walked along. A hearing ear. A warm heart. I watched an elderly British couple consulting a map, at the corner of Broad Street. Probably Bill and Doris, up from the provinces for the day. It was only as I passed them that I realised they were speaking some sort of Slavonic patois. I slipped into a little Chinese restaurant off Gerard Street and took out the Motorola. Wollenweider was his usual gay gay self.

"So, where are we going from this point, Barrett?"

"You can pull in Bruno and his friend now."

"That shouldn't be any problem."

"We have enough evidence to extradite. I'll be in touch again this evening."

The Peking duck arrived, a greasy, spiced up duck, fit for a king. I lashed into it wondering, in the back of my mind, whether I shouldn't be in touch with Dublin again. There was just something nagging at me as I crunched on my oriental fowl. The little waiter bowed at me.

"Everything all right, sir?"

"Grand. Any chance of a glass of water?"

"Glass of water on the way, sir."

Fuck it – phone and be done with it. Miss Katie would be the next to be hit anyway, whether she was cleaning up in Les Charmettes, sucking her boyfriend's appendage in the apartment in Ballsbridge or doing another runner. But we could cross that bitch when we came to her. Now that the Manchester deal was over and Brian Toomey's friends, in high and low places, had been sidelined, I assumed we were almost there. I don't know why I felt I had to phone Miss Katie. It certainly wasn't to gloat or to mark her cards. I just had an uneasy feeling that, if I took off the blindfold, I might find an altogether different chessboard in front of me. Intuition: a twinge somewhere between the oesophagus and the duodenum. I took out the regular mobile from my right pocket. I was beginning to get mixed up at this stage. Binary matters always confused me. I could never do calculus or German grammar in school. Der and die. Dis and dat. Fuck and forget.

Miss Katie was on the premises when I phoned Les Charmettes. The little lesbian let out a roar for her. The restaurant was starting to fill up now with tourists and office people. I stabbed at the duck again. I could hear Miss Katie tramping down the corridor to the phone, in her high heels. It was a cut-your-throat voice, a voice that knew the posse was on its way. But there was something else beneath, a subtext of threat.

"You think you're so fucking smart, don't you Barrett?"

"You doublecrossed me in Manchester, darling. I don't like that."

The couple at the next table sat up in their chairs, sensing some juicy chat to share later on, in suburbia.

"Just watch out, Barrett, you and yours."

"I beg your pardon?"

The line went dead. I glanced around me at the other customers and smiled wanly. Maybe this was what I had wanted from Miss Katie, a hint that the beast wasn't dead yet. Just to keep the juices going. I put my regular mobile away slowly and took out the Motorola. Now, more than a few eyes were on me.

It was Saturday noon. Anna should be back from the morning run, dancing classes and drama, with her legs up on the coffee table in the sitting room, nibbling away at the *Irish Times* crossword. Or browsing over the latest letter from her legal reptile.

"Hello?"

"Anna, it's me, Barrett."

"Hi."

"Is everything all right there?"

"What do you mean?"

"No funny phone calls. . . . no?"

"No, and anyway, your lot are across the road in one of their very conspicuous unmarked cars."

"There's not supposed to be anyone there in a car."

"What?"

"Get the fuck up the stairs with Aoife and hit that panic button!"

Squirrel's mobile was powered off. Great. I found myself

throwing caution to the wind and using the Motorola to call Mulhall. His voice was crisp and clear for a Saturday morning.

"None of ours, Barrett. Don't worry. We'll get there first."

"No! Mulhall! Don't!"

Mulhall's phone cut off from his end. What had I started? I kept my eyes away from the tables around me. Time to focus. I stood up, pulled out a twenty pound note and threw it on the counter as I walked out.

"Keep the change."

"Sir?"

I stopped a cab on the corner as I was punching in Squirrel's home number. He had done a late shift and was just getting up.

"Barrett?"

"There's something happening at Anna's . . . two guys in a car . . . she's pushed the button . . . and Mulhall is on his way."

"Great! I'm gone."

I heard Squirrel shout to his wife as he barrelled down the stairs and out the door. And there I was, sitting in the high seat of a black taxi, heading for Victoria, able to do sweet shag-all, satellite communications or no. I saw the whole scene before my eyes in Ashbrook Close in little snapshots. Anna and Aoife lying on the floor at the far side of the bedroom. Trajectory and cover. Hit the ditch. Basic training. Anna with the mobile still in her hand. Two mutts sitting outside in the car, sizing up things. Common-or-garden lowlifes, the sort that hovered on the edge of the paramilitaries while keeping their hand in a few tills. Our own Irish Mafia, in embryo. My old mobile rang. It was Anna's voice.

"We're OK, Barrett. There's another car pulling up."

"Get your fucking head down! Now!"

The taxi driver ducked instinctively and pulled over to the kerb. I saw his frightened eyes turn to me, Paddy, in the back.

"Look, I don't want no trouble, my friend. Forget the fare."

I stared back at him, a stupid grin on my face, ignoring his panic.

"Anna, there might be some kind of a shoot-out, so keep tight and low . . . right?"

And then the mobile went dead. Some blip in an electronic turkey, in geostat orbit above the earth. The taximan was in panic. I saw him eye up a policeman standing near the pull-in zone.

"Just go, squire! I don't want to get involved."

I took out a tenner and smiled. Bloody Irish. Bloody ceasefire. Think it's all over and the buggers start up again. I headed straight into Victoria and lost myself in the crowd. Nothing I could do now, I told myself. You don't have any control over the situation. Lap of the gods. After picking up my ticket, I grabbed a sandwich and coffee and stood under the great electronic notice board. I took a couple of deep breaths and tried both phones at once. The Motorola came up trumps. Contact. Anna's voice was on the line.

"We're all right; there are guards in the house. Everything's OK. Do you want to talk to Aoife?"

In a second, it was all teddy talk and where was I and would she see Angelina before she went back to Milan?

Squirrel was to fill me in on the details the next day about the snappy Toyota Landcruiser in Ashbrook Close, with Mulhall's boys in it. How they took the other two by surprise and got into the back of the car just as the ERU came around the corner. Then the standoff, with Squirrel arriving on the scene in the middle of it all, getting Daly to hand him over authority, through O'Leary. Mulhall's men stepped out of the car with the other two. Squirrel told the ERU boys to let Mulhall's men back into their own car to head off.

"What's going on here, sir?"

"Special operation. Here's Inspector Daly on the line."

It wasn't Daly, but Dennehy, the commissioner, a soft spoken graduate from a new era. A man to bury yesterdays. And a few of yesterday's men too. So Mulhall's men got to head off in their legally held car while the ERU "purified" the other car and found the handgun Mulhall's men had planted. The two lowlifes were put face down on the warm summer concrete of Ashbrook Close. A garda helicopter joined them overhead now. Pure street theatre. It was Squirrel who found the gun under the seat.

"It's not our fucking gun, man!"

"Well, like we found it in your possession, lads . . ."

It was changed times. The farmer and the cowboy must be friends now. The lion had to lie down with the lamb and, if he didn't, his balls would be forfeit. Squirrel told me later that the two buckos were from Bruno Downes's stable all right, by way of various buddies, probably including Miss Katie and, by extension, Brian Toomey. The main thing was that Anna and Aoife were all right. I put out of my head the what-might-have-happened scenario, just like I had outside the Dunevin Lodge. It was the past.

Anna's voice was on the line: "It's OK, Barrett. I know it's not your fault this time."

"Thank you."

I was being called Barrett again. No more Thomas. Once I heard Thomas this and Thomas that, I felt cold. Distant. Barrett. I smiled to myself. A cartoon was forming itself in my mind. I was fourteen again. Fourteen and courting. Nothing to lose. Only an ex-wife. I headed for the train.

As the train pulled into Epsom station, I switched the phone back to Mulhall. Danny Mulhall was his usual avuncular self. There was no mention of the incident in Ashbrook Close, because Mulhall had as much a stake in the new status quo as I did. Peace meant profit, political or otherwise. My message was simple.

"I want you to move on Pat McDonagh now."

"And has it been cleared, with your side?"

"It's all in place – security clearance to get inside Mountjoy. We're using the Irish form of your name. Even the computer won't recognise you."

I stepped out on to the platform as the crowd swarmed by me to their waiting cars.

"And Miss what's-her-face?"

"She's going down now."

"And the other lady?"

"We're going to give her another little bit of rope, just to be sure."

"So I can tell McDonagh everything else is in order?"

"Apple pie order."

I snapped the mobile shut, wondering just where Alannah Harris, the woman in the corner of the Manchester photo that I had assumed, at one stage, was some sort of badly made-up Dublin TV, until Squirrel had confirmed my suspicions, was at that point. Miss Katie had blackguarded me once too often. The voice of Charles Begadan would rise from the grave to give her grief in court, and the small matter of the touting for rent boys for Alannah Harris's brother, Brian Toomey, would now come into play. Wollenweider had done enough work on that from his end. And now for the seventies. Reed and d'Alton. And one dark night in Belfast, in January 1973. And the murder of a young man called Phillip Keane.

Chapter Twenty-Five

EPSOM WAS THE usual hodgepodge of W.H. Smith, Marks and Spencers and Boots High Street culture, though the real dosh lay outside the town, behind well-mannered hedgerows and well-manicured lawns. There was an easiness about this part of Surrey; not old money exactly, but oldish. Make the bacon in London and drag it home to Epsom and environs. I still felt uncomfortable as I crossed the threshhold of the White Hart. Even in these times, an Irish accent was still an Irish accent. I sipped at my light ale and buried my nose in the *Guardian*, among the *Daily Mail*s and *Daily Express*es. No Irish town would ever be Epsom. They might get their Boots and Marks and Spencers in the main street, but that air of civility and deference couldn't be faked, for love or money. Someone was always a step away from calling you a bollox in the bar of an Irish town, even if you were the doctor's son. Especially if you were the doctor's son. The type of mute indifference I saw in Epsom took years of breeding. Crookedness – that was the Irish mark of Cain. Contrariness. Be awkward. Be difficult. And that's what I was used to, like a lame leg or a birthmark. I spoke softly into the Motorola. Mr Reed was expecting me. I shouldn't leave it too late as he tired easily. Better not pull out the second mobile to contact Squirrel here or I would really have eyes on me.

John Reed was holed up in a small private hospital, about ten miles outside Epsom. The "Éire Politician Admits to Homosexual Affair" interview had been farmed out by the *Guardian* to Reed, all those years ago, precisely because he was a shirt lifter himself. All very liberal. All very seventies. Yawn. Fortunately, my taxi driver wasn't the mouthy Dublin sort I was used to. Nose up your arse and moan and groan about his sorry lot. I was dropped outside the great red-brick building in behind a mass of pine trees. At the reception desk, I was told that Mr Reed could see me now. A chatty little tea lady, who smelled as though she had been doused in lavender, led me along the corridor. Was I Irish? Thought she recognised the accent. Nice to see all that trouble was over, wasn't it? Nice. Everything was nice. There was a lot to be said for Surrey. It was nice.

"Mr Reed was a famous man, in his day."

"So I believe."

"Do you take the *Guardian* in Dublin yourself?"

"No, not personally."

The Cedar Court was somewhere between a small clinic, a convalescent home and an old folks' home. It looked a bit like pot luck; some would come out of it walking, others in a box. I had neglected to ask about Reed's precise state when I made the arrangements. Likely as not, he wouldn't be called to testify in a future trial of Brian Toomey.

John Reed was immediately recognisable. He had that *Guardian* look about him all right. Just as Epsom couldn't be an Irish town, John Reed couldn't have been an Irish journalist. He was sitting in an easy chair, in tartan dressing gown and slippers, playing a game of chess with another patient. I remembered the sallow skin, the slicked back hair and the slight stoop from that night, in 1973, in our house in Drumcondra. From his wheezy breathing, it was clear that things weren't looking good in the chest department. My eye fell on the yellow oxygen bottle on the wheelie stand. The alert eyes turned to me.

"Jack Barrett's son, right?"

"That's me."

"I'd know you out of your father, a mile away."

Because it was such a pleasant day, we sat out on the balcony. It was just after lunch, and as most of the regulars were either snoozing or strolling about the grounds, we had the balcony to ourselves. Just the two of us and the yellow oxygen bottle. Our whole demeanour said, to anyone who might approach, "Keep Out!"

Reed was still sharp as a needle. He didn't need any prompting to slip back in time. Reed had one-and-a-half legs in the grave and nothing to lose by telling me the truth, a truth he wasn't allowed to publish in the seventies. I wished Reed hadn't insisted on bringing the chessboard out to the balcony though, confuddling me with all sorts of clever feints and checks. Still, I suppose it was his cigarette substitute. Or maybe he just didn't want me looking into his eyes too much. John Reed grinned across the devastated board at me.

"Everyone underestimates the rook, even Spassky."

Reed had one of those awful phlegmatic coughs. It was like he was going to deliver his lungs into the handkerchief. But he ignored the oxygen bottle. That would be for later.

"OK, let's get down to business, Thomas. It's like this, you see."

The thin hand deftly moved a knight into position.

"Master Brian Toomey was up to his balls in the bombs-for-property thing, and our lot were threatening to expose your crowd because they wouldn't agree to military overflights and hot pursuit. Early 1970s . . ."

"This we know."

Reed put me in check again. My team was already decimated, pawns blown away by slack thinking. Both bishops had been compromised and were virtually useless. Reed's hand suddenly reached across the board and seized mine.

"No more moves, Thomas. Accept defeat with grace."

"Which my father should have done."

"Journalists hate conceding defeat, like policemen."

I could image the scene in 1973: furious phone calls between British and Irish mandarins over border incursions and the rest. Lots of shouting in the Dáil and argy-bargy in the House of Commons. Lots of posturing. Then rumours of the bombs-for-property business filtering through to the upper echelons of the British establishment. Now they had a lever. But the Irish government threatened to drop their support for any power-sharing government if the Brits persisted. So the Brits decided to go for the minister for justice himself, Brian Toomey. But the Irish weren't ready to hang out their dirty washing just yet, especially not when it was the Brits who were doing the laundering with a homosexual smear. I looked down at the chessboard.

"And then, John?"

"Then they came up with the gay smear. The dogs in the street knew Brian Toomey's preferences. Teenage boys, in a word."

"And the Brits threatened to destroy Toomey with the story?"

"Through the *Sun* or the *Daily Mail*, with this British former lover they had found."

"But Toomey got in first and came out a hero, as a common-or-garden gay."

"Exactly, but none of us knew of the Willington Lodge at the time. Any of us who noticed the news of the murder thought it was just another Protestant sectarian gang, albeit a crowd who liked chopping up young men. The boy wasn't found in the Willington Lodge, you see."

A nurse appeared with a tray of tea and ginger snaps. I slid the chessboard to one side and poured. We sat sipping tea for a few minutes. Reed told me then that the *Guardian* had offered him the gig of interviewing Toomey for his "coming out", knowing full well that they were giving the British establishment a toe in the bollox in the process. Being full of liberal woolly thinking, they missed the point that they were really helping to scupper Arland 1. In their haste to be even-handed, they were stopping the Paddies from laundering their own dirty washing, stopping us from growing up. Reed's hands were shaking. It was clear that his energy was finite, seriously so. The effort of holding the cup to his lips seemed almost too much for him.

"In the end, the Brits and the Irish fell into bed together, Thomas."

"Mutual interest, and you were codded, like my father."

"Difference was, I didn't get bitter. You shouldn't take a game of chess personally, Thomas. Can't think straight for the next game."

"Did you not suspect . . . ?"

"If we had . . . the murder of a young man . . . the Willington Lodge, I swear . . . I would have shouted it out from the rooftops . . . threats of libel or no."

"I know, John, I know."

"Anyway, Martin d'Alton has chapter and verse on the Willington Lodge . . . and all the documents . . . I only wish I could join you this evening . . ."

I handed Reed the oxygen mask and turned on the bottle. His

face flooded with relief as the oxygen penetrated through the thick layer of mucous encrusting his alveoli. John Reed wasn't too long for the world. Some night soon, his heart would fail, and he would slip away. I left Reed shortly after that. He was tiring quickly. I promised to phone him to tell him how things worked out. He might read about it in the papers anyway.

"Not really. We don't pay much attention to Ireland, except when you lot are making mischief, which was part of the problem in the north all along . . . indifference on this side."

He had done his duty. Told the truth. All the news that wasn't fit to print in 1973 but now must see the light of day. I thanked him and left him the little present I had brought him, a book from my father's library: Dorothy McCardle's *The Irish Republic*. First, dog-eared edition, from 1930 something.

"Very thoughtful of you, Thomas. I'll treasure it."

I needed some time before heading out to the Royal Automobile Club, with its plush hotel and restaurant, so I took a taxi back into Epsom, had a bar lunch in another lookalike pub and did some serious newspaper reading. When I checked on the old mobile, I found a few messages. Jon Wollenweider had phoned to say that Bruno Downes had been lifted, along with Gerry McGuckian, his northern buddy – the one who had actually pulled the trigger and killed Larry McMenamin. Miss Katie had been picked up in her boudoir and was being detained for questioning in the Bridewell. She was having the full weight of the evidence in the Charles Begadan case dropped on her padded bra in order to pressurise her into coming clean on the Alannah Harris connection with Manchester and McMenamin and other matters. There was no one much left for Brian Toomey to hide behind. Word was that people were trying to distance themselves as much as possible from their erstwhile hero. The Brits and the Paddies were back together on this one now, but, this time, they weren't involved in obfuscation. Brian Toomey's second outing would be part of a greater trawl through such matters as certain unexplained murders in the murder triangle of Mid-Tyrone, but the only murder that concerned me was that of Phillip Keane, in the Willington Lodge, in early January of 1973. Old times were coming back. The current taoiseach and the British prime minister were opening up the old account ledgers, but all the evidence would have to be in black-and-white, like the seventies themselves. And the black-and-white evidence, in the case of poor Phillip Keane, lay in the hands of Martin d'Alton, QC, because the British police had long since shredded any original evidence on the investigation into the murder of Phillip Keane. I dug out the second message on the mobile. Anna's crispy voice chirped out of the little speaker.

"I know you've done your best, Barrett. I hope you're all right over there. Please phone me."

Yes, I was being called Barrett again. It hadn't been a mistake the first time. I might have phoned Anna there and then if it hadn't been for my appointment in the RAC Club, but I had to keep a clear mind for Mr d'Alton. A chess-clear mind. No feelings, no footsie.

Chapter Twenty-Six

THE RAC WAS situated at the foot of the Epsom Downs. As I stepped out of the taxi, a fine summer mist was settling on the belly-soft rolling hills. I looked out across the golf course and felt even more alien than I had done in the town. Behind me, the taxi driver signed off.

"Have a nice evening, sir."

A well-seasoned, elderly couple was strolling in off the golf course with a tall, confident-looking man, who must have been the resident golf pro. I could hear their cheerful, clipped chat in the distance. It was all gentle and common sense and English and know-your-place. I wasn't a Christian Brothers' boy for nothing. Feeling inferior came naturally to me. I slipped up the steps of the hotel and made for the restaurant. A porter opened the door for me.

"The reservation is in the name of?"

"A Mr d'Alton."

"Ah. Mr d'Alton is here already."

I glanced across the restaurant floor to where Martin d'Alton, Queen's Counsel, was sitting, smoking a cigarette and reading a newspaper. The last of the summer light, through the window next to his table, lit up his soft features. There was the same ease in his face as you saw in the Epsom Downs. Or in Epsom itself, for that matter. Order in the hedgerows. The Middle East might pull itself apart and schoolchildren mow one another down in American towns, but Middle England would sail on regardless, peacefully, purposefully. A Norman pâté of Anglo-Saxon meat-and-bones. The one and only time I had seen Martin d'Alton in the flesh had been at a session after the Fianna Fáil Ard Fheis in Dublin in 1974. My father had dragged me along to meet a British parliamentary group over to discuss the demise of the power-sharing government in the north. My father had gone out of his way to avoid Martin d'Alton that evening. The memory was still fresh in my mind. Now, my father wasn't a difficult man. If anything, he was too eager to please by far. But something about his stand-offishness, when introduced to Martin d'Alton that day, at this Anglo-Irish lovefest, seemed odd to me. I thought, for a long time afterwards, that it was the same thing I felt when faced with that certain suave British self-assurance – a two-stroke mixture of resentment and admiration. But as Martin d'Alton stood up to greet me in the RAC Club restaurant, I knew deep down that I had got it all arseways. Seriously arseways.

"Nice to meet you, Thomas."

"I appreciate you taking the time."

"Always glad to help out the son of an old . . . acquaintance."

D'Alton waved his hand vaguely and a waiter called Mr Marconi appeared out of nowhere. His head tilted solemnly as though he was waiting for a reprimand.

"Grigori, myself and Mr Barrett here will start with a couple of Black Bushes."

"On the way, Mr d'Alton."

I could see how the Irish prisoners Martin d'Alton defended would have felt total faith in him. He knew the system. He screwed the system. He was the system. Still and all, the first Black Bush dissolved any residue of touchiness I felt in the grey-haired lawyer's company. We thrashed about a bit for a while, discussing this trial and that. All those highly charged headlines in the British papers, in the seventies.

BASTARDS!

Martin d'Alton threw back the last of his Black Bush nonchalantly.

"You do know that the chap I defended in the Staines bombing charge was later convicted of murder?"

"We all get something wrong. I've been gulled too, once or twice."

It was decent of Martin d'Alton to show me he could screw up too. By the time the main course came, we had reached back through time to the seventies. Wedges and loon pants, tank-tops and glam rock. This, strictly speaking, was Papa's territory. Dark talk in darkened rooms. Memoranda from P. O'Neill about the latest Provo hit. Toasted bodies lying on pavements in Belfast. Ordinary people killing ordinary people. A woman beaten to death in a romper room by a couple of teenage girls, with bricks, while her child cried outside in the hall. And Bloody Friday – someone's ribcage found up on a rooftop, weeks after the bombing, when it had been picked clean by seagulls. The rare old times.

"It was a nightmare, wasn't it, Thomas?"

"You must have been very popular, defending Irish suspects."

"I did what I thought had to be done. Mind you, we shouldn't cover up the past, in our natural haste to forget."

"How do you mean?"

Then Martin d'Alton, with all the theatricality of a high court performance, lifted up the plastic envelope at his feet. He grinned at me.

"*C'est tout.*"

"*Tout* what?"

"These are copies of the original police files on Mr Brian Toomey."

"How?"

"Now, Thomas, no one asks a journalist for his sources. Come! Come!"

Martin d'Alton proceeded to open the file. There must have been thirty or more pages, along with a couple of dusty affidavits.

"These are court documents?"

"Ah, yes, but the case never came to court, of course."

"Any more than Arland 1."

"And for the same reasons."

Martin d'Alton's hand reached under the sheaf of papers. What he pulled out was a series of photocopies of photographs of a young man. Before and after. I covered the photos with my hand, in case the waiter was hovering about. The body of Phillip Keane looked like it had been worked over by a complete lunatic, with hatchet, knife and hammer. It was clearly more than a murder; more an attempt to cover up the cause of death and dispose of the body.

"That's Mr Pat McDonagh's handiwork you're looking at, Thomas."

"And we're sure of that?"

"There's evidence in statements he made to your lot and ours, from the eighties."

"And we both know who committed the . . . murder, Martin."

"But was it murder or manslaughter, Thomas? There's the rub."

Grigori was back at the table again. Was everything all right? Perhaps Mr d'Alton would like his usual Cointreau after the meal? When Grigori buggered off with himself, I turned back to Martin d'Alton. Now I was talking to the real QC. Martin d'Alton set down his knife and fork, side by side, to signal to the world that he had eaten his fill. He was summing up now, jiggling his eyes about in his head like the Lord High Executioner before the chop. Grigori had already appeared with the two glasses of Cointreau, and the plates were cleared away before my companion spoke.

"It's like this, Thomas: proving manslaughter is one thing; proving murder is altogether another thing."

He tapped the plastic file.

"We have evidence and witnesses to support the first charge."

"Witnesses, plural?"

"Mr McDonagh and . . . ."

"Let me guess. Danny Mulhall."

"Yes, and it's peacetime now, and even the ones who lived behind the sectarian smokescreen, in the seventies and eighties . . ."

Martin d'Alton took out an original photograph from an envelope in his inside pocket, a birthday photo. Phillip Keane standing in front of his mother, with a birthday cake, blowing out candles. Ten, in all. Six years before his life was snuffed out. No sign of a father anywhere in the picture.

"These things must be paid for, one way or the other."

"So, what Dick Keegan told me is true then."

"Say again, Thomas?"

"That this boy was Mulhall's nephew, his sister's illegitimate child."

Martin d'Alton lit up again.

"Bit of a wild child, it seems. Fell by the wayside, then, before you know it, he's being passed around like . . . what's that charming phrase you have in Ireland?"

"Snuff at a wake?"

"So to speak."

"And Pat McDonagh?"

"Well, he was involved in the bombs-for-property business. Of course, Brian Toomey was owed a few favours by Mr McDonagh."

"But McDonagh wasn't a murderer . . . we're sure of that?"

"No, your key witness was simply involved in the unlawful disposal of the body."

"Then we have a clear run?"

"As long as you have the PSNI in Belfast on your side, yes. You must be sure of them."

"And you're not so sure?"

The restaurant began to fill up. Post-golf syndrome. There was talk of money and more money at the next table. A woman in a blue tracksuit was talking into a mobile phone and saying something about meeting the last train from Victoria, darling. But I hadn't finished with Martin d'Alton just yet. There was something else I needed to know. I called for another round of Black Bush to get to the nub of my own quest. Sink or swim. Martin d'Alton knew where I was heading though before I even asked the question. He had second-guessed too many prosecution lawyers and was a couple of steps ahead of me. He steepled his hands and looked into my eyes.

"And yes, I did tell your father the truth. After that Fianna Fáil Ard Fheis in 1974. I offered him the same material I am offering you now."

"And he funked it."

"Those were different days. You mustn't be too hard on him."

"That's decent of you to say so."

I knew that whatever material Martin d'Alton handed me across the table, there was a shitload more waiting in some archive or other. Once he knew both the Brits and the Irish were singing from the same hymn sheet, he would deliver. That was the difference. D'Alton's Irish equivalent would have had a far lighter conscience, after all this time. Burnt the lot years ago. It was easy enough to be hard on my own crowd. But it was hard being hard on my father, realising that the great Jack Barrett, champion of the liberal left, had sold the pass.

"You know, Thomas, none of the Irish papers would have published such a story, in those days."

"We were too busy punishing perfidious Albion to see the skidmarks on our own underwear."

"It's a different day."

"Maybe it is and maybe it isn't."

"And now, I have something to share with you, about your father."

"About my father . . . ?"

"Something you should know. Something that will help explain why he kept his silence all those years ago. It was because of you . . . because of you and your mother."

"I don't understand."

"Just listen and you will."

I took a sip of Black Bush and sat back, as instructed. And d'Alton began. It was a murky story. A story of the late seventies, after Arland 1 had been sunk and Brian Toomey had "outed" himself. It was the tale of a late night meeting in a pub out in WOMA, before there was an M50 and all the housing estates that

straddled it. My father had been called out on a tip-off by a political go-between. It must have been shortly after he learned Brian
Toomey's dirty secret, the one I was now privy to. He met up with
the avuncular, political gofer in the back bar of the hotel. It all
started very palsy-walsy, until the host mentioned the Willington
Lodge and "certain events". My father's journalistic nose must
have sniffed the air then, thinking that he was going to be given
chapter and verse; that he had just met a fellow soul who was
interested in that rare commodity known as "the truth". What
came next shocked and frightened him to the quick. It had the
tone and texture of an old parish priest's curse, backed up by the
clunk-click of a Kalashnikov behind the ditch. The heavily built
heavy leaned over to my father and whispered in his ear.

"I've been told to tell you . . ."

"By whom exactly?"

"I've been told to tell you that if you proceed with this investigation, that your family will never have a day's luck, so they
won't."

"They'll never have a day's luck? I don't believe in witchcraft."

"We're not talking about witches here, so we're not."

Your family will never have a day's luck. The phrase must have
haunted my father, day and night, night and day, until the resolve
that lay behind his journalistic nerve was stilled and he took to
self-pity, the bottle and self-loathing. I suddenly felt I owed the
old man a second hearing. And a third hearing, for that matter.
And I didn't give a tinker's fart for the tears that welled up in my
eyes, in the Royal Automobile Club, Epsom, Surrey.

When we left the RAC that night, it was around eleven. Cars were
pulling away across the gravel: heavy Rovers and Daimlers whose

doors closed with a genuine clunk, not cheap disposable Japanese cars. Martin d'Alton dropped me at my hotel, not far from the White Hart. He declined a late-night drink, but let it be known again that, if needed, he was available.

"There'll be a lot more dirt dug up on the seventies, Thomas."

"Yours or ours?"

"Both. No one comes clean out of the north."

I watched the Volvo pull away and headed indoors. It had suddenly gotten cold, and there was a late summer dampness in the air. I imagined John Reed struggling to breathe out in the home, an abandoned chess battle on the board beside the bed and a night nurse checking his breathing as he lay there, slowly cruising towards death. I put all this morbid stuff out of my mind then and phoned Squirrel. Miss Katie would go all the way. Witness protection scheme and all. Bruno Downes and Gerry McGuckian were already in the clink, in Amsterdam. Extradition papers were being prepared. They were just waiting for the word to lift Alannah Harris, who was probably, at that moment, sitting like a frightened rabbit out in her Rathgar house. But they couldn't touch her before the prima facie evidence in Brian Toomey's case had been lined up. Squirrel's voice was soft.

"Are we ready to roll, Barrett?"

"Just about. I'm going to e-mail some copies of this stuff to O'Leary tomorrow morning."

"And Belfast?"

"I'll be there by noon to meet with McWilliams tomorrow."

Angelina was still awake when I phoned the house in Drumcondra. Nothing unusual had happened at that end. No odd visitors or strange phone calls. I was glad she had decided to stay on the couple of extra weeks to see me through.

"Oh, and Thomas . . ."

"Yes?"

"Your wife phoned – Anna."

"She's not . . ."

"She said you should phone her when you get back to Dublin."

"But she has my number."

"You are such an innocent man sometimes, Barrett. Don't you know girls are always giving messages to one another?"

And that was probably why, when I was e-mailing the stuff to Daly the next morning from a little office in Heathrow, I took the liberty of firing off a cartoon I had drawn a couple of nights before to Anna's home e-mail. It showed a boy and a girl peeping out from behind two bushes. The man was saying, "You show me yours first!"

It wasn't original. And that helped. I left the girl's balloon empty, so that the woman could have the last word. It was coy. It was courtship. And what had I to lose? Angelina had spoken.

Chapter Twenty-Seven

THERE WERE NO helicopters swooping low over Belfast streets any more. No Saracens screaming around corners or gentlemen walking away slowly from car bombs primed to gut a street in a microsecond. It was a strange thing though, peace. You couldn't see it, touch it or smell it, but it was like a woman's mood in a darkened room – you could feel it all around you. For the younger ones, it meant a helpful dose of amnesia. For the older ones, it was the hope that things wouldn't ever go back to the bad old days they used to talk about.

"Left him out to die in the laneway . . . what you wouldn't do to a dog . . ."

I drove out of Tennant Street with Inspector Terry McWilliams at the wheel of an unmarked car. The Provos were still trainspotting, of course, still filling in their little notebooks with car regs and addresses, just in case peace turned sour again. McWilliams didn't entirely trust the whole business.

"They're just sick of bating one another up, if you ask me."

"Isn't that a start?"

"It is, I suppose. But you boys down in the south, with all due respect, didn't have to scrape people off walls like we did."

I glanced at McWilliams. Tight grey hair and clean-shaven face. Mid-fifties. Not old enough to remember the border campaign, of course, which my father had written about, which was a pantomime in comparison to what was to follow, in the seventies. We headed north, up by Carlisle Circus, in the general direction of the Cavehill and Napoleon's nose. McWilliams nodded to the right.

"New Lodge Road. Lost a mate of mine near here."

"Really."

"This is where the real crazy stuff went on . . . lifting people and torturing them to death. We picked up a chap once on the peaceline, and they had peeled back his scalp, like you'd peel back a banana."

"Jesus."

"Aye, before they took the liberty of driving a few nails down through the poor man's skull."

"How did you survive it all?"

"I'm not sure I did; I'm divorced ten years."

We were on the Cavehill Road now. There was an almost British order to things here now. Unlike a German one, it was slightly tatty, but warm; well-ordered street furniture, but with the kerbing not quite regular. Somewhere past the remains of Belfast Zoo, we turned left off the main road. The site of the Willington Lodge wasn't far away. I imagined what it must have been like up here in the seventies. The army patrols tearing up and down the Limestone Road. Sniper attacks from the waterworks on the Antrim Road. The distant thud of a bomb down near the city centre. And that special North Belfast fear – the nine o'clock knock.

"Is your da in, son?"

Blam! Blam! Blam! Another sectarian hit. Still, better than being lifted, wheeling home top-heavy from booze, and taken to the local romper room for customising. Darkness, dampness, fear. Fear of footsteps in the dark.

"They killed a fellow near here, one time. They put a ladder up to the bedroom window, at three or four in the morning. Tapped the window and blew him away when he got up to answer. Aye, brave boys, great men."

The car swung into a tidy little street. It might have been North London rather than North Belfast.

"There you go."

At first, I didn't know what McWilliams was on about, then I realised that he was pointing to a row of spruce trees to the left of us. We got out of the car. No need to lock it here. The locals might have been fond of killing one another, but, oh dear, they didn't do quite as much tea-leaving as they did in Dublin. And they were way behind altogether when it came to drug dealers and junkies.

"Peace will bring all that, Thomas, don't you worry."

"I'm afraid you're probably right."

"And our lot and your lot are going to have to see a lot more of one another. Like it or lump it, the criminals already have a United Ireland."

There was a little gateway set into the middle of the row of trees. A sign on one of the gates said "LINGTON LOD".

This was the place then, the Willington Lodge. The arse end of the Arland investigation. I followed McWilliams in and focused my eyes on the empty space and the wild grass, an empty space where the Willington Lodge had once stood. There was scarcely a stone left upon a stone. After the bomb, according to McWilliams, the whole building had been condemned and pulled down. No connection had been made, at the time, with the death of Phillip Keane, the young male prostitute. The site had recently been sold, and now it was a peacetime goldmine. In a few months, work would start on a new apartment block. We walked about the site for a few minutes, not that there was anything much to see. I suppose, without getting too New Age about it, I wanted to seal my relationship with the site, and, by implication, with McWilliams. When Brian Toomey was finally dragged into court, all this would be important.

"What's your reading on what happened?"

"Well, it's clear enough that Toomey used this place as a glorified whorehouse when he was up in Belfast on Arland business. He had a fondness for young men. But things went too far that night. Whether it was asphyxiation during some rough play or he actually had some sort of a brainstorm and murdered the boy . . . Maybe Phillip Keane had threatened to rat on Toomey."

"And McDonagh?

"Well, McDonagh was in our books by then anyway. He was up to his oxters in the whole bombs-for-property thing, of course, so Toomey dragged him in to clean up the mess. McDonagh made it look like another loyalist murder, then dumped him in the Lagan, but we knew from the start that it didn't fit."

"How?"

"Well, it wasn't that the loyalist gangs had anything against castrating people and that sort of carry-on, just that they tended to do it on older men, ones they could torture so-called intelligence out of, before killing them."

I still felt uneasy in Belfast, peace or no peace. Not physically afraid. More unconvinced and ill-at-ease. I felt the whole circus was still just under the surface. The tracer bullets and the bombs were, by and large, gone, but walk into the wrong bar and you might still end up as stiff meat.

We drove back down towards the city, crossing the Lower Shankill, in the general direction of the south side. We cut down across the Ormeau Road then and across the Queen's Bridge, where we pulled up near a couple of blocks of flats.

"Wouldn't do to be opening your gob in this neck of the woods, Thomas."

We left the car and made on down towards the river bank. We didn't go as far as the shore of the Lagan itself. Just far enough for McWilliams to point out where Phillip Keane's body had been washed up, at a bend in the river where a bank of mud and gravel and broken branches was gathered. Same river, different water.

"In a fertiliser sack, like butcher's offal. That's how we found him. We near emptied our stomachs that night; had to get the A squad down to give us a hand."

"I can see how it seemed like a loyalist killing."

"Well, some of us thought there might be satanism behind it, Thomas."

"Isn't it illogical to believe in the devil?"

"Just as illogical as it is to believe in God. And I believe in both, so I do."

"So, how was the Brian Toomey connection made?"

"That came from the Provies. And when we didn't get our act together, legally speaking, they obliged us by blowing up the Willington Lodge. Only Danny Mulhall's say-so saved McDonagh. He headed south after that. The Provies, of course, wouldn't touch a southern politician as high up as Toomey.

"And now?"

"Ah, sure we're all friends now, Thomas. Didn't you hear that?"

Terry McWilliams smiled at me sardonically. Back in Tennant

Street, I handed photocopies of Martin d'Alton's material over to him. Then I took the six o'clock Enterprise south to Dublin, a Dublin which seemed slightly more summery than Belfast. I thought of the gable wall slogan I had once seen at the Protestant end of the Limestone Road, many years before, on a brief trip to Belfast at the height of the troubles, as the pisses of rain ran down the wall:

WE WONT FORSAKE THE BLUE SKIES OF ULSTER FOR THE GREY SKIES OF AN IRISH REPUBLIC

Yawn.

Squirrel met me at Connolly Station, and we went for a pint in Rathgar. Miss Katie was even more eager to deal now, it seemed. The word was that Bruno Downes's extradition from the Netherlands would be fast-tracked. The Dutch had enough of their own scumbags about.

"What about Alannah Harris?"

"Tomorrow, 6 a.m."

"Why are we leaving it so late, Squirrel?"

"We didn't want to rattle either Toomey or her. We're going to get him tomorrow at the opening of a day centre."

"Isn't that a bit theatrical?"

"We just want someone to say "*That's the man*". Then it will all roll from there."

"And that's Pat McDonagh's job?"

"Sure is, pardner."

When I turned into Ashbrook Close an hour later, I told Squirrel to keep the engine running, that I would only be a minute. I hadn't been inside the family home in over a year. The usual drill was that I would collect Aoife at the door. No complicated stuff.

When Anna opened the door, ponytail and reading glasses and all, I had to hold myself back though. And then Aoife ran past her and grabbed me. My ex-wife looked over my shoulder.

"Do you want to come in, Barrett?"

"Squirrel's waiting."

"Is he?"

I turned around in time to see Squirrel's white Mondeo pulling away.

"He must have picked me up wrong."

I sat in the dining room then, like a confirmation boy waiting for the bishop's question or the clatter on the cheek. We chatted cautiously about nothing much. Nothing much except the events of the previous couple of days.

"Ashbrook Close isn't usually that exciting."

"I'm glad you're all right. I was worried."

"I was worried for you too, Barrett."

My mobile rang. It was O'Leary, with a little word in my ear. I was to be in the station by 7 a.m. the following morning. Myself and Squirrel would be picking up McDonagh from Mountjoy. I was to be fresh and ready for the important day ahead. I felt even more like a confirmation boy now, with O'Leary as the bishop.

"Your sick leave's officially over, Barrett. You do realise that?"

"Thank you, sir."

I glanced across at Anna. Aoife was playing away at the jigsaw of windmills and canals I had brought back from my last visit to Amsterdam. I wanted to be back home. Woman, home, warmth. I would do anything to get back home. I had to get a date with my ex-wife. Fuck pride. Fuck the past.

"How about a coffee at the weekend, Anna, to talk things over."

"I don't know."

"Or whenever suits, soon."

"Look, phone me at the weekend, Barrett."

"Fair enough."

When the taxi dropped me in Drumcondra, Angelina opened the door to me. I didn't get an early night that night at all. I sat up skulling whiskey with my Italian guest until two in the morning. Maybe I just wanted to talk to her about my courtship, about the girl I was wooing. About my ex-wife with the pony-tail and the funny glasses and the new smile on her face.

"What can you lose, Thomas?"

Chapter Twenty-Eight

To tell the truth, Pat McDonagh, with his straggly ginger hair and greasy moustache, looked more like an out-of-date rock drummer than someone who might topple a government. You needed a long spoon to sup with his like though. He had finished a year of his four-year sentence for extortion, and he was ready to cut a deal, under the auspices of Danny Mulhall. Now, I hadn't been inside Mountjoy in years. Angelina would have loved the damp brick and crumbling mortar. The deal we were doing with McDonagh had to be honoured on both sides of the border, especially as the northerners were probably going to have the privilege of trying Brian Toomey, after his extradition hearing. It went against the grain that the likes of McDonagh should be considered for early release, but the greater good demanded it. The national interest. But that still didn't make Pat McDonagh a nice guy in my book.

Myself and Squirrel were at the gates of Mountjoy at 8 a.m. sharp. We were led through the maze of ancient doors into the governor's office. I glanced at my watch and whispered, "Alannah Harris should be singing by now."

And that's the way it worked out, it seemed, with a pre-breakfast raid on a splendid Rathgar home, left over from the time of the Raj. When Alannah Harris realised that the forces of law and order had surrounded her house, she raced up the stairs in an attempt to erase the hard drive of her laptop, the one whose address we had found on the Clondalkin computer with the rent boy lists and contacts. But it wasn't to be. Both Alannah Harris and computer were taken, virgo intacta, to Rathmines Garda Station. The ragged ends of the web that stretched from Dublin to Manchester and Amsterdam and God-knows-where had been saved. Miss Katie was selling everyone down the river, by the new time.

Pat McDonagh was led into the governor's office by the prison warders. I saw the long hands, the steely eyes, the eyes that wouldn't let you in. I reminded myself that we had a tough one on our hands here, but no one would be coming to snatch Pat McDonagh. He was, politically speaking, in a negative equity situation. It was peace-and-flowers time now, and everyone was anxious to cut themselves in on the deal and get brownie points. Once we had him in the car, we went through our own protocol with him, just to see he was on message. As in, do a runner and we'll put a bullet in your hole. I checked my watch. It was about nine o'clock.

"Are you clear about the routine, Mr McDonagh?"

"Clear as a bell, Detective Barrett."

I swallowed hard, wondering whether the shit wouldn't hit several fans when it was found out that the likes of Pat McDonagh was the star witness. Still, set a scumbag to catch a scumbag.

Back in the station, myself and Squirrel busied ourselves with other matters while Pat McDonagh was kept in confined quarters, with a couple of packs of John Player Blue. I phoned Jon Wollenweider to tell him that the extradition affidavits were on the way. If necessary, and I hoped it would be, I could travel back to Amsterdam myself. Larry McMenamin's killers would be sorted, just as soon as Brian Toomey was. It was a quiet morning in the station, but myself and Squirrel were both on edge. The usual couple of passport applications appeared at the hatch. Then there was the reported abduction of a child by a separated father in Ranelagh. Harkin, the barrel of beef from Galway, took the details in the back room, then sent out the usual alerts. He glanced at myself and Squirrel as he came back into the office.

"Any strange, lads?"

"Divil a thing."

"Fair enough, Barrett. But I know be the gimp of you that there's something on."

This was High Noon. This was the day I got to serve notice on the man who had driven my father to an early, humiliating death. A bottle of pills by the bedside. A did-he-or-didn't he sui-cide when I was over working in England in a double-glazing fac-tory for the summer. Squirrel spoke into the radio.

"They're still at breakfast in Jury's. Toomey and his secretary."

"Well for him he has time for breakfast."

"Let's get everything in place, Barrett."

I stuck my head through the door of O'Leary's office. He was on the phone. I reckoned he was speaking to Daly or Commis-sioner Dennehy. Last minute details. He put his hand over the receiver.

"Superintendent Daly has asked me to stay in the station for this one. It's just you and Detective Murray then."

O'Leary smiled at me.

"Cartoon forming in that brain of yours, Detective Barrett?"

"No, I was just . . ."

"You've had a good rest, Sergeant Barrett. I'm sure you can handle it on your own."

It was just after ten when we put Pat McDonagh into the car and headed for town. I glanced at McDonagh's no-see-no-say eyes in the mirror, but there was nothing to read there. Of course, McDonagh had nothing to lose. If the scenario backfired, he still got remission of sentence. If Toomey's counsel ended up querying McDonagh's reliability as a witness, there were more who would step into the breach now that the first stone had been cast. John Reed had already drafted a submission that would stand up in court. I still felt edgy though. Brian Toomey had wriggled out of too many situations before. I took out the photograph that Martin d'Alton had given me in Epsom, the photograph of Phillip Keane as a young man, fresh-faced and naïve. I slipped it back into my pocket again. I hadn't been in touch with Danny Mulhall since the stand off in Ashcroft Close. I was back off the sick, of course, which meant that unofficial channels had been shut down. We had Miss Katie and Bruno Downes and McGuckian and Alannah Harris was cooling her arse in Rathmines Garda Station while forensics went through her house. And yet it still didn't feel right. I wouldn't feel things were in order until Brian Toomey was finally sent down and Arland 3 could get up and running over his broken bones.

We crossed Harold's Cross Bridge and swung right up the canal. I contacted the mobile patrol again. They had Toomey in sight.

"Suspect has just left hotel . . . in blue Mercedes . . . heading into town on Northumberland Road . . . pursuing . . ."

There was a bit of a buzz around town that morning. The sun was out and all was right with the world. As we drove along Pearse Street, for Ringsend, we saw the blue Merc swing in from Fenian Street.

"Gotcha!"

Squirrel hung back until Brian Toomey's car was over Irishtown Bridge, then we followed on, leaving the car on a double yellow, near a row of shops. There was no great security that day. Brian Toomey, after all, was now only a humble backbench TD. No matter what he had been in the seventies. It had been decided not to bring the uniforms in on the thing, just in case of loose lips. I let McDonagh out of the rear and watched him stretch himself. It would be the longest walk on free soil he had taken in a year. I rested my hand on his shoulder.

"Please don't do a runner, Mr McDonagh. I'd take a very dim view of it."

Pat McDonagh's charming blue eyes looked back into mine. Bomber, hitman, extortionist and body disposer.

"I'll not give you any cause for bother, so I won't, Sergeant Barrett."

"I'm glad to hear that, Patrick."

There was music coming from inside the little hall. Abba babble.

"Mama Mia, here I go again."

The work had scarcely finished on the drop-in centre, a big breeze-block building with double glazed windows and an anonymous, all-purpose look. I had done a recce the night before and figured out where to make my stand. Squirrel and McDonagh slipped on down the side of the building while I had a quiet word with the garda on the door, a slightly built young fellow with rosy cheeks. I didn't see him lasting long on the force. He would deal with his share of drugs and RTAs and domestics before he quit though. That was for sure. The garda spoke into his radio. I could hear the clicks as he was passed up the line to Daly. And Daly's voice then.

"Detective Barrett is now in charge of the situation."

"Right, sir."

I left the uniform where he was and headed on down, past the builders' planks and the busted cement bags, for the little kitchen at the rear of the building. The second garda, standing near Toomey in the hall, would now be aware of things. O'Leary would have spoken to him. Myself and the boys stood waiting until the push bar was opened and we could slip into the kitchen. The Abba song died away. I could hear the MC speaking.

"It's a great honour to have Mr Brian Toomey with us, a man who has survived the slings and arrows of outrageous fortune himself . . ."

I heard the laughter of the crowd. The laughter of an idiot who has scorched himself in the flames and is letting on the joke isn't on him. I scanned the kitchen and sat McDonagh over in the far corner. He took up a discarded newspaper and snuggled up behind it. No advantage lifting Brian Toomey in public. Only give his defence a chance to work on unlawful arrest and all that fiddle-faddle. I heard Brian Toomey speak briefly then. He too was delighted to be here. He used strange words like honour and hard work and dedication. I smirked at Squirrel.

"What a greasy little bollox!"

"Steady now, Barrett. Don't go getting personal on us."

McDonagh was tucking into the racing page. Not a word out of him.

"Are you a betting man, Mr McDonagh?"

"All life's a gamble, Detective Barrett."

"Is that a fact, now?"

I took a couple of deep breaths. When Brian Toomey's

speechifying was done, I spoke into the radio and peeped out through the door into the hall, where I could see the second garda take Toomey's arm. A look of surprise flitted across the TD's face. I read his lips.

"Is there a problem, garda?"

None, you bad fuck, I thought in my own mind. *Only the murder of Phillip Keane, the bombing of the north for profit and the murder of Larry McMenamin.* I ducked back into the room and had a final word with Squirrel. Eyes straight ahead. *Settle down, Barrett. Steady as she goes.*

I didn't hear the footsteps until they were almost at the door. Like most dramatic moments, the actual details were fairly mundane. The door swung open and Brian Toomey entered, followed by the second garda. Toomey stopped dead in his tracks, the colour draining from his face. He turned and glanced around at the garda who was keeping his eyes firmly on the wall in front of him. Then Toomey regained his composure. Tugged at his little polka-dot tie.

"What's going on here?"

I coughed. Pat McDonagh slowly lowered the newspaper so that his ginger hair and moustache could be seen. And the eyes that could stab your heart at a thousand feet.

"That's the man from the Willington Lodge, Detective Barrett."

"What's all this about? I demand to know!"

Brian Toomey tried on his snotty voice then, the one that got him special service in south Dublin restaurants. It was the fairest of cops though. In your face, baby. Daddy's boy was back. I stepped forward in to the fire. My eyes were steady. I would have been happier putting a bullet up Brian Toomey's backside, but this one was for Papa. Papa and the massive overdose of Nembutol he had taken one rainy Friday night in 1975.

"Mr Brian Toomey, I am arresting you, under the Criminal Justice Act, in connection with the death of Phillip Keane, in Belfast, in February 1973."

Brian Toomey's face was flushed with contempt, the contempt of a Gonzaga College boy for a Christian Brothers' boy. Tough titty. The muck were on the way up now. I sort of wished Toomey had made a run for it then. We would have given his royal podginess a little head start and taken him down with a big crowd around him, in the middle of the street. But he knew the game was up. Arland, Phillip Keane and McMenamin. The 1970s were back again, and I was politeness itself.

"I hope handcuffs won't be necessary, Mr Toomey."

Christ, how I would have loved a photograph of that moment, to e-mail to my father in the next world, but I had to be content with the banner headline in the following day's *Irish Times*.

Toomey Arrested on Suspicion of Involvement in NI Death

It was straight back to Mountjoy for McDonagh and straight to the station for Mr Brian Toomey, TD. O'Leary did the processing and initial questioning of Toomey from there. I smirked a second time when I saw Toomey's tub-of-guts lawyer arrive at the station.

"I'm here on Mr Toomey's behalf."

Myself and Squirrel had a late afternoon pint in Rathgar before splitting. It was all a bit of an anti-climax, in a way. A day I had waited for, for over twenty years. Squirrel skedaddled off early, letting me stew in my self-righteousness. I dropped out to the nursing home before going home to Drumcondra. My mother looked well enough. She was sitting with a gaggle of old ladies in the conservatory. The general talk was about the threat of an ESB strike and whether the power in the home would be affected. My mother looked across the room at me. She had obviously heard the news about Brian Toomey's arrest. I took her outside in her wheelchair, while there was still a bit of heat in the day. We went down by the rockery and out on to the little fenced path facing the sea. With the sun, the sea and the sky, you could almost fool yourself, for a moment, into thinking you were in a European country with a climate. We have to cherish our illusions, of course, even if they are fleeting. I stood beside mother as we watched a huge ship pass along the horizon.

"Where would that be going now, Thomas?"

"God knows. Further than England anyway, I'd say."

"Is that a fact, now?"

"France, Spain . . . North Africa, maybe."

"Isn't it grand for them."

I looked down at the age-freckled face. I didn't really want to drag my mother into celebrating my victory when she wasn't ready for it, but the little smile that crept into her face said it all.

"Wasn't your father the right fool to take his own life for that pup, Thomas?"

"He was soft, Mam, not foolish."

"And that gouger Toomey's been arrested, then?"

"He was taken in this morning."

"Is that so?"

I could feel the laughter rising up in my belly as I spoke. Christ Jesus, a boy had to have a break sometime.

"I arrested him, Mam."

"Isn't that grand, and tell me something, Thomas."

Her eyes looked out towards the bay again, towards the ship on the still, blue sea.

"Would you say that ship is carrying cattle or goods?"

That evening, I took Angelina out to dinner at a little place off Merrion Square. It wasn't the sort of place I was used to going. I said please and thank you far too often, and I didn't have a bull's notion about the wine list. Angelina, looking up from the menu, hooshed away the fussy little waiter.

"Give us five mintues, eh?"

"Certainly, madam."

He scuttled back down his hole like a hurt crab. We got stuck into talking about Angelina's little adventures over the summer, but my mind was really somewhere else – and Angelina knew it. There was nothing, at the end of the day, quite like unrequited love for an ex-wife. By the time I had seen Angelina back to her door that night, I had promised to give it all another serious bash. I was really making that promise to myself.

I sat up late that night, still a little high from the morning's doings in Ringsend, mooching through old photographs and files of my father's until I finally gave in at around two o'clock in the morning. I slunk into my bedroom and, in the pitch black, opened the bottom drawer of the tallboy and took out the envelope sellotaped to its base. The envelope contained the letter given to me, years before, by a friend of his, a letter my mother had, mercifully, never seen. I locked the sitting room door behind me, just in case Angelina should wander in. Under the old standard lamp, I opened the buff-coloured envelope. The paper felt dry and brittle, but the words in the faded ink were as fresh as they had been the day I first read them.

My Dearest Ina,

I am sorry I have to take this step. I cannot let yourself and Thomas suffer any more, but neither can I live with the shame of failing in my duty to reveal the real truth behind Arland.

MALO MORE QUAM FOEDARE

Death rather than disgrace. I hope you and Thomas will one day come to understand my actions. I cannot live with the bitterness of defeat and the indignity of watching my enemy rise again. To tell the truth, I have failed. And there is only one honourable course. I hope my God will forgive me. I hope, most of all, that you and Thomas will forgive me, in time.

Your loving Jack

It took me less time to make up my mind than I usually spend puzzling over whether to have a pint or a small one. I rummaged about in the bureau drawer and found a little green disposable cigarette lighter. I held up the letter by the corner and set fire to it, watching my father's last words go up in flames.

MALO MORE QUAM FOEDARE

I dropped the paper in an ashtray, turning it over and over with my silver Parker until it had been consumed. Then I ground up the ashes, so that none of the words could escape. Not even the Latin ones. When Sky news came on at 3 a.m., with something about storms in the Caribbean, I felt myself slipping through the floorboards with sleep, so I headed for bed and, in a moment, was gone into the land of forgetting. But somewhere in my dreams, my father must have winked at me, because when I woke, I felt such a relief sweep over me that I started to cry silently as I lay in bed. Big, slobbery tears of relief rolled down my cheeks on to the cotton sheets. And another bit of Latin floated into my head: "Ego te absolvo . . ."

And, even if it was sacrilegious, I meant it.

Chapter Twenty-Nine

IT WAS A cold autumn and the winter was worse. Real snow and real ice. Oodles of car crashes, power failures and hypothermia. Christmas itself was almost on the doorstep by the time the book of evidence in the Phillip Keane case was ready. The shops were full of tinsel and aerosol snow, and the airwaves were polysaturated with carols and Christmas medleys. John Reed passed away in Surrey around the middle of October, but not before he had made a detailed submission, on tape, for the court in Dublin. It was easy enough to stitch Bruno Downes and McGuckian into the picture. Miss Katie, no stockings and knickers to match, was on the witness protection scheme, somewhere in England. Ireland just wasn't big enough to hold a gal like her. Even I wasn't entitled to know her whereabouts, just in case I might try one last squeeze of those plastic dugs.

Brian Toomey didn't get to spend his remand down in the gentlemen's jail in Wexford, as I'm sure he would have preferred. Instead, he was made slop out his cell in Mountjoy with the junkies and all the other losers. Very traditional, in a Dickensian sort of way. His sister, Alannah Harris, all scowl and dark glasses, was nobbled for soliciting rent boy cannon-fodder for her brother, among others. *Le tout* Rathgar turned out to see the trial. My mother, unfortunately, didn't last long enough to see Brian Toomey in court. One day in early November, she went under for the last time. There was a big turn out at the funeral in the church with the winged roof on Ballygall Road. Many of them came back to the house in Drumcondra after the funeral. Anna stage-managed the whole thing: the cold buffet, the beer, the tea and the whiskey. Anna and I were talking by then, meeting every week or so, informally. I treated each meeting like a first date, presuming nothing and assuming everything. I was courting my ex-wife again, but there was still a long way to go, cartoons or no cartoons. Still, my father had been avenged. It was a burden that seemed to have blighted everything for more than twenty years that no amount of thinking could resolve – only revenge, pure and simple.

The cameras were out in full force on the final day of Brian Toomey's trial. It was a bone-chillingly cold day.

Toomey Trial Verdict Today

The great and the not so good packed the public gallery. Traffic diversions were in place along the quays. Sky television had a sandy-haired man speaking to camera just outside the gates. Everything was in place: the band, the choir, the solo singer. Myself and O'Leary were together in court that day, with Inspector Terry McWilliams sat to one side of us. There was a great air of anticipation: Brian Toomey was about to be sentenced for a heinous crime, committed over thirty years before, in another jurisdiction. I was so busy listening to McWilliams and O'Leary that I scarcely noticed Toomey enter the courtroom. It was as though a nobody had entered the room. I looked across at him. The silken skin was the same, as were the slicked back hair and the soft eyebrows, but the golden boy smirk was gone for ever. Gone, never to return. Brian Toomey knew that, when he was sentenced in a few weeks, he would be seeing out the remainder of his years inside.

There was a muted murmur when Justice James Doran, a silver-haired patrician with a Midlands accent, entered the room. I looked across at Brian Toomey again, at the face that might yet sink a dozen reputations. I had the uneasy thought then that a lot of people would like to see him dead, a lot of *Who's Who* sort of people. Like me, they would have no doubt but that Toomey still had plenty of venom left. Out of the corner of my eye I became aware of someone watching me. When I glanced around, I saw the gaunt face of Tom Hunt in the public gallery. He was here on a wing and a prayer, with just enough lease of life left to see his adversary getting a roasting. I noticed Brian Toomey glancing in Hunt's direction a couple of times, a look of angry disdain etched into his face. The opening was over almost as soon as it had begun. Mr Justice Doran called the foreman of the jury, a dapper little creature, to pronounce the verdict. There was a murmur around the room when the guilty verdict was announced. Brian Toomey had been found guilty of the premeditated killing of Phillip Keane, because, it was revealed in evidence, the young man had threatened to reveal the southern politician's predilection. A murder verdict – wonderful!

Brian Toomey was led out of the building on the end of a chain, and we all began to make our noisy way out. I caught Hunt's face as he pushed his way through the crowd towards me, the shaky hand outstretched.

"A great day, Thomas."

"True enough. You know Sergeant McWilliams here, of course."

"'Deed and I do. It's all a bit *déjà vu*."

"Hopefully the outcome won't be *déjà vu*, Mr Hunt."

I left Hunt and McWilliams to chew the fat and went to catch Squirrel out at the side entrance to the court. We were just in time to see Toomey being helped into the prison van and the click of a hundred cameras. I could see the next morning's headlines in *The Irish Times*.

Toomey Convicted of Murdering Belfast Rent Boy

Squirrel stamped his feet on the icy ground and lit a cigarette while the uniforms swarmed around. I heard the two back-up cars revving up for the trip back to Mountjoy. As I caught a glimpse of Toomey as the van pulled away, I smiled back at the angry face. It was unprofessional, but it was the very least I could do. The van took off with its posse, down towards Smithfield for the south quays. It seemed only a moment later when I heard what sounded like a car crash, somewhere behind the Four Courts. Terry McWilliams was at my side in an instant. The old dog for the hard road. Thirty years of northern troubles resurfaced in his face.

"What was that, Thomas?"

We were all standing there, waiting for someone to ask the question officially when the radio broke in.

"Blue Unit! Blue unit! Incident in Smithfield . . . prison van intercepted . . . armed elements . . . please copy . . ."

Of course, our car was parked a quarter of a mile away, so we had to climb into one of the squad cars and leave Hunt and McWilliams on the steps. There were sirens in the air now. A couple of units had been called in along with any ERU that was in the vicinity. I heard someone order in air support from Baldonnel. Myself and Squirrel were suddenly haring off around the corner in a squad car, with no back-up and no Uzi nestling at our feet. Just regulation pea-shooters. Fuck knows what was around the corner. Last season's hand-me-down Kalashnikovs.

"Is someone trying to take out Toomey, do you think?"

We bounced against a kerb as we turned the corner. It looked as though a bomb had gone off. The prison van holding Brian Toomey had been pinned against the wall by a big yellow low-loader, lifted from the markets. A couple of dazed prison officers were pulling themselves together in front of the van.

"Go right, Squirrel! Go 'round!"

We swung around and did a loop, arriving at the north entrance to Smithfield. There was pandemonium everywhere, with tourists and yuppies scattering this way and that. A shot had been fired. A Dublin reg car, with Toomey in the back and a couple of companions, had made off towards the river. I looked up to see a garda helicopter breast the houses on the south side of the plaza. There was a further scattering of panicky souls as the helicopter put down. I raced in under the rotor blades.

"We're coming with you . . . blue Dublin reg . . . Passat . . . headed off towards the Quays . . ."

"We had a sighting near the Green."

I held my stomach as myself and Squirrel climbed into the whirlybird. I didn't like this sort of thing at all. It was all too LA for me. I put on my helmet and spoke into the headpiece.

"Head for the Green, then."

Sightings were coming in thick and fast now. First it was Balls-bridge, then Donnybrook, then Rathfarnham. But we still hadn't IDed anything ourselves yet. I nudged Squirrel.

"Best guess?

"The mountains or the M50. Maybe they're heading to WOMA."

"Which?"

"I'd say the mountains; M50 is too crowded this time of the day."

The last two sightings were in Rathfarnham. If they hadn't switched cars already, that is.

"What are they up to? Who is it, Squirrel?"

"Maybe taking him out."

"Why?"

"Fuck knows."

"Why not do it back in Smithfield then? Or before he was jailed at all?"

I thought back to Mulhall's curious comment that night in the Dunevin Lodge, a while before: "I believe in people being tried and convicted before . . ." But I said nothing to Squirrel about it as the helicopter veered away from WOMA.

We followed Ballyroan Road up towards the mountains, weaving over and back across the ditches on the off-chance of finding the blue Passat around the next hill. Down below us, I spotted a white car racing towards the mountains with a clamp-on light on the roof. Squirrel glanced back in the direction of the detective car.

"How the fuck did he get up here so quickly?"

We looked at one another.

"That's them! Hey!"

I shouted into the mouthpiece.

"Suspicious-looking White Nissan with a garda light heading in the direction of Rockbrook . . . maybe decoy . . . radio back."

We must have gone over every hill and hollow between Johnny Fox's and Kilmashogue in the next couple of minutes, even swooping down low over one of the forest car parks, looking for a white car on a snow-covered mountain. But there was no sign of the car. The trail was cold. We pushed on a bit further and came over a snow-covered ridge near Glencree.

"There's the Passat, Barrett!"

The blue Passat had been abandoned at the side of the road, halfway down towards the reconciliation centre. It was an idyllic scene down below: snow-covered trees and frozen roads. The co-pilot turned to us.

"Well?"

"Carry on into the German cemetery."

"It'll be very tight."

"You won't wake anyone."

As we passed over the wall, myself and Squirrel pulled off our headsets. The helicopter stood poised in the air of the cemetery and did a fussy little pirouette. There, over near the scrubby face of the cliffside overlooking the cemetery, a couple of men standing with their back to the action were playing hide-and-go-seek. Hear no evil, see no evil, say fuckall. I looked over my shoulder past the little rows of stone crosses, the resting place of First World War and Second World War dead, the named and the unnamed, to where the portly figure of Mr Brian Toomey was kneeling in the soft, white snow.

"Bring us down!"

"No can do. You'll have to go from here."

The helicopter motors were whoomp-whoomp-whoomping in my ear as I shouted at Mulhall and Toomey. Mulhall looked across at me, but he kept the pistol to Brian Toomey's noble skull. I crouched at the open door of the helicopter with Squirrel shouting in my ear. We were both watching Mulhall's eyes, wondering whether a sudden move on our part would push Mulhall to pull

the trigger. I couldn't see Toomey's face at that point. He was leaning forward in an obscene attitude of contrition. Those Latin
words ran through my mind again. My father's motto.

MALO MORE QUAM FOEDARE

I couldn't allow Mulhall to take Toomey out, though, even if
my twisted heart said otherwise. I tried to shout over the din of
the rotors.

"Don't, Mulhall! It's not worth it. . . ."

But Danny Mulhall just stared straight past me and kept the
pistol to Toomey's head. I glanced over my shoulder.

"Cover me, Squirrel . . ."

I jumped down on to the cold, unkind earth. I rolled when I
hit the ground, but I still managed to do my shoulder an injury
on the kerbing of one of the graves. I pulled myself up and drew
my gun.

"Drop the gun, Danny . . . come on, now!"

Mulhall's smile was almost mystical in its serenity. *I believe in
people being tried and convicted before* . . . I was so sure he was
going to pull the trigger. So sure, in fact, that I could already picture myself standing over the dead politician's body, the sweet,
musty scent of *schadenfreude* in my nostrils, as I handcuffed Mulhall.

But then Mulhall's smile changed to something else. Maybe
some programme kicked in that I didn't recognise, or he might
have simply done a quick inventory of the pros and cons of the
situation. Danny Mulhall turned away from me slowly then and,
standing behind Toomey, put him in an armlock and whispered
something in his ear. Mulhall might have been an old priest whispering an act of contrition to a car crash victim. He held Toomey
tightly with one hand while holding the gun to his temple. I

watched in astonishment then as Mulhall took Toomey's right and placed his fingers around the butt of the revolver. It was clear then what Mulhall was doing. He had given Toomey the option of doing the decent thing – of topping himself rather than spending the rest of his natural in a cell. That way, everyone would be happy. Brian Toomey's squat fingers fixed on the gun. I didn't move, bracing myself for the blast that would come as Brian Toomey took his own worthless life. There was a strange pause then, like a glitchy moment on a DVD screen when everything breaks up into pixels.

My memory is a sort of a jumble after that, a series of grainy, jumpy shots taken from different angles and spliced together by a man with cataracts. From the side, I saw Toomey's face change suddenly. The taut, terrified expression of a moment earlier turned suddenly to a snarling mask of savage contempt. I caught a glimpse of Danny Mulhall's startled eyes from the side. I saw Toomey wrench the gun around, over his shoulder. Then Brian Toomey, without a moment's fluster or hesitation, put a nice warm bullet in Danny Mulhall's chest. A stop-me-and-buy-one sort of bullet. A bullet that wove its way in through his companion's breastbone and tore out half his heart. I caught Mulhall's stunned smile as he swung round to face me, mortally wounded. It was the stupefied smile of an ageing schoolmaster scrambling to field an unexpected question from the brightest boy in the class. Then I was suddenly moving forward, shouting like a lunatic. There was no *Armed Garda, please leave down your weapon* sort of bullshit.

"Drop the gun, Toomey! Drop the gun or you're fucking dead!"

The truth is, I wanted Brian Toomey to raise the gun to me,

so I would have an excuse to send one flying into his soft, sensuous cheeks. But Toomey threw himself down on the ground beside the blood-covered snow, his arms raised in an attitude of mock surrender. I heard Squirrel's footsteps behind me.

"Barrett, lower the gun. Put down the gun, Barrett."

Myself and my father had been foiled at the last hurdle again. The Barretts, *père et fils*, screwed again by the cream of the class. When the back-up teams began to arrive, their roaring engines replacing the noise of the helicopter that had just taken off with Danny Mulhall's body, we dragged Brian Toomey to his feet. There was an unquenchable smugness in his bloodshot eyes. He couldn't resist stopping a moment as the uniforms dragged him away, a smirking Christ on the way to his own little Calvary.

"*Quis audat vincit*, Detective Barrett. Or didn't you Christian Brothers' boys master Latin, hmm?"

I drew out at Brian Toomey without thinking too much, a long-forgotten Shotokan punch from my old unarmed combat classes. My fist found a sensitive place south of his pampered solar plexus. At least I had the pleasure of seeing the bastard spit blood into the snow at my feet before I was dragged off him by Squirrel. If I had left well enough alone, arrived a few minutes later or just turned my back on Danny Mulhall's gun and let him get on with it instead of being Mr High Moral Ground, then it might have been Toomey lying in the snows with open-head surgery.

I stood there in the white, white graveyard, in the company of the German dead of the two world wars, smoking my second cigarette in over twenty years. I like to think that my father's spirit was hovering over the little gap in the hills just then, looking down on the whole scenario. And, who knows, maybe it was.

The papers didn't put a tooth in it that evening. Printer's ink was thicker than blood.

TOOMEY KILLS PROVO KIDNAPPER

And all the animals of the plain sighed a sigh of relief over their coffee and croissants, but their relief was only temporary. The whole dirty mess of Arland would come out in the end, with or without Brian Toomey's co-operation, and he had no reason not to co-operate now: he would never see daylight on a public street again. Pat McDonagh's deal still had to be honoured though. He would be out on the streets in short order, free to pursue whatever livelihood an out-of-work Provo might take up. We didn't really see McDonagh lasting too long on the outside. He had too much twitchiness about him. Bruno Downes and McGuckian would eventually be put away for the murder of Larry McMenamin. Phone records, e-mail intercepts and Miss Katie's evidence were crucial there, of course. There is always a woman behind every successful man, of course, even if she is wearing false breasts and a crotch strap. Alannah Harris, as expected, was the one who had set the wheels of Larry McMenamin's murder in motion. She would have to sweat out the next five years in the unsalubrious company of even rougher females than Miss Katie in the women's prison at Mountjoy. And Brian Toomey would go down on three counts: Arland, McMenamin and the killing of Danny Mulhall. All in due course.

I sometimes imagined Miss Katie, in some British housing estate, dressing up to go out for the evening, rolling up her suspenders and applying a little extra rouge, so that her rough, mannish skin wouldn't show too clearly under the bar lights as she nursed her regrets. After a while though, even Miss Katie vanished from my mind, even if Alannah Harris, with her beehive hairdo and killer shades, never quite did. The thought of her discomfort in the confined quarters of the women's prison gave me good cheer on many a winter's evening. It made up for her brother escaping Danny Mulhall's bullet. Just about.

The following spring, when the cold winter rain turned to warmer spring rain, I moved back in with Anna. Weekends only, on a sale-or-return basis. I began drawing cartoons and caricatures feverishly. *Phoenix* and *Magill* started buying again, and the stuff wasn't bad at all. And not bad at all is good enough for me these days. Even if we never get back to looking at one another seven days a week, I'll be happy enough with that. Having someone who gives a shit about you: what more can you ask of the world? That summer, Angelina rented a room in the Drumcondra house for a month. This time it was Beckett she was after. Beckett and Joyce. The southside and the northside. I offered to do a few walks with her, as long as I didn't have to read anything. There was quite enough literature in cartoons, from my point of view, to last me a lifetime. And in watercolours too. I didn't need words. Pictures were enough for me. Big time.